To Maureen,
all best
J.C. Brown

Heaven's Rage

Tiffany Craig Brown

Outskirts Press, Inc.
Denver, Colorado

Heaven's Rage
All Rights Reserved.
Copyright © 2010 Tiffany Craig Brown
v3.0

Author Photo © 2010 Steve Gladstone - www.stevegladstone.com

Outskirts Press, Inc.
http://www.outskirtspress.com

ISBN1: 978-1-4327-5695-6
ISBN2: 978-1-4327-5696-3

Outskirts Press and the "OP" logo are trademarks belonging to Outskirts Press, Inc.

PRINTED IN THE UNITED STATES OF AMERICA

To all the survivors; you know who you are.

"Heaven has no rage like love to hatred turn'd,
Nor hell a fury like a woman scorned."

William Congreve
The Mourning Bride III, 2

Chapter 1
San Diego, California;
July 21, 2003

Ian was jarred awake by a shrill beeping. His arm jutted out from the sheets, his hand reaching toward the bedside table where he'd tossed his pager just a few hours earlier. Still half asleep, he groaned with agitation as the urgent peal pulsed through the room. He fumbled around for a minute before knocking the pager to the floor.

Ian rolled out of bed, picked up the pager and saw *187PC*, the code for homicide, glaring back at him. He jumped up and ran to the living room to grab the phone, tripping over a pile of clothes on the way. He hurriedly dialed the number for the San Diego Sheriff's Department dispatcher.

"Buchanan," he barked into the phone.

"Detective Buchanan, we've got a one-eighty-seven gunshot victim at 1550 Elm Avenue, Chula Vista," said a female voice on the other end.

"Male Caucasian . . . no suspect information at this time," the dispatcher continued, "Call received at oh two thirty hours.

Officers are on scene and securing the crime scene. Detective O'Reilly will meet you there. Can you give me an ETA?"

Buchanan sighed, briskly rubbing his hand over his face in an attempt to wake up. Feeling the roughness of the stubble on his cheeks, he realized it had been nearly a week since he had last shaved. Recalling his supervisor's most recent admonishment for his disheveled appearance - the sternest yet - he briefly considered running a razor over his face. He discarded the idea just as quickly.

Ian Buchanan's disdain for shaving had earned him a reputation for slovenliness throughout the Sheriff's Department. Just last week he'd overheard one of his fellow homicide detectives refer to him as *Columbo*. He'd chuckled to himself, thinking, *Nah, I don't wear a raincoat.*

Realizing that the dispatcher was still waiting for an answer to her question, he said, "Notify the on-call D.A. and Forensics. I'm on my way . . . should be about thirty minutes," and abruptly hung up the phone.

Ian hurriedly donned the now-wrinkled blue jeans and T-shirt he'd shed onto the bedroom floor last night before falling into bed and then dashed out the door.

After a quick stop for coffee at a nearby convenience store, Buchanan pointed his white Ford Taurus toward the entrance for the I-8 freeway headed west. Chula Vista was a little over twenty miles southwest of his small house in El Cajon.

He passed his parents' house and realized that though they lived only a block from him, it had been nearly a month since he'd seen them. *I'll try to stop by on Sunday*, he told himself.

As he thought about his parents, his mind wandered back to Alaska. He'd lived there until the age of fifteen, at which point his father had retired from the Anchorage Police Department and moved the family back to the San Diego area.

As if on autopilot, Ian's car flew down the freeway while memories of a land overflowing with breath-taking ocean coasts, majestic mountain peaks, glaciers, rushing rivers, green rain forests and a myriad of wildlife called to him like a seductive lover.

I will return to Alaska one day, he vowed, smiling to himself.

Returning his attention to the present, and the prospect of another macabre crime scene awaiting him, his nostalgia turned melancholy.

——— ‹‹�()›› ———

Chula Vista, which means "pretty view" in Spanish, sits about halfway between downtown San Diego and the Mexican border and about ten miles southeast of Coronado Island.

The bright lights, TV crews and bath-robed onlookers engulfing a townhouse in the middle of Elm Street's 1500 block left no doubt in Ian's mind as to the location of the crime scene.

"Fucking media," he grumbled to himself as he maneuvered his car through the crowd. "It's bad enough dealing with one of you, but get you all together and you're like a pack of vultures with drool dripping from your beaks just waiting for your next meal."

He glanced toward the townhouse and saw Mike O'Reilly, his partner and best friend, talking to a uniformed officer inside the yellow police-taped area. His lips curled into a smile.

As he approached the scene, someone yelled, "Detective Buchanan!" causing local reporters to swarm around him like flies on honey. Suddenly blinded by the bright lights, he bristled

— 3 —

at the cacophony of reporters trying to out-shout each other with their questions.

Waving his arms at the crowd and raising his voice to be heard, he yelled, "I just got here. I know nothing. When I have something for you, I'll let you know. In the meantime, back off and let me do my job."

He turned and walked toward his partner, who was grinning at Ian's discomfort. As Ian drew near, Mike slapped him on the back and cracked, "Better you than me!"

"Thanks pal," Ian groused.

Mike pointed toward the townhouse and said, "Neighbor found the body . . . claims she was awakened by what sounded like a gunshot. She looked out her window and saw the front door open so came over to see if the owner, a male Caucasian who was apparently a friend of hers, was okay. She walked in and found the body in the middle of the living room floor. Looks like multiple gunshot wounds. So far, no weapon's been found. The criminalists got here about fifteen minutes ago."

"Is the medical examiner here yet?" Ian asked.

"Yeah, she's in there now," Mike answered as the two walked through the front door.

Surprise registered on Ian's face. Then with a wry grin he said, "No shit? Must be new."

Mike chuckled as he led his partner through the small entryway to the back of the house. Most investigators from the Medical Examiner's office left them cooling their heels for an hour or more, so this was a pleasant surprise.

As they entered the living room, Ian raised his hand and then nodded at the criminalists who rounded out their investigative team. They were busy snapping pictures, taking measurements and collecting other forms of evidence.

Jim Ritter, the Crime Scene Investigator, spoke from the other side of the room. "Well, if it isn't Mutt and Jeff," he said, referring to the differences between Ian's slight stature and thinning hair and Mike's big, burly build and full head of curly hair.

Buchanan shook his head as he recalled the first time Sergeant Moore had attributed the names of the comic strip characters to them. The title had stuck and though Ian feigned annoyance, he secretly got a kick out of it. He recognized how different he and his partner were – and that it went beyond their physical traits. While Ian tended to be a loner, Mike thrived on the company of many, especially women. Ian often joked that he'd never seen Mike with the same woman twice.

He hid his smile as he continued to study the scene.

The body of a slightly gray and balding man appearing to be in his early fifties was sprawled out in the middle of the room. A pool of blood had seeped into the beige carpet. Two spent casings lay on the ground, about a foot apart and to the right of the body. Ian took note of the fact that they were in full view. *Not only was the perpetrator in a big hurry to get out of here, he was no professional,* he surmised.

The only sign of a struggle was the tall, rattan princess chair lying on its side just to the left of the body.

A petite brunette, unfamiliar to Ian, was on her knees examining the corpse. He gingerly walked around the body to stand on the other side. Looking down at the woman, Buchanan said "You're from the Medical Examiner's office," more as a statement than a question.

The woman, wearing a ball cap which read SDME across the

front, stood and held out her gloved hand for Ian to shake. He ignored it.

She cleared her throat and, with evident discomfort, quickly dropped her hand.

"Dr. Sarah Epstein - and you are correct, I'm with the M.E.'s office."

Ian's eyes darted around the room to take in the entire scene as he spoke. "What can you tell me so far?"

"Well, I can give you my preliminary assessment."

Sensing a chill in her voice, Ian softened his approach. He didn't mean to be gruff and over the years had learned to check himself, to alter his behavior. He also knew that in order to do his job he would need this woman's help.

"That would be great," he said with a smile in his eyes that had not yet reached his lips.

"I see two entry wounds, one in the lower left quadrant of the abdominal area and another in the right anterior chest wall," Sarah began. "No exit wounds - and so far no bullets found. That, along with those cartridge casings suggests a low-velocity bullet from a semi-automatic pistol."

She pointed toward the dead man's mid-section. "The soot on his shirt here indicates he was shot at contact range."

Motioning upward, she continued. "On the other hand, the scattered gunshot residue here in the chest area indicates a medium range shot. In other words, it would appear the perpetrator was anywhere from one and a half to three feet from the victim. My guess is that it came from above . . . the victim may have fallen after the first shot and, wanting to be sure he was dead, the shooter stood over the body and fired a second bullet. Of course at this point that's just conjecture . . ."

"Thanks. Time of death?"

"This lividity is post-mortem and I see no signs of rigor mortis so I'm estimating one to two hours."

Upon entering the room, Ian had smelled a foul odor. As he stood there, the stench seemed to worsen.

"What the hell is that smell?" he asked, wrinkling his nose.

"Smells like vomit to me," said Jim.

"Vomit? Did you find vomit?" asked Buchanan.

"I haven't gotten that far, but it appears to be coming from the bathroom over there."

Ian looked down the hallway, just off the living room, toward which Jim was pointing. He walked to the bathroom but only got as far as the doorway before the putrid stench hit him full force. He grabbed the hem of his jacket and pulled it over his nose and mouth, trying not to gag. The toilet bowl was filled with a thick, brown-tinged liquid. Peering down at the toilet, he could see remnants of dried vomit stuck to the side. "Damn, that stinks!" he muttered. He walked back into the living room, lowered the jacket from his mouth and said, "What do you think, Doc, is our vic responsible for that?"

"I don't smell vomit on him, but I can't say for sure until we get him back to the morgue."

Buchanan noted a door that led from the kitchen to what he assumed was the garage. Glancing toward the front door, he spoke to all in the room as he asked, "Any sign of forced entry?"

"I've checked all points of entry into the house and found no disturbances whatsoever," replied Ben Li, the other forensics specialist assigned to Ian's team.

Ian looked in his direction. Ben was preparing to pour the contents of one of two wine glasses sitting on the coffee table into a plastic evidence container. Both glasses were full of a deep burgundy-hued wine. Mike chimed in. "From all appearances, our victim knew his assailant."

"Who hopefully left prints behind," Ian replied. "Any luck, Ben?"

Li spoke without looking up. "Latent prints are visible, but the glasses need to dry before I can attempt to lift any."

"Looks to me like nobody imbibed," Ian pointed out.

Ben nodded. "I think you might be right but we can hope."

Ian turned to his partner and pointed toward the body. "What do we know about him?"

"Well, I just got here myself . . ." Mike began.

Ritter spoke up. "According to his wall of glory over there," indicating the wall at the back of the room covered with framed certificates and plaques, "he was once a military helicopter pilot – for both the Navy and the Army. Name's Richard Tate."

As Mike and Ian walked over to get a closer look, Mike added, "The neighbor who found him told the uniform he lives alone." He looked down and flipped through the pages of his tablet then continued, "Woman named Maryanne Tripp. Has lived across the street for ten years. . . ." He motioned toward the body with his chin. "She said Mr. Tate here moved in a couple years after her."

"Let's go have a little chat with Miss Tripp . . ." Ian suggested, turning toward the front door.

Mike followed, "Yeah, one of the patrol officers is at her house with her. As could be expected, she was pretty shook up."

The two walked across the street, staying inside the yellow tape as long as possible to avoid the reporters who once again were shouting questions in their direction. Ian simply waved his hand at them as he picked up his pace.

Chapter 2
July 21, 2003

Maryanne Tripp was a tall, plump blonde who looked to be in her mid-to-late-forties. As Ian and Mike entered the townhouse, they could see her slumped on a faded, blue plaid couch. She looked up at them with red, swollen eyes still rimmed with tears.

A young female police officer stood near a window that looked out on a grassy area and beyond to the home of Richard Tate. As she glanced their way, both detectives flashed their badges in her direction. She nodded in acknowledgement then turned to leave.

Buchanan and O'Reilly focused their attention on the witness.

"Miss Tripp, is it?" Ian asked softly, "or is it Mrs.?"

The woman peered up at him and quietly said, "Miss, but you can call me Maryanne."

"Okay Maryanne," Ian said as he sat down on the couch next to her, "I'm Detective Ian Buchanan and this is my partner, Detective Mike O'Reilly. We'd like to ask you a few questions."

Maryanne nodded. Her bottom lip began to quiver as she

asked, "Who could have done such a thing? Dick was such a nice guy."

"Did you know him well?"

Maryanne's eyes welled up with tears. "Yeah, I guess. We talked a lot. He used to be in the Navy, retired a few years ago. I don't know what his job is right now . . . or was. I asked him once and he said it was top secret, with the federal government. I kinda got the impression maybe he was with the FBI or CIA or something like that."

"When was the last time you saw Mr. Tate prior to discovering his body?"

"Well, I was working in my yard . . . pulling weeds from my flower bed out there," she said as she waved her hand toward the front yard. "That was about, um . . . oh, 3:30 or 4:00. Anyway, he pulled into his garage and then started unloading some bags from his car - groceries I think. I said hello and he waved at me," Maryanne explained. "I came inside and didn't see him after that."

"Did you see anyone else at that time?" asked Ian.

She shook her head. "No."

"He lived alone?" Mike questioned.

Maryanne nodded.

"Do you know if he had a girlfriend or any female friends that visited him on a regular basis?" asked Mike.

"No, not really . . . not that I know of."

Maryanne paused for a moment and then continued, "I know he had ex-wives and some kids. He mentioned his kids a couple of times – um, boys I think. I don't know how old they are or where they live. But I think he had a lot of trouble with the ex-wives. He did tell me that they wouldn't let him see his kids. He was real upset about it."

Ian and Mike exchanged glances.

"You said, 'ex-wives' – plural - how many are we talking about here?" Ian asked.

Maryanne shrugged, and then glanced upward as though trying to recall a conversation. "I know he had at least two, but I don't remember exactly what he said that gave me that impression. I'm sorry. I wish I could tell you more."

"You're doing great," Ian reassured her. "I know you told the officer what happened, how you discovered his body, but would you mind describing it to us?"

"Okay," she replied. She fixed her gaze on the floor and began.

"I got in bed around 11:00 but I couldn't sleep so I read for awhile. I think I was dreaming because I woke up suddenly. I guess I must have dozed off. A few minutes later I heard a loud bang. It was almost like . . . well you know when you blow up a paper bag and then pop the air out of it? That's kind of what it sounded like, but real loud," she explained.

"So, you heard just one shot, is that correct?" asked Ian.

"Yeah."

"What time was this?"

"Well, I didn't look at my clock so I'm not sure . . ."

Ian had interviewed many witnesses over the years who had trouble recalling time. He also knew that she would probably remember more that would trigger her memory on that later, so he let it go.

"Okay, what happened next?"

"I laid there for a minute and then the dogs on the next street started barking – there are several that live over there," she said, pointing to a row of houses the next street over. "So then I got curious. I looked out my bedroom window but couldn't see anything. So, I walked out to the living room and looked out my front window. I could see that Dick's front door was open because his lights were on."

Ian sat forward and turned his body, his knees pointing toward Maryanne, then asked, "Did you see anybody?"

She shook her head. "No, I didn't see anybody – just his door open. His sidewalk was lit up but that may have come from the lights inside. I don't know."

Once again her eyes welled up with tears, her breathing quickened.

"I thought Dick might be hurt . . . like maybe he fell or something, so I went back and put on my robe and then ran over there."

Maryanne stopped talking. She wrapped her arms around her abdomen and doubled over as if she were going to be sick, triggering Ian's next question. He leaned toward her and queried, "Maryanne, did you get sick at Mr. Tate's house?"

She slowly lifted her head and peered at him through puffy eyes. "I felt sick, yes."

"Okay, let me put it this way," said Ian, "did you throw up?"

Maryanne looked at him curiously and answered, "No, I felt like it but no, I didn't. Why?"

Ian didn't answer but continued with his questions. "What did you see when you got there?"

"I saw D-Dick lying on the floor. There was blood everywhere," she described as tears streamed down her face, "and it smelled awful."

Ian was quiet a moment, giving her some time to compose

herself. Trying not to show his discomfort with her tears, he cleared his throat and looked away. He spied a box of tissue on the coffee table so picked it up and offered it to Maryanne. She pulled a few sheets out of the box and used them to dry her eyes and then blew her nose.

Maryanne swallowed hard then continued. "I rushed to the phone and called 911. The woman who answered kept me on the phone until the police . . ." she looked at Ian and then Mike, "um, the other police . . . got there."

"Other than the phone, did you touch anything in Mr. Tate . . . er . . . Dick's house?" asked Ian.

She looked thoughtful and then whispered, "I don't remember."

Ian's head bobbed up and down as he said, "Okay, that's okay. But we'd appreciate it if you could come down to the Sheriff's station tomorrow to be fingerprinted - at your leisure . . . I'm sure you could use some sleep."

Maryanne's eyes grew wide. "Am I a suspect?"

Ian shook his head. "No, not at the moment. Maryanne, you've been very helpful. We just need your fingerprints so we can exclude them. That will, hopefully, help us to distinguish any fingerprints of the person who did this."

She heaved a sigh of relief but then her cheeks reddened. "Oh, okay. I understand. Yeah, I'll go down tomorrow."

Ian handed her his card. "Here's the address. And, Maryanne, if you can think of anything that you think will be helpful, please don't hesitate to call, okay?"

She agreed that she would, then stood and walked them to the door.

Ian reached for the doorknob and then turned back to face

Maryanne. "One other thing . . . you mentioned the smell in the house when you entered . . . can you describe it to me?"

"Bad . . . kind of sour," she said through pursed lips, "not like I would have expected blood to smell at all."

"Could it have been vomit?"

A look of understanding suddenly registered on her face. She raised both eyebrows and murmured, "Ah, that's why you asked me if I had thrown up. You know . . . now that you mention it . . . it could have been vomit. At the time, I thought it was the blood … or the smell of death. Yeah, I think vomit may have been what I smelled."

Mike and Ian thanked her for her time and headed back across the street. Ian noted that, although several reporters were still milling about, the TV crews appeared to have left. He sighed with relief.

"So, what's with the vomit obsession?" Mike asked wryly.

Ian grinned at him. "No obsession. Just wanted to be sure it didn't come from one of San Diego's finest - you know, some rook feeling a little squeamish…" He then reached up, slapped Mike on the back and quipped, "Knowing the way you guzzle alcohol, I had to rule you out as well."

Mike threw back his head and laughed. "Nah, that would be a waste of good booze!"

⸺◦《◉》◦⸺

Buchanan and O'Reilly returned to the crime scene as the body was being lifted into the van that would transport it to the morgue. Sarah Epstein walked out the front door carrying a heavy-looking aluminum case in which she kept her investigative equipment.

The case bounced against her calves as she walked, giving her the look of a small child struggling with a large, full suitcase.

With a gleam in his eyes, Mike walked toward her and inquired, "Need some help with that?"

She stopped and looked up at him. Irritation flashed across her face, her voice dripping with sarcasm as she responded with, "Gee, Detective, I think maybe I can manage all by my little-bitty self. But thanks so much for the offer."

She turned on her heels and stomped away; the case continued its awkward leg thumping.

Mike grinned like a Cheshire cat and said, "She's crazy about me!"

Ian shook his head and chuckled. "Yeah, you're quite the lady killer."

The two squeezed side-by-side through the front door and found the criminalists still working the scene.

Ian snapped on a pair of rubber gloves and spoke out of one side of his mouth. "What say we have a look at the rest of the house?"

Mike reached for his own gloves. "Sounds like a plan."

Mike turned down the hallway toward the bedrooms while Ian headed into the kitchen. A pile of dirty dishes filled the kitchen sink and a half-full wine bottle stood on the counter. Otherwise, Ian was impressed to see the room was fairly neat.

A lighted number two was displayed on the face of an answering machine next to the telephone. Buchanan reached down and pressed the play button. A mechanical male voice said, "You have two old messages," then, "Message one."

He cocked his ear as a male voice emanated from the black plastic box, "Hey Dad, it's me Brett . . . I'm gonna come down this weekend when mom goes to her high school reunion. I thought maybe we could spend the weekend together. Give me a call, okay?"

The mechanical voice followed with, "Tuesday, July fifteenth, 8:23 p.m.," then, "Message two."

This time it was a female voice, "Dickie . . . it's Mom. You said you were going to call me after your dinner with Gina. What happened? Call me as soon as you can. I'm anxious to hear."

"Sunday, July twentieth, 6:15 p.m.," declared the mechanical voice. Ian glanced at his watch, noting that it was now Monday morning.

"Gina, huh? Wonder who Gina is . . ." he muttered. He opened the little door next to the message display light, removed the tape, dropped it into a paper bag and wrote a description on an evidence tag.

A small brown leather-covered book was open on the counter on the other side of the phone. Buchanan picked it up and looked at the open page which had a tab on the edge that read "G". He saw only one entry, *Gallagher, Jordan and Asshole*.

Ian chuckled and murmured, "Something tells me that's either an ex-wife or an old girlfriend."

He flipped through the book until he came to a page full of hand printed addresses and phone numbers for people whose last names began with the letter "T".

He placed his index finger at the top of the page and read, *Tate, Allen & Debbie* . . . Moving both his eyes and finger down the page he saw listings for *Tate, Brett* . . . *Tate, Carter* . . . *Tate, Caitlin (and bitch)* . . . *Tate, Gina* . . . he paused, realizing that this was probably the Gina mentioned on the phone message. He made a mental note of the fact that her phone number was local, then continued reading, *Tate, Miriam (Mom)* . . . *Tate, Richard (Dad)* . . . The list went on to enumerate several more Tates.

Buchanan snapped the book shut, then pulled out his notepad and made notations as to the condition and position of the book when he found it.

He was just finishing when Mike entered the room. Pointing over his shoulder with his thumb, he said, "You gotta see this…"

Ian peered up at his partner. "See what?" then without giving Mike the chance to respond, held up the address book and said, "I think we got next of kin in here . . . along with a few interesting side notes."

O'Reilly cocked an eyebrow, "Oh, yeah?"

"We can get to that later . . . what are you so amused about?"

With what appeared to be a mix of fascination and self-satisfaction, Mike bounced on his toes and said, "I'm beginning to think our vic was a fucking nutcase. C'mere!" He motioned for Ian to follow him, spun on the balls of his feet and headed toward the back of the house.

"Now there's something to cheer about!" Buchanan muttered sardonically as he trailed behind his partner.

As they walked past the bathroom Ian held his breath in anticipation but found the odor had diminished substantially. Black fingerprint powder was scattered across the floor, making it apparent the criminalists had finished their collection of evidence in that area. Mike led him to the first of two bedrooms and stood in the doorway allowing Ian to enter first.

The room was obviously a home office. A large oak desk sat below a window that covered the width of the back wall and nearly half the height. To the left of the desk was a small table that housed a computer and printer.

Buchanan turned to face the wall opposite the desk. It was covered with large photos; he walked over to get a closer look. Ian noticed that two different women were portrayed in the photos and that all the pictures appeared to have been taken from afar. One of the women pictured was a short redhead and was accompanied by a young girl who looked to be about 12 or 13 years old; another displayed a tall blonde woman with her arm around a man. The man's face had been scratched out with a black ink pen, leaving deep grooves and some tears in the paper.

"Neither of these women seems aware of a camera," Ian murmured, "and the pix look as though they were taken by a professional . . . maybe a PI?"

Mike's head bobbed up and down as he said, "Yeah that was my thought." He walked over and pointed at a photo of the woman who had been with a man in the other picture. "On this one, he wrote the word bitch across her face – what does that tell you?"

Buchanan was thoughtful for a moment and then softly uttered, "Interesting." Looking up at Mike, Ian proceeded to tell him about his findings in the address book.

"I was just getting ready to hit redial on the kitchen phone when you walked in," he explained.

Buchanan glanced at his watch to find it was now 9:45 in the morning. Satisfied that it was not too early, he motioned toward the office phone with a jut of his chin.

Grasping Ian's subtle hint, Mike walked over and picked up the telephone receiver. He studied it for a moment and then pressed a button. Ian looked on in anticipation.

Mikes' eyes suddenly lit up and he spoke into the phone. "Yes, this is Detective O'Reilly with the San Diego Sheriff's Department . . . may I ask who I'm speaking with?"

He was quiet a moment, then said, "No Ma'am, as far as I know your children are fine. Actually, I'm calling about a Mr. Richard Tate . . . can you tell me how you know him?

"Uh huh, oh I see . . . your ex-husband? Yes Ma'am, well I'm sorry to have to inform you that he's been murdered."

O'Reilly glanced at Buchanan, who had begun to roll his fingers against his palm, and smiled. Then his face grew dark as he spoke into the phone again. "I see. Yes, we would like to speak with you further." Another pause. "Well Ma'am, you never can tell." He stopped and then nodded as if the woman on the other end could see him. "Okay, we'll be in touch. Yes Ma'am, thank you."

Shaking his head while hanging up the phone, Mike peered at Ian.

"Well?" Ian exhorted, "what the hell did she say?"

Mike cocked an eyebrow and related, "Her name's Meg. As you heard, she's his ex-wife . . . She said the bastard finally got what he deserved."

Ian's eyes grew wide. "No shit?" A hesitant smile touched his lips as he asked, "You're thinking *suspect*?"

Mike didn't answer. The partners stood and looked at each other for a minute. Both were fully aware that homicide statistics lean heavily toward male perpetrators and that the rare case in which a woman committed murder was usually in self defense. They also knew there were exceptions to every rule.

"If so," said Buchanan, "defense attorneys will be chomping at the bit to take this one on."

Mike nodded and muttered, "No shit."

"Tell you what," offered Ian, "while you finish up in here, I'll try the phone in the kitchen. I'm assuming you haven't checked the bedroom yet?"

Mike shook his head.

"Okay, I'll be back . . ." Ian threw over his shoulder as he started out the door, "then we'll take a look . . ."

Buchanan walked back down the hallway, re-entered the kitchen and immediately reached for the phone. He found the re-dial button and pressed it. He looked at the digital readout as the phone automatically dialed the number. It was long distance. It rang twice before a woman answered. Like his partner, Ian explained who he was and asked her name.

"This is Miriam Tate . . . what's this about?" the woman asked nervously.

Ian instantly recalled her name from the address book and realized he was speaking with the victim's mother. Clinching his eyes shut, he began to massage his forehead. This was the thing he hated most about his job. He gingerly explained the situation. The woman gasped but, to his relief, did not become hysterical.

"I'll get a flight down as soon as possible," she spoke rapidly, her voice shrill. "I'll have to find someone to take care of my dog . . . I guess I should call the other kids . . . oh, and my boss . . . she's not gonna like this . . ."

Buchanan waited while the woman related her "to do" list as if she were preparing for vacation. He found her demeanor somewhat disconcerting. Now he almost wished she had been hysterical, if only because it would have seemed a more natural response from a mother.

When she finally took a breath, Ian expressed sympathy for her loss then asked, "Mrs. Tate, who is Gina?"

The phone was suddenly quiet. Just as he began to wonder if

she were still on the line, she softly answered, "One of Dickie's ex-wives . . . why?"

He explained about hearing her message on the answering machine. He thanked her and started to say goodbye, but before he could end the conversation she interrupted by blurting, "They finally did it . . . those evil women . . . one of them is responsible for this, I just know it!"

Ian's ears perked up. If she had reached through the phone and grabbed him by the collar, she couldn't have seized his attention any better.

"Who are you talking about?"

He heard a long sigh as though she were exasperated with his ignorance.

"One of those women he married . . . Dickie was . . . addicted to marriage . . ." she continued without taking a breath, "they're just awful people . . . but they're all going to burn in hell anyway . . ."

Sorry I asked, Ian thought, as she continued her rant.

Finally, no longer able to contain himself, he raised his voice. "Yes Ma'am, I understand and we certainly want to discuss this with you further . . . "

Miriam became quiet so he persevered, "Please call as soon as you get into town."

He explained how she could reach him, then quickly said goodbye and hung up the phone. He was standing in the middle of the kitchen pondering her words when he heard Mike say, "Earth to Buchanan . . ." He slowly raised his head and peered up at his partner.

"Where were you?" asked O'Reilly.

Ian shook his head to clear the fog. "I was talking to the vic's mother. She's flying down from Sacramento." A slow smile formed on his lips as he said, "I don't think she likes me much so I'm gonna let you interview her . . ."

Mike grinned sideways. "What's wrong with her?"

Buchanan burst into laughter and slapped his partner on the back. "Haven't I warned you about taking this detective thing too far? You're so suspicious . . . geez!"

The two men searched the bedroom together. The only thing of interest they found was a framed picture of the same blonde woman portrayed in the photos discovered in the victim's office. This one was in the top drawer of the bedside table. As with the others, the picture had been taken from a distance, but in this one she was alone.

Ian studied the picture for a moment then wondered aloud, "Could this be Gina?"

Mike peered over Ian's shoulder and said, "Well, whoever she is, this guy has some kind of obsession with her . . ."

"This is one area in which *Mommy Dearest* can be of assistance," remarked Buchanan as he slid the wooden frame and its picture into a paper evidence bag.

O'Reilly grinned and said, "*Mommy Dearest*, huh? I thought you said there was nothing wrong with her!"

Ian turned his back to his partner to hide the smile on his face. "Why, I do believe your cynicism is showing again . . . you assume I wasn't just using a term of endearment?" he bantered.

Eying the remote-style phone on the bedside table, Buchanan changed the subject. "You know this redial thing has been fairly helpful . . . shall we give this one a shot?"

"Go for it," replied Mike.

Ian picked up the receiver. Once again, the detective pressed the redial button and for a second time the digital readout indicated a long distance number. He waited through five rings before a machine answered. A woman's voice invited him to leave a message.

He began speaking to the machine, "Yes, this is Detective Ian Buchanan with the San Diego Sheriff's Department. . ." when he was abruptly interrupted by a male voice on the other end.

"This is Nick Gallagher," the man said, anxiety evident in his voice, "what's happened?"

In an attempt to calm the man, Buchanan softened his tone. "Nothing to panic about, Sir . . ."

"Is my wife, okay?" the man asked with seeming dread.

"I'm sure she is . . . Sir, I am not calling about your wife . . . Actually, I'm trying to find out your connection to Richard Tate. . . ."

After an audible sigh, Gallagher said, "The son of a bitch is my wife's ex-husband . . ."

"I see," said Buchanan, "I take it the relationship was not amicable?"

"Hardly, the guys a lunatic . . ." Nick started then paused before asking, "Detective, what's going on? Why are you investigating Dick? What did he do?"

"Well, he went and got himself murdered," replied Ian.

There was a long silence before Gallagher murmured, "Oh . . . shit."

"Yeah, well, from the sound of things, I have the feeling this won't be devastating news to your wife," declared Ian. "I'd like to talk to her . . . Where can I reach her?"

"She – she should be on her way home from San Diego . . ."

Gallagher stopped in mid- sentence.

Buchanan picked up on his hesitation. "Your wife has been in San Diego? Where do you live?"

"For her high school reunion . . . We live in Sacramento," the man said tentatively, "I, uh . . . if you give me your phone number, I'll have my wife get in touch with you."

"That would be a good idea," Ian said, "the sooner the better. In fact, if you can, you might want to try to reach her before she gets home. We'll probably need to speak with her at length and it would be simpler for all if she were here in San Diego."

Gallagher said he would try then asked, "You don't think Jordan had anything to do with this, do you? I mean, that's impossible . . ."

"Mr. Gallagher, we've just begun the investigation and will be talking to anybody and everybody who might be able to provide clues as to who might have done this. That includes your wife - Jordan, you said?"

Before Nick could respond, Ian inquired, "By the way, were there children from their marriage?"

"Yes," answered Gallagher quietly, "two boys . . . One is with my wife. I'll call the other one . . . It might be better if he heard this from me."

"That'll be fine," Buchanan agreed, "but we'll want to talk to them as well."

Ian relayed his phone number and then asked, "One other thing . . . have any idea why Mr. Tate would have called your home recently?"

Raising his voice, Nick growled, "Who the hell knows with that maniac? Somebody has been calling here and hanging up for years . . . we always suspected it was him."

"Could your wife have spoken to him?" Ian asked casually.

"Not on your life, Detective," Gallagher answered hotly, "Jordan hasn't spoken to him for a very long time . . . and believe me, if she did she would have told me about it. She detests the man."

"I see."

"But not enough to kill him," Nick immediately added, "if that's what you're thinking."

Ian quickly responded, "I'll be looking forward to hearing from Mrs. Gallagher. Thanks very much." Without hesitation, he gently placed the phone back on its base.

"Another ex-wife?" Mike asked from behind him.

"Yeah . . . another one that thinks highly of him too," Buchanan remarked wryly, "and this one just happened to have been in San Diego this weekend."

"Holy shit, that means three ex-wives so far . . ." O'Reilly marveled, "Wonder how many more we're gonna run across!"

"Well, according to the vic's mother, he was . . . how did she put it . . . addicted to marriage?" Ian replied. "And in the meantime, our suspect list grows."

Buchanan's lips stretched to their limit as he yawned noisily. He raised his arm to get a better look at his watch. "No wonder I'm so fucking tired," he declared, "It's twelve twenty! Let's get the hell outta here. I could use some coffee – and some food too, come to think of it."

"I could use a beer, myself," O'Reilly remarked, then seeing Ian's furrowed brow added, "But we're on a case and upstanding guy that I am, I'll wait – at least until the cocktail hour!"

Although Ian was concerned that Mike's drinking was getting out of hand and had expressed as much, he couldn't help but chuckle at his partner's words. "What a guy!" he joked.

Chapter 3
July 22, 2003

After re-energizing themselves with food, Detectives Buchanan and O'Reilly had spent the previous afternoon pouring over Richard Tate's address book. They'd also left a message for Gina Tate and were hoping for a return phone call soon.

Jordan Gallagher had called shortly after Ian spoke with her husband and left her cell phone number with Cheryl, the Detective Secretary. When Ian returned her call, she was at her home in Sacramento. Much to his disappointment, Jordan told him she'd be unable to return to San Diego for several days, saying she would wait until her husband could accompany her.

He couldn't tell if the distress he'd detected in her voice was over the death of her ex-husband or out of concern for herself. That was just one of the reasons he was anxious to talk to her face-to-face. He'd expressed that desire to his Sergeant this morning. But when he'd asked for permission to get on a plane to Sacramento so he could interview her sooner, Sergeant Moore had reminded him of the county's shrinking budget.

"I understand your urgency," Moore had told him, "but it's not as if you don't have other people, including suspects, to interview . . . at least this one is cooperating so you know she isn't going anywhere. Sorry, Detective."

Now, as he ruminated over his frustration with one of the victim's ex-wives, he was informed that another was on the phone.

He grabbed for the handset and barked, "Detective Buchanan."

A woman's voice with a slight Latin accent said, "Detective, this is Gina Rodriguez. Why are you calling me?"

He was taken aback by her name.

"Uh, Miss Rodriguez, are you the same Gina who used to be married to Richard Tate?"

Her voice took on an adversarial tone as she replied, "Yes . . . a very long time ago." Then, after a brief pause, inquired, "Why, what's happened to Dick?"

Mike, returning from the break room with a cup of coffee, raised a questioning eyebrow in Ian's direction. He responded by raising one finger as if to say, *hold on a minute.*

A smirk settled on Buchanan's lips as he redirected his attention to the woman on the phone. "What makes you think something happened to your ex-husband, Gina?" he asked, placing emphasis on her name for his partner's benefit.

Mike's eyes widened. He perched himself on the edge of Ian's desk to better hear Ian's side of the conversation.

"Because," Gina shot back, "You are the Sheriff, no? You are asking me these questions . . . so either something happened to him or he committed a crime!"

"I see," he said charily.

"So are you going to tell me?" she asked tersely.

Buchanan cleared his throat.

"Yes Ma'am. As a matter of fact, I'm a Homicide detective with the Sheriff's department. Dick is dead."

The line went silent.

Just as he started to ask if she was still there, he heard her whisper, simply, "How?"

"Well, it appears he's been murdered . . ."

Gina's voice cracked as she began to ramble, "What do you want with me . . . why are you calling me . . . why aren't you out there finding the person that did this?"

Buchanan interrupted. "Gina, calm down. This is routine. In order to find out who did this, we need to talk to anyone who knew him well. You were married to the man . . . you can help us."

"Are you talking to his other wives?" she asked curtly.

He continued to speak softly, replying, "Yes, we are."

"Okay," she spoke again, raising her voice an octave, "When? . . . I'll have to plan it around my work schedule."

"Sure, I understand. What would be a good time for you to-day or tomorrow?"

They arranged to meet at her home, which was located on Coronado Island, at 7:00 that evening. After jotting down the directions, Ian said goodbye and hung up. Turning to Mike he said, "Shit, I have the feeling this one's gonna be a tough nut to crack."

Buchanan had just begun to describe Gina's demeanor when his phone rang. He answered in typical brusque fashion. This time it was the receptionist informing him that a Mrs. Tate was there to see him.

"Oh?" he responded, "Okay, I'll be right there."

"I'm not sure which Mrs. Tate it is, but one of them is out front," he explained to Mike. He turned and walked out of the office toward the stairs that would take him down to the reception area.

Upon reaching the landing at the bottom of the staircase, his eyes scanned the room, settling on a gray-haired woman who looked to be at least seventy. She was busy cleaning her glasses with a soft cloth. Since the woman was the only visitor in the lobby, he assumed this was his caller. As he walked toward her, she stood up.

"Mrs. Tate?" he inquired.

"Call me Miriam," she replied as she shook his outreached hand.

"Nice to meet you . . . I'm Detective Buchanan."

Miriam nodded. "Have you found my son's killer yet?"

Pointing in the direction of the staircase he said, "Uh, no Ma'am . . . tell you what, though, let's go upstairs and we'll fill you in on what we know so far. I'm sure you also have a lot of information that will be helpful to the case . . ."

Miriam ascended the stairs first. When she reached the top, she turned to him as if to say, *now where?*

Buchanan led her into a room so small they had to walk sideways to reach one of the metal chairs encircling a large, gray table. He invited her to sit and then told her he would fetch his partner and return, but Mike's sudden appearance in the doorway, armed with legal pads and a tape recorder, made that unnecessary.

After Ian made the introductions, all three sat at the table - Miriam on one side and the detectives on the other. Buchanan nodded at his partner to indicate he wanted him to handle this interview.

"I just got in," said Miriam with a sigh, "and I'm tired. So I hope this won't take too long. The rest of my family will be here tomorrow and I have a funeral to plan."

"Uh, yes Ma'am, we understand and may I say that I'm very sorry for your loss," O'Reilly murmured, deep compassion etched on his face.

Buchanan smiled inwardly at the caring posture Mike had affected. His partner had a fairly cavalier attitude toward life in general so Ian knew this was mostly an act. He'd seen O'Reilly use this approach often when speaking to witnesses - or anyone else he thought could help solve a case - and although Ian recognized the phoniness of Mike's tactics, he'd seen them work time and time again.

It appeared to have the desired effect on Miriam Tate as she gazed into Mike's eyes, her lips curling into a curious smile. "Thank you," she uttered softly.

Buchanan placed his hands behind his head and leaned back in his chair while Mike continued, "Now, Mrs. Tate, I understand you believe that one of your son's former wives may have had something to do with his demise."

The smile vanished from her face. She sat up rigidly, her muscles tensing before their eyes. "I don't just believe it, Detective, I'm sure of it," she said sharply.

"Okay." Mike tilted his upper body in her direction. "Please explain what makes you so certain?"

"Well, they've gone out of their way to make him miserable. The first two, that would be Jordan and Meg, have made it nearly impossible for him to see his kids, all the while demanding more money."

O'Reilly smiled at her and suggested, "Why don't we back this up a bit. Give us the background on these women . . . I mean, when he was married to them and for how long, how many kids

– that type of thing, okay?"

Miriam dipped her head in acknowledgement of his request then began to narrate her version of Dick's marriages.

Jordan had been his first wife, she told them. The marriage had lasted three or four years and had produced two children – boys named Carter and Brett, both of whom were now grown men. According to Miriam, Jordan was the worst of the three wives. She described a vicious woman who had sued Dick for child support increases on a regular basis, taking him to court at least ten times. In addition, Miriam reported, Jordan had kept Dick from seeing the children and had poisoned their minds against their father.

Ian interrupted at this point to say, "Miriam, there was a message on Dick's answering machine from his son, Brett. I didn't get the impression of any animosity there . . . "

"Well, no, not now. Once the boys grew up they began to see what kind of person their mother truly is. They both love their father. But you see, that's one of the main reasons she hated Dick so much. There was no end to that woman's vengeance."

Mike placed his hand atop Miriam's and in soothing tones asked, "So you think Jordan hated him so much she was driven to kill him?"

"Yes," she answered.

"More so than his other wives?"

Miriam shrugged and hastily said, "Ah, they are all a bunch of heathens, who knows what any of them are capable of." Then, in an offhanded manner, she added, "You know Dickie told me that Jordan and Meg were friends . . . maybe the two of them conspired against him!"

"Tell us about Meg," Mike prodded. Ian knew his partner was

anxious to know more about this wife because they had set an interview with her for the following day.

According to Miriam, Dick had married Meg soon after his divorce from Jordan was final. Meg had a son from a previous marriage whom Miriam said she didn't know very well. A few years into their marriage, she'd given birth to their daughter Caitlin, who was now about seventeen years old. Dick's mother went on to describe a spiteful woman who had virtually denied Dick any access to his daughter.

"He rarely even speaks to her," she lamented, "and it's all because of that woman."

"In this case, it sounds like she won," Ian pointed out. "I mean Meg succeeded in keeping him away from his daughter . . . so why do you think she'd be motivated to kill him?"

Miriam turned her eyes toward him and in a conspiratorial tone said, "Well, as a matter of fact Detective Buchanan, I happen to know she threatened him. She said he was traumatizing the girl. Dickie told her he was going to take her to court again and, because she was in violation of the court order, he would get custody of Caitlin."

A smug smile crept onto her lips. "You know what her response was to that?" she asked rhetorically, "She said . . . 'over your dead body!'"

"Okay," Mike murmured, "It sounds like neither Jordan nor Meg was very fond of your son. Explain how Gina fits in here."

Before she could answer, Ian interjected, "That reminds me Miriam . . . I heard your message on Dick's answering machine, the one where you were asking him about his dinner with Gina . . ."

"Oh that," she remarked with a toss of her hand, "Gina recently returned to San Diego. Dickie said he had talked to her and that they were going to have dinner. He seemed to think there was a chance for reconciliation."

"Returned from where?"

"Well, from . . . I don't know . . . she went to Puerto Rico right after they split up, then I don't know where the Navy sent her. Dick told me she'd returned to the San Diego area a couple of months ago." She shrugged.

"I see . . . and when was this dinner supposed to happen?"

Glancing down at the table, Miriam lowered her voice and replied, "This weekend . . . I don't know which day."

Ian threw a knowing look in Mike's direction then sat back in his chair and waited for his partner to continue the interview.

O'Reilly acknowledged Ian's look with a nod of the head then turned to Miriam and prodded, "Okay, tell us about your son's relationship with Gina."

Gina, Miriam told them, was Dick's third and last marriage. When he met her, Dick was still in the Navy, as was Gina. At the time they were both stationed at Coronado Naval Air Station. Miriam seemed to think that Dick's relationship with Gina had been the least stressful.

From her tone and the way she described her interactions with Gina, it was apparent to Ian that Miriam had felt kindly toward her daughter-in-law and that surprised him.

Ian didn't like this woman. He found her cold and her behavior odd. Compared to the hundreds of grieving family members he had dealt with over the years, Miriam Tate was a definite anomaly.

"I know my son began to drink too much during their marriage and though I didn't approve, I could understand. Because of Meg and Jordan, his life had become hell on earth," she defended.

"Although Gina loved him, she couldn't take anymore so she left."

"You see," she continued, "he had even lost some of his faith . . . but over the past few years he has returned to the church. So, he was ready to make amends to Gina. He planned to talk to her about that over dinner."

"Do you know if he actually had dinner with her?" Mike inquired.

Miriam shook her head, "No, I don't. Dickie didn't return my call." She shrugged.

Buchanan sat up in his chair and questioned, "Are you including Gina when you say one of his ex-wives murdered your son?"

Miriam's head jerked in Ian's direction, her eyes rounded as though mystified by his question. Then she averted her eyes and spoke so quietly he had to strain to hear her, "Dickie told me that the day Gina left she threatened his life."

Ian glanced over at Mike. O'Reilly's eyes were trained on the ceiling in introspection; his index fingers pressed together, tapping against pursed lips. An awkward silence ensued.

Ian briefly explained their planned course of action, telling Miriam about their appointments with Dick's ex-wives – or in Jordan's case, an expectation of one.

At her request, the detective recommended a nearby hotel. He thanked her for coming in and asked her to keep him informed of funeral arrangements, letting her know he planned to attend.

Chapter 4
July 22, 2003

Buchanan and O'Reilly ate sandwiches at their desks, leaving their office at 6:40 for their meeting with Gina. While driving south on I-15, the two detectives reviewed the evidence they had accumulated so far.

"We still don't have anything on the latents lifted at the scene." Ian lamented. "In fact both Ritter and Li are working hard to get the forensics data pushed through the lab but as usual they're overwhelmed."

"Yeah well, this isn't a heater case so it's been pushed to the back burner. But as you well know, our crime lab is one of the best – they're worth waiting for," said Mike.

"Oh hell yeah," Buchanan replied, "Shit, you and I don't need any fucking statistics to tell us that crime in this county is at an all time high. But that doesn't alleviate my frustration at having to wait."

Mike nodded his head in somber agreement. "If it helps any . . . Ritter told me he sent the vomit sample from the scene to the DNA lab for testing. So, as soon as the M.E. forwards samples from the victim, they can run the comparison tests," he explained.

At least that way we'll know whether or not it came from him," O'Reilly added, then grinned as he quipped, "I know how important this puke issue is to you!

Buchanan chuckled as he merged the Taurus onto I-5 headed north.

"Well, that'll probably take weeks to get as well," he muttered. "And something tells me that our vic's not responsible for the puke. That means we'll have to obtain a DNA sample from our suspects in order to place them at the scene, which will no doubt turn into a legal battle. We can only hope that none of these ex-wives run out and get themselves an attorney and dummy up on us too soon."

"Fucking attorneys," Mike uttered with a shake of the head, adding, "They might even be worse than reporters."

Buchanan parallel parked on Isabelle Avenue, about a block from Gina's home. As the two detectives approached the front door, a gentle breeze wafted from the ocean and fluttered softly across the veranda that graced the front of the cottage; wisps of air delicately danced around their heads and softly tickled their faces and necks. A profound sigh escaped through Ian's lips as he breathed deeply and sniffed the fresh, salty air with appreciation.

Ian turned to his partner, and with rare sensitivity murmured, "How could anyone who woke to this every morning possibly be guilty of murder?" He swept his arm toward the beach.

Mike smiled back and answered abstractedly, "Makes you

wonder, don't it . . .?" then reached up and pressed the doorbell button.

Within moments the door opened and they were greeted by a dark-haired woman with a slight but athletic build, still dressed in her naval uniform. The detectives displayed their badges then introduced themselves.

Gina glanced at her watch and declared, "You're right on time, Detectives. Please come in. I'm afraid I only arrived home a few minutes ago and have not had time to change."

Ian eyed the silver oak leaf on her khaki uniform collar signifying her commander's rank. "We'd be happy to wait if you'd like to change. It's been awhile since I've worn a uniform but I do remember how much I enjoyed getting out of it at the end of the day."

She smiled stiffly. "Thank you . . . I'll feel much more comfortable once I've done that. May I get you something to drink while you wait?"

Both detectives declined her offer and made themselves comfortable on the brown leather sofa in her living room. While they waited for her to rejoin them, Buchanan took in the room's décor of earth tones, ornate wrought iron and Latin memorabilia and was inwardly surprised to find what he considered somewhat masculine furnishings.

Gina returned a few minutes later with her long black hair flowing over her shoulders. She wore a red and white striped tank top with matching running shorts. Ian glanced in Mike's direction and, as expected, saw his partner ogling Gina's tanned legs. Gina's look of discomfort indicated she'd also noticed his stare.

She quickly walked over and dropped onto a brown leather easy chair and turned to face Ian.

"How can I help you, Detective?"

Ian scooted forward until he was barely perched on the edge of the sofa and somberly replied, "You can start by telling me when you last saw Richard Tate. . ."

Gina answered quickly, "That's easy . . . nine years ago when I left him."

She sat back in the chair, crossed her legs and folded her arms across her chest. The large chair dwarfed her, giving her the appearance of a small child playing at being a grown-up.

"Really? Was that when you went to Puerto Rico?"

Gina's eyes widened and she asked uneasily, "How did you know that?"

"Well Ma'am, it's my job to know these things . . . I'll take that as a yes." "When did you return to San Diego?"

Her jaw set stubbornly as she leaned forward, her arms still crossed. "Well Detective, since you know so much, why don't you tell me?" she challenged haughtily.

Ian was rapidly becoming aware that this woman liked to remain in control. Out of concern that she would view him as the enemy and clam up, he softened his tone and smiled at her.

"I'm sorry, Ma'am, I didn't mean to be flip with you. Let's start over, shall we?" He shifted his eyes in Mike's direction.

O'Reilly, who was seated at the other end of the sofa, got his partner's drift and spoke up. "I love Puerto Rico. I vacation there all the time . . ."

Gina's brow furrowed as she glanced at Mike. Flipping her hair over her shoulder, she abruptly turned her body toward Ian in an overt attempt to ignore Mike.

Ian realized his partner had blown it earlier with his lascivious stares, thus effectively disabling their ability to play *good cop, bad cop.* He frowned at his partner then awarded Gina with the most ingratiating smile he could muster.

Her shoulders lifted as she sighed heavily. A reluctant smile formed on her lips.

"After Puerto Rico, I was assigned to the Pentagon for three years. From there, I went to Whidbey Island, in Washington. Three months ago, I returned to Coronado. . . Okay?" she asked smugly.

Buchanan nodded. "And how long after that did you talk to Dick?"

Gina started to speak then stopped, *as if,* Ian thought, *catching herself.* Her eyes narrowed when she looked up at him and cagily asserted, "I told you . . . I haven't spoken to him for nine years."

"So you said." He paused and scratched his head in feigned puzzlement before uttering, "It's just that his mother . . . is under the impression you and Dick had a dinner date this weekend."

Gina's head jerked up so quickly Ian was surprised she didn't get whiplash. She shook her head from side to side then firmly declared, "I did not have dinner with Dick. As I said, I have not spoken to the man for nine years."

Glancing to his right, Ian caught a glimpse of Mike's facial expression, one of obvious disbelief.

"I understand," murmured Buchanan. A brief silence ensued.

Ian cleared his throat then gingerly asked, "Would you mind describing your marriage to Dick . . . including why you're no longer married?"

He couldn't have been more surprised when she agreed.

~ GINA ~

"O woman, woman, when to ill thy mind
Is bent, all hell contains no fouler fiend."

Homer
The Odyssey XI, 1.531

Chapter 5
Coronado Island, California;
Spring, 1989

Gina leaned over and touched her toes, then came back up, arching her back and raising her arms above her head. This was part of the warm up routine she went through each day before her early morning run.

It was important to her to stay in shape and she loved to run, especially along the ocean shoreline. She started running on the beach in her beloved Puerto Rico while in high school, one of only two girls on the cross-country team. Gina was used to being a "minority" female on *the team* – whether with sports or in her military career.

Her running abilities had helped her in the ROTC program at the University of Puerto Rico as well. There she was the *only* woman in the program. She shook her head, remembering the smirks on her fellow cadet's faces as they looked her up and down, as though she was there for their pleasure.

Like dogs in heat, she thought.

As though she would have anything to do with the likes of them! After all, she reminded herself, *she was a princess.*

Although unable to prove it, Gina had been told by her great Uncle Miguel that she descended from royal blood. He told her that her name, Regina, meant "queenly" and she should always remember that. She didn't disappoint him. Gina knew she was regal and lorded it over anyone who deigned to get in her way. She also had a temper. Make her angry and she would come at you like a lioness protecting her cubs.

As Gina reached down to tighten the laces on her running shoes, she was startled by a man's voice behind her.

"Now there's a true athlete for you. Knows how important it is to warm up the ol' muscles before hitting the track."

Swinging her head up and around, Gina looked into the bluest eyes she had ever seen. She rebuked herself for gazing at him with what must be a sappy-looking grin.

"I'm Dick," he said, reaching his hand out for her to shake.

Although she responded with a firm handshake, she was surprised by the tremor in her voice as she answered, "Gina Rodriguez".

What is wrong with me? she thought. *Geesh, you're acting like one of those silly Anglo bimbos who hang out at the O' Club hoping to hook a Navy pilot!*

"I was just getting ready to take a quick jog along the waterfront,' Dick offered. "Care to join me?"

"Want to race?" Gina challenged.

"You're on!" Dick responded with a chuckle.

Gina noticed he wasn't still laughing after she quickly beat him to the edge of the pier.

"Okay, Mister, want me to slow it down a bit?" Gina teased.

Dick was leaning over, breathing heavily. He glanced up at her and nodded.

As they continued their run, Dick told Gina he was a pilot attached to HS-4, an anti-submarine squadron better known as the Black Knights. She watched his chest puff up with pride as he described the SH-60 Seahawk helicopter he flew for the Navy.

"The Seahawk evolved from the Sikorsky-built UH-60A Black Hawk which is flown by the Army," he explained. "Better known as the LAMPS - which stands for Light Airborne Multipurpose System - Mk III helicopter, it provides all-weather capability for detection, classification, localization, and interdiction of ships and submarines. Its secondary missions include search and rescue, medical evacuation, fleet support, and communications relay."

"Only the best helicopter pilots are allowed to fly this machine," he boasted.

It wasn't until the end of their six-mile run, outside the base gymnasium, that Dick asked anything about her. She didn't mind, though, for she was totally taken with this self-assured, cocky guy. Gina was thrilled when he asked her if she would have dinner with him that weekend.

"Then you can tell me all about yourself!" he exclaimed with a grin so big his gums showed.

After discovering they both resided in the Bachelor Officer's Quarters and arranging to pick Gina up at 6:00 on Saturday evening, Dick swaggered toward the men's locker room throwing her another grin over his shoulder.

Not a bad start to this assignment, Gina reflected as she released her gleaming black hair from its pony tail.

<hr>

Gina tried to hide her disappointment with Dick's choice of

restaurants. Although the rustic Ocean Beach café had an unso-
phisticated charm, this was their first date and she thought he
might try a little harder to impress her.

The menu was written in colored chalk on a blackboard hanging on the wall behind a dingy counter that appeared unchanged
since it was originally built – probably sometime in the 1930s or
'40s. It was a good thing she liked seafood, Gina thought, since
that's what her choices were limited to.

After ordering their meals, scallops for Gina, halibut for Dick,
she explained that she had only arrived in Southern California
three weeks ago. As a Lieutenant previously stationed at the Naval
Training Center in Great Lakes, Illinois, she was now the aide to
Admiral Harry Miller at Naval Air Station, North Island.

True to form, Gina had studied up on her future Navy home
soon after receiving her orders. She related some of her findings
to Dick, starting with the fact that the 5,000-acre air station en-
compasses the city of Coronado from the entrance to San Diego
Bay to the Mexican border.

He listened as she went on to explain that North Island derived its name from the original geography. In the 1800s, the sand
flat was referred to as North Coronado Island. The Coronado
Beach Company purchased Coronado Island for development of
a residential resort in 1886. Famous for its Hotel del Coronado,
the southern part of the island became known as the city of
Coronado. North Coronado wasn't developed, but leased to the
owner and operator of a flying school until the beginning of
World War I.

North Island is known as the *Birthplace of Naval Aviation*. The
Navy began training pilots there as early as 1911 – just eight years
after Orville and Wilbur Wright flew the first manned aircraft at

Kitty Hawk, North Carolina.

In 1914, an aircraft builder named Glenn Martin took off and demonstrated his pusher aircraft over the island with a flight that included the first parachute jump in the San Diego area. The jump was made by a ninety-pound civilian woman named Tiny Broadwick – to Gina one of the most interesting facts she uncovered.

"Yeah well, one thing I know is that American Navy pilots are the best in the world and I'm proud to be one of 'em,'" Dick added.

Gina smiled inwardly. She was competitive by nature and particularly enjoyed it when she could outsmart a man. She told herself to go slow with this one, though, because she liked him and didn't want him to run the other way just because she was smarter than he. And she *was* smarter, she told herself. She was brainier than most men, except maybe her father.

Gina's father, who was a language professor at the University of Puerto Rico, had insisted that Gina and her brothers learn to speak several languages. So, in addition to Portuguese, her native language, she was fluent in Spanish, English and French. Except for her Latin accent, no one would have known that Gina had not been born and raised in the continental United States.

After dinner, Dick suggested they drive back over to Coronado Island for a stroll on the beach.

While Dick maneuvered his grey Toyota Celica over the Bay Bridge, Gina marveled at the panoramic view - a spectacular array of pinks and lavenders from the setting sun cast a halo over the Pacific Ocean.

Central Beach, the site of Dick and Gina's morning run earlier that week, lies between the Hotel del Coronado and the naval air station. Flat, wide and expansive, the one-and-a- half-mile-beach has long been a popular running spot for Navy personnel.

Listening as the waves slapped against the shore, Gina could almost imagine she was home in Puerto Rico. A sudden chill in the air that brought goose bumps to her arms and set her teeth to chattering told her otherwise. Dick saw her shiver and placed an arm snugly around her shoulders. Gina nestled into him and felt the warmth flow through her body.

"I grew up in Napa Valley but graduated from high school in Alameda, which is up north, near San Francisco. Last year, my dad retired from E. F. Hutton, where he was a very successful stock broker," Dick related as they walked.

Gina listened with contentment, as she watched the final remnants of the amoeba-shaped sun disappear over the horizon.

He told her he had attended San Jose State University on a swimming scholarship.

"I didn't need my college paid for. My ol' man could afford to send me to college but he was a San Jose State alumnus and got a kick out of me attending the same school."

After describing his brief stint as an Army helicopter pilot and his Navy career, Dick told Gina about his two previous marriages and his children.

"My kids are great, but I'm not sure why, since they are being raised by a couple of real bitches."

Gina was a bit taken back by the venom with which Dick described his ex-wives but judging by the pain in his eyes as he spoke, supposed that it was deserved. She sensed that he had truly suffered at the hands of these women. Because of how important her father was to her, she began to resent these two strangers as Dick told her of their efforts to keep him from his offspring.

"I would go for custody and probably win if I were married," he claimed, plopping down on the sand, "But, as long as I'm not, no judge will let me have them – no matter what those bitches do or say to *my* kids!"

Dick reached up and grabbed Gina's hand to pull her down beside him.

"It really hurts me so much not to be able to spend more time with my kids. But both those bitches do everything they can to get back at me for leaving. I thought about staying for my kids' sake but they were suffering so much seeing us fight all the time. If I had had any idea that either one of my ex-wives woulda taken' it out on my kids, I swear I woulda stayed! Shit, my first wife won't even let my sons talk to me on the phone. I can hear them in the background begging to talk to me, too!" he raged.

Gina placed her hand on his shoulder and peered into his deep blue eyes.

"It's not right," she said, "every father should be able to be with his kids. My Papa is very important to me, I know. I'm sure your kids want to be with you – their mamas should not do this to them!"

Dick smiled at her, but she sensed his suffering and felt a pain in her heart.

Chapter 6
Spring; 1989

Over the next few months, Gina and Dick spent all their spare time together. They had even traveled to Sacramento to meet Dick's mother. Coincidentally, that's also where his children from his first marriage lived.

Dick had arranged to have his two sons there for the weekend. Surprised because she had heard time and again about his inability to see his children, Gina had questioned him about it.

"The bitch fought tooth and nail to keep me from seeing them, but my lawyer called her lawyer and reminded him that there is a court order for visitation. He told him that unless she wants me to quit paying her all that damn money in child support, she better comply! She didn't have much choice, did she?" he'd crowed.

———⊷⟨⟨◉⟩⟩⊶———

Not only was Gina the only girl in her family, she was the youngest. She was used to being the center of attention and had not spent much time around children. So, although Carter, 11, and Brett, 9 were nice kids who treated her with respect, Gina wasn't comfortable around them.

She tried to give Dick some time with them, figuring she would take the time to get to know his mother better.

Miriam Tate was a tall, thin woman with hair and eyes of steel. Although friendly enough, Gina detected a coldness about her. It was as though she was going through the motions but didn't really *feel* anything.

She did have plenty to say about Dick's ex-wives.

"I know my son can be difficult to live with sometimes – hey, I lived with his father mind you," Miriam explained to Gina, "but Dickie was a good husband and provided for both his families. He still does the right thing by them and those children - I don't care what those women say.

"Besides, marriage is sacred," she went on. "I think all of them, Dickie included, should have worked harder to keep their families together. My marriage was very difficult for years, but Jesus came to me one night and said, 'Miriam, you have to try harder to make this work; so I stayed until Dick, Sr. took off with that tramp and left me high and dry. But, Jesus will forgive me, I know, because *I* wasn't the sinner, Dick was.

"Neither of those *women* was right for Dickie. I tried to tell him that but he wouldn't listen to me. Neither of them are good Christians like he is. You know, John 3:36 tells us 'All who trust him' - God's Son – 'to save them, have eternal life. Those who don't believe and obey him shall never see heaven, but the wrath of God remains upon them'."

Dick had told Gina that he was a born-again Christian; however he rarely went to church. Gina, on the other hand, attended Catholic Mass every Sunday. Dick had joined her on a couple of occasions. He told her that, because he was raised as an Episcopalian, he felt very comfortable with the Catholic religion. He had even expressed an interest in the possibility of converting. Besides, he'd explained, his second wife had been Catholic and they had been married by a priest.

Even to Gina, Miriam seemed a bit extreme, but she respected everyone's right to practice his or her religion. *Believing in God is the most important thing*, Gina reflected.

Based on all she had heard from Dick, and now his mother, she was beginning to believe Dick's ex-wives were truly evil people. She wondered how poor Dick could have gotten mixed up with such horrible women.

That evening, they all sat down to enjoy the spaghetti dinner Gina had helped Miriam cook. Gina's cooking repertoire held much to be desired, but she was trying to learn and after all Dick had told her about his mother's wonderful cooking, she figured Miriam would be a good teacher.

Dick sat across the table from her, with Carter next to him. Miriam was at the head of the table. Brett, who was a study in constant motion, sat to Gina's left.

Several minutes into the meal, Brett looked up at her with puppy-like innocence and inquired, "Are you going to be our new step-mommy?"

Dick almost choked on his iced tea and then began to laugh. Gina instantly felt the heat rise to her face.

"Shut up, Brett!" Carter rebuked, "You're not s'posed to ask questions like that."

Carter was the more serious of the two and verged on being shy. He also made it quite clear that he was the older brother, frequently providing "instruction" to his carefree, younger sibling.

"Yeah, Son," Dick chimed in, "Give me a chance to pop the question first, will ya?"

Gina was so startled she didn't know what to say. She realized her jaw was hanging open as she stared incredulously at Dick.

"Who wants some chocolate cake?" Miriam asked, clapping her hands together.

That was enough to claim the attention of Brett, Carter *and* Dick. Gina could have kissed Miriam but was still frozen in place, mulling over Dick's last comment. *Did he really just say what I thought he said?* she asked herself. *We've only known each other a few months.* Admittedly, she felt a slight thrill at the suggestion.

———⚫———

During the drive home, Gina noticed that Dick seemed inordinately quiet. She glanced over at him and saw a rigidity to his jaw. His mouth was set in what she could only describe as a pout – bottom lip protruding and the outer edges turned downward in a frown.

"Is something bothering you mi amor?" she asked.

"Damn right it is!" he retorted, alarming her.

"Well, if I have done something to upset you, you should talk to me about it, not snap at me," Gina stiffly rejoined.

"Oh, it's not you, it's that whore Jordan," he referred to his first wife, "the boys told me she is getting ready to move them all in with some asshole she's sleeping with! I've got to figure out a way to stop her from subjecting my kids to her sluttish behavior!" he snarled.

Considering his intense anger, Gina wasn't sure if she should respond or just let him vent. She briefly touched his arm in an effort to let him know she understood he was upset and that he could talk to her.

"You know, Gina," he turned and looked at her intently, "if we were married, I could get custody of my kids and get them out of that immoral environment their mother has created for them."

Gina jerked her hand away, stunned.

"Is that supposed to be a proposal?" she replied angrily.

"Now, babe, don't get your panties in a bind," he assuaged, "you know I was getting ready to ask you to marry me. I guess it just came out wrong because I'm upset about my kids."

Gina still felt stung and wanted to reach up and slap his face. But seeing his pleading look, she softened and gave him a glimmer of a smile.

That appeared to be all Dick needed for encouragement. He pulled the car over to the side of the road, cut the engine and turned to her.

"I wanted to buy you a nice engagement ring. But you know I don't have much money because of all the child support I have to pay. If you'll agree to be my wife, I'll find a way to get that ring for you. I promise."

"Do you love me, Dick?" she asked.

"You know I do, babe."

"I can't have children," she told him, "so if you want more, I won't be able to give them to you."

Without asking why she couldn't have children, Dick chortled, "I have enough kids to last me a lifetime. No, I don't want any more, I just want to protect the ones I have from their miserable excuses for mothers."

"Then, si, Senor Tate, I will be your wife!" Gina gleamed. "And I will hold you to your promise to buy me a beautiful ring."

She thought she detected a shadow cross his face but then it was quickly gone so she figured it was just her imagination.

Chapter 7
Summer, 1990

"Oh Papa, Mama," Gina shouted, "I'm so glad you are here!"

"Como esta mi princesa?" beamed Augusto Rodriguez, wrapping his arms around his only daughter.

Gina reached out for her mother, who stood next to her husband smiling warmly. Isabel was all too aware of the special closeness between Gina and her father. She understood because she felt that same bond with Eduardo, her eldest son. Now, she welcomed her daughter's embrace.

"Welcome to California!" Gina laughed, throwing her arms out to her sides as though she herself were the state opening itself up to its visitors. "I must warn you that you will both have to speak English here. Dick and his familia don't speak Portuguese or Spanish," she informed them.

"Where *is* my future son in law?" Augusto asked.

As if on cue, Dick spoke up, "Welcome to America Mr. & Mrs. Rodriguez."

"Oh please Deek, you must call us Mama and Papa," said Isabel quietly.

"Okay, Mama!" Dick laughed.

After picking up their luggage, Gina and Dick led her parents to Gina's white Ford Bronco.

"We brought my car," Gina explained, "because it has more room. Dick has a sports car."

On the way to the hotel, Gina filled her parents in on those wedding plans they hadn't discussed on the telephone. Her parents would be lodging at the same hotel as Dick's mother, while Dick's three kids would be staying with the couple in their newly-rented home near Ocean Beach.

The elder Dick had refused to come to the wedding because Miriam would be there. Although it really hurt Dick that his father wouldn't be there, Gina told him it was probably for the best. Miriam was always making cracks about her ex-husband and his new wife and, considering all the problems Dick had with his own ex-wives, Gina figured they had enough drama to deal with. Dick reluctantly agreed with her.

Gina explained to her parents that the couple wouldn't be taking a honeymoon right away because the Navy wouldn't allow them to take leave at the same time. She didn't want to tell them the truth; that Dick thought they couldn't afford to because, as he put it, he was paying so much in child support to "those two bitches." Gina didn't want to discuss the details of Dick's problems, which were now *her* problems, with her parents. Moreover, she knew her father would insist on giving them money for a honeymoon if he knew the circumstances, and that he couldn't afford it either.

Gina also didn't mention the absence of an engagement ring

and was grateful that her mother hadn't asked to see it. Dick had backed out on his promise to buy her one, citing his "current state of poverty."

"You'll have a nice wedding ring. Isn't that what's most important?"

Gina had previously told her parents about Dick's kids and now detailed their roles in the wedding. Carter, Dick's oldest, would be his best man, while Brett would be an usher. Caitlin, Dick's daughter from his second marriage, would be their flower girl.

"Caitlin looks so pretty in the little pink dress she is wearing for the wedding," Gina exclaimed to her parents.

Gina felt closer to Caitlin than to Dick's sons, probably because she was only four years old and a girl. To her, Caitlin was like a little doll; Gina was always buying her new clothes and styling her wispy blonde hair.

Caitlin lived in Poway with her mother, only twenty minutes away from Dick and Gina. Dick had somehow managed to arrange visitation with Caitlin for every other weekend.

He had been divorced from Meg for two years when he met Gina, but they were still fighting over custody and visitation.

Although Dick had kept Gina informed of the difficulties he was experiencing with Meg in the courtroom, she had not met Meg until a couple of weekends ago; that was the first time Gina had gone with Dick to pick Caitlin up for their visit.

Gina had been appalled at the rudeness Meg displayed toward both of them. She hardly looked at Gina and shouted, "Make sure you bring her back on time, asshole!" to Dick as he helped Caitlin put her overnight bag in the car.

Now Gina thought she understand what Dick had been telling

her all this time about his ex-wives.

Although she had not met his first wife Jordan, Gina had heard Dick's side of their shouting matches on the phone. Judging from what he was saying, she could only surmise that Jordan's behavior was at least as disturbing as Meg's.

Gina had spent many a night holding Dick in her arms, trying to comfort him as he lamented about the unfair treatment he received not only from his ex-wives but the courts.

She had grown to despise both of Dick's ex-wives for what she perceived as their despicable treatment of him both during and after the marriages and was determined to show him how much she loved him and just how wonderful a relationship could truly be.

Gina put these thoughts out of her mind now, reminding herself that in two days *she* would be Dick's wife - and sharing her joy with her parents, who had traveled all the way from Puerto Rico for the occasion.

Unfortunately, none of Gina's brothers could make it to the wedding. Her only regret was that she could not be married in Puerto Rico with all of her family around her, but she was especially happy that her parents were here.

Her mother had helped her plan the wedding through phone calls and letters and had even hand sewn her long white gown. She had insisted on wearing white though Dick said he didn't like the idea because it was his third marriage. *It will be my first -and last,* she told herself. She had always dreamed about the day she would dress like the princess she was.

She was planning to wear the crystal tiara her mother brought from home as well. It had belonged to her great grandmother, the one from whom she had inherited her royalty; the legendary relative about whom Uncle Miguel had told her as a child.

This was going to be her special day and no one could ruin it, even Dick's ex-wives.

Gina and Dick made arrangements with her parents for the rehearsal dinner that evening and headed back to the airport to meet Carter and Brett, who would be arriving in an hour from Sacramento.

———— ((O)) ————

The ceremony had gone off without a hitch; the kids had all performed their roles splendidly and looked nice in their formal attire. *And I did look and feel like a princess*, Gina thought.

The reception afterwards was where everything began to fall apart. It was held in the main ballroom at the Officer's Club. They had hired a local band that specialized in Latin music.

When she was a teenager, her mother had insisted upon dance lessons and Gina had balked, thinking her mother old fashioned. She was glad for her mother's resolve now though because, after the wedding dance with her new husband, she had tangoed splendidly with her father. Isabelle had simply looked on with pride.

It was soon after that dance that everything went awry.

She had heard Dick over in the corner with some of his pilot buddies talking loudly.

Not only was it obvious to Gina that he'd had had a lot to drink but, judging by the sympathetic looks she received, several of the guests had noticed as well.

As Gina approached her raucous husband she was horrified to hear him slur, "Yeah, at least now I have someone to pay *my* bills while I'm busy supporting those two sluts —one of 'em who's screwing some jerk in the bed I bought and paid for!"

As she thought about it later, she wasn't sure if the stress of the wedding had affected her or if she too had consumed too much champagne. Even now, she felt the heat emanate from her face as she recalled her reaction to Dick's words and the pitying looks on his buddies' faces as they realized she had heard him.

Without a second thought, Gina had stormed over to Dick, brought her arm back and leveled him with a hard fist to his nose!

After that, everything was a blur. She vaguely remembered the stunned gasps from the crowd. In a haze, she recalled her mother swiftly taking her by the shoulders and leading her away. When they had reached the ladies room, Gina had crumpled into her mother's arms.

"Oh, Mama, what have I done?" she'd cried.

Isabelle had simply shushed her, rocking Gina in her arms.

"Sometimes the men we love do things that hurt us deeply but we must remember that they are our husbands forever and learn to forgive them. They do not understand what they do. And, besides, Deek is drunk. I'm sure he did not mean to hurt you, my darling," Isabelle murmured.

Aghast, Gina had peered up at her mother. "How can you say that, Mama? I won't be like you and let my husband mistreat me my whole life while I crawl at his feet!" she'd fumed.

Isabelle had pulled back as a look of horror caused by her daughter's words filled her eyes, but Gina mindlessly continued.

"Oh, I love my Papa, but I have seen the way he has treated you! He never would have done those things if you had not let him! No, Dick will not treat me like this and he better realize that right now!"

As she reflected upon it now, the day after her wedding and that horrendous scene, she felt sorry that she had hurt her mother, and embarrassed by her own actions, but was still determined that she would not be dominated and abused by her husband.

Now she heard Dick out in the kitchen with Carter and Brett. He was shouting at them about something; she couldn't make out the words. She heard Brett crying and decided maybe she'd better get up and check out the situation.

As she entered the kitchen and saw Dick's face, she stopped in her tracks. His right eye was swollen and the skin around it was a dark shade of blue. A wave of guilt rushed through her.

The kitchen suddenly went silent and she felt all six eyes on her.

"Hi Gina," uttered Carter, breaking the silence.

She murmured, "Good morning," to the room and awkwardly looked away, taking in the state of her kitchen.

The sink was piled high with dishes, and toast crumbs, which at first glance looked like an ant colony marching across the counter top, were scattered everywhere. A stream of milk ran from a tipped-over glass across the counter, down the face of the cabinets and onto the floor.

She glanced down at Brett's tear-streaked face and raised a questioning eyebrow.

"Dad is mad because I spilled my milk," Brett sniffed, "I told him I didn't mean to."

She glanced at Dick, who looked at the floor and muttered, "The boys were just telling me about the asshole their whore mother is living with."

As was usual when he referred to Jordan that way in front of the boys, Gina frowned at him. She was too exhausted to belabor the point though and, with one last glimpse of his black eye, turned to leave the room.

I will not apologize, she thought. *Hopefully he's learned he can't mistreat me and get away with it!*

———※◎※———

Later that day, Dick told her about his telephone conversation with Jordan.

"She's busy screwing her latest and doesn't want the kids back for a couple more weeks," he said.

Gina was appalled. "What kind of mother is she?" she asked.

She realized she was shouting and lowered her voice so the boys wouldn't hear.

"She's a selfish, evil bitch who doesn't deserve to have custody of her children," he replied.

Chapter 8
Sacramento, California;
Summer, 1991

Gina and Dick sat in metal chairs in the lobby of the Sacramento County building that housed several mediators, one of which Dick was waiting to see.

"I don't know why this room needs to be so uncomfortable," she complained.

Dick just shook his head and continued to look at the floor. Gina stood up to stretch her legs. Carter and Brett sat on the other side of the wall with their mother and new stepfather. As she peered around the partition to see what they were doing, she was startled to see Jordan watching her and quickly stepped out of sight.

Six months into their marriage, Dick had followed through on his threat to file for custody of his sons. Hearing of Jordan's impending marriage had provided him the impetus to get the ball rolling.

Jordan, who had been married to Nick Gallagher for only a few months when served with the court papers, had countered by requesting that Dick's visitation with Carter and Brett be supervised. The court required Dick, Jordan and the two boys to attend mediation, which is what they were waiting for now.

Gina was angry at the notion of supervised visitation and had expressed that to Dick on several occasions. Although Dick had told her he thought the whole idea of supervised visitation was ludicrous, it seemed to Gina he didn't feel the same sense of outrage as she.

Actually, it's as though it's some sort of competition he simply has to win. This thought was a bit unsettling to her.

"Why can't you spend this time with your kids?" she asked him now. "You have come all this way to Sacramento and you can't visit with them?

Dick jerked his head up and looked at her.

"You know, you're right, Gina. I should be able to see my kids. One more time that bitch is trying to control things and now she has that asshole spurring her on. Who the hell does he think he is anyway – trying to horn in on my relationship with my kids?"

About that time, a clerk came out and told them the mediator was running late.

"Why don't you go get yourself a cup of coffee and come back in an hour?" she suggested, "Mr. Hansen should be ready for you then."

Dick got a sudden gleam in his eye. He rushed over to block the way of Jordan, Nick and the boys as they headed for the door.

"Hey guys, why don't we go get some breakfast?" Dick asked the boys.

Jordan got a panicked look on her face and turned to Nick.

Nick said, "Let's not make this tougher than it already is, Dick.

We're not here to socialize, nor is this a planned visitation for you. We're leaving now."

Gina was outraged. *How dare Nick interfere?*

As the group turned to leave, she shouted, "You're not their father!" at Nick.

Nick shook his head at her and steered the group out the door.

"You're not their father!" Gina shouted again at their backs.

Her anger was getting out of control, she knew. She was incensed, though, not only out of frustration for Dick's sake, but at the very idea that anyone would have the audacity to turn their back on her.

Just then, normally quiet Carter turned to her and, with what seemed a ferocity she would never have expected from him, declared, "You're not our mother either."

Gina was so startled that she froze and watched them continue out the door. She felt Dick's hand on her shoulder and looked up at his crimson-colored face and neck. Gina wasn't sure if he was angry with Nick or embarrassed by what she had said.

As if he had heard her thoughts, he answered her question by decrying, "You see, that bitch is even brainwashing my kids! Carter never would have spoken up like that if his mother wasn't telling him lies about me. And that asshole, Nick, who the hell does he think he is? You're absolutely right, Gina, he's not their father! When you talk to the mediator, I think you should tell him what you've just witnessed . . . How they kept me from even speaking to my kids . . . how this man is trying to take my place as their father. It will probably come out better if you tell him, rather than me."

Gina glanced over her shoulder to see the clerk standing there, arms crossed, glaring at them as though she were the librarian and they had shouted across the library at one another.

"Let's go eat breakfast, Dick," she mumbled as she pulled him through the door by his arm.

After breakfast, Gina found herself back in the lobby trying once again to get comfortable in a metal chair. This time was worse than the last because of the earlier confrontation with Nick, Jordan and the boys. Her discomfort with having to sit in the same lobby with them was even more unpleasant than the rock-hard seat.

Dick and Jordan had been meeting in the mediator's office for nearly an hour. *What on earth is taking so long?* she wondered. She had flipped through all the magazines on the table while she waited, but found nothing of interest. "All these magazines were written for housewives or women looking for a man," she muttered under her breath, "Nothing for a woman with brains."

She glanced up to see Jordan walk out into the lobby, with Dick close behind her. Jordan looked angry, as she crossed the lobby toward Nick and the boys.

Gina's breath caught in her throat when she noticed that Dick was staring after Jordan with a look of longing and hurt.

Oh dear God, she thought, *he is still in love with Jordan! He could not look at her with such desire, otherwise. Is that where all his anger is coming from? Is it because of the hurt he feels at losing her? But, he told me he had left Jordan! If that were really true . . .*

"Gina!" she heard Dick calling her name through a fog.

She looked at him questioningly.

"Mr. Hansen is ready to talk to you," he said, and then with a look of concern, asked, "Gina, what on earth is wrong with you?"

"N-nothing," she stammered. She rose and then followed the clerk down the long hallway to the mediator's office.

Mr. Hansen was a small man. He wore glasses too large for his pinched face and what hair was left on his head was a mass of gray wires growing every which way. Gina felt the urge to offer him her comb.

"Sit down, Mrs. Tate," he said while pointing to a chair in front of and facing his desk.

As she lowered herself into the orange and green striped fabric chair, she sighed with relief. At least this chair was somewhat comfortable.

"As you know, Mrs. Tate," he began, "I've been asked to assist the courts with a decision as to the custodial and visitation arrangements for your husband's children."

"Please, Mister Hanson, you must speak of me as Gina, or Lieutenant Tate," she directed.

He raised an eyebrow but nodded his head in agreement.

"Okay, Gina, please give me your thoughts as to your husband's relationship with his children."

Gina didn't hesitate. She told him all she had heard about Jordan's refusal to allow Dick to spend time with his children, her rudeness and spitefulness.

"I think she is trying to hurt him for leaving her," she said by reflex.

As she said the words, though, Dick's earlier reaction to Jordan flashed through her mind. Afraid Mr. Hanson would see the doubt she felt at her own words, Gina looked down at her lap.

"How do the children react toward their father?" he probed. "Do they appear to be afraid of him in any way?"

"Oh no!" she cried, "his sons love him very much. You must believe that, Mr. Hanson! Dick would never harm his kids."

———⟫•⟪———

The drive to Miriam's house would take awhile, not only because she lived in the suburbs of Sacramento, but because they were stuck in rush hour traffic. Dick was swearing and muttering and banging the steering wheel.

"Shit, that Jordan is such a liar," he grumbled for what seemed the tenth time, "I just have to hope that mediator is smart enough to see through her. What did you talk to him about?"

"Dick, we have been over and over this! I told you everything I can remember. Please, stop it now. Why do you make so much of what I said? Why do you care so much what Jordan thinks? You still love her, don't you?"

Dick's face crumpled like a piece of paper wadded in a fist. His lips pouted as they often did when he was hurt or upset; she had seen that look so many times before.

Without warning, the back of his open hand smashed across her face, causing her head to jerk back against the seat's head rest. She tasted blood and reached up in horror to touch her lip.

"Goddamn it Gina, why are you such a fucking bitch?" he spat, whirling his head in her direction.

"You do not ever hit me, you bastard!" she screamed. "How dare you do that to me? Did you do that to Jordan? Is that why she divorced you? She did leave you, didn't she Dick? I saw it on your face today – you wish you were still married to her. But you are not – you are married to me. I have helped you every way I know and you call me a bitch and hit me!"

As he averted his eyes, she felt the rental car lurch forward. Dick's foot had pushed the accelerator all the way to the floor. Gina grabbed the harness above her head with her right hand and pushed the other down on the dashboard to keep from flying toward the windshield.

"Dick!" she shrieked, "What are you doing? You're going to kill us!"

"What difference does it make? You're a bitch and you hate me and what is the point of either one of us living? Huh?" he snarled.

Gina panicked. She could feel every beat of her heart, drumming against her chest as if imprisoned inside her and trying to break out.

"Please Dick, please. You know I love you; everything will be okay, please stop!" she pleaded.

He suddenly took his foot off the accelerator and slammed on the brake, just inches from the vehicle in front of them. Even with her hand on the dashboard, Gina was thrown forward with a force she felt in her neck muscles.

The driver of the pickup truck he'd nearly hit suddenly jumped out and ran back toward them. He began screaming at them, calling Dick a "fucking moron," while pounding on the driver's side window. Dick didn't look at the man and Gina saw genuine fear in his eyes.

The stalled traffic began to move again, so the infuriated man turned and ran back to his truck.

Gina wanted to yell at Dick. She wanted to tell him what a coward she thought he was - to point out that he felt no qualms about backhanding his wife, but trembled with fear when another man yelled at him. But her own distress forced her to bite her tongue. All she just wanted was to reach Miriam's house and to get out of this car, away from this maniac who was her husband.

She felt the bile rise in her throat. *What is happening to my marriage?* she asked herself. Dick had never laid a hand on her before. She then recalled when she had punched him at their wedding reception. She had been hurt by what he had said. Now he had been hurt by what he saw as her lack of support of him.

He is under so much stress with this custody suit, just trying to be a father to his kids. Maybe I only imagined the look he gave Jordan. Maybe it wasn't desire I saw, just sadness about his children. I should not have said what I did. Maybe we are even now. Still, I can't let him do this again.

Gina remained quiet for the rest of the ride. Dick seemed to have calmed down as well and was driving at a normal speed. She felt his hand caress her face.

"I'm sorry babe, I don't know what came over me," he said.

She looked up into those blue eyes she loved so much and saw his pain.

"I know Dick, I know you are upset. But please promise me you will never hit me again."

"It won't happen again," he pledged. "Please forgive me."

Gina was glad to see Miriam was still at work. She did not want Miriam to see the dried blood on her mouth. She quickly went into the bathroom and washed her face.

Chapter 9
Coronado Island, California;
Fall, 1994

Three years later...

Gina saw her reflection in the mirror above the fireplace mantel and cringed at the swelling around her eyes. As strong as she usually was, she had been crying at the slightest provocation lately.

She and Dick had argued again last night. The arguments were becoming a part of their weekly ritual. He was the most maddening creature she had ever known.

His violent nature and the physical abuse were beginning to wear on her. Of course it had continued. She should have known it would after the first time he struck her, all those years ago in Sacramento. And of course, he always apologized afterward, crying and pleading with her not to leave him.

"You're different than those other bitches I was married to before," he'd claimed more times than she could count. "I really love you and I know you could never be as evil as they are. Besides, if you leave, who changed – you or me?"

Gina had heard it all. "Just let me finish this court battle," or, "have the child support lowered," or, "get more visitation," or, "gain custody of my kids" - whatever his latest crusade was. She now understood that Dick liked to portray himself as a victim.

She realized his main goal was to beat Meg or Jordan, that for him his battles with his ex-wives were a struggle for power, pure and simple. Beating them was as important as any athletic victory had ever been, if not more so. He could not stand for either of them to "win" anything.

She also was beginning to see why they hated him so much, though she would never admit that to Jordan or Meg. She knew the two of them had been talking, comparing notes, trying to band together against Dick. But the fact that they had always been rude to her – Jordan had even called her crazy once – kept her from feeling any alliance with them.

Gina had stuck by Dick through thick and thin. Through the custody battle with Jordan, which only resulted in his keeping the visitation rights he'd had before but not attaining his sought-after custody of the boys. That episode had actually driven the boys away, which of course Dick blamed on Jordan and "that asshole" Nick.

She had gone with him to the court hearings, held his hand, stuck up for him to judges and lawyers and, most of all, to Jordan and Meg.

She supported him in his attempts to increase his visitation time with Caitlin, an effort in which Meg fought him like a bulldog. He lost that dispute as well, along with Caitlin. His daughter had made it abundantly clear she didn't want to spend any time with him.

Initially, Dick had forced Caitlin to come to his house every other weekend, citing the court order and his "right to spend time with his children." But Caitlin had moped around, locked herself in her room and told Dick how much she hated him every chance she could. She had devastated Gina by telling her that she despised her as well. Finally, Dick relented. They had not seen Caitlin in several months.

Everything was a mess. And Dick never stopped. He always had some new scheme up his sleeve. He had even convinced Brett to come live with them a couple of years ago, promising him the moon and, of course, not delivering. Dick had been unable to hide his glee while Brett described Jordan's extreme anxiety over his decision.

Dick had not spent any time with Brett the whole time he lived with them. Gina had been left with all the parenting responsibilities, on top of her work. Most evenings Dick was at the club with other pilots from his unit, stumbling in well after Brett and Gina were asleep.

She had begun to resent Brett, who had been homesick and unhappy since shortly after his arrival. Instead of staying for the agreed-upon year, he went back to his mother after six months.

Enraged, Dick had stormed around the house, yelling at Gina, telling her it was her fault, accusing her of driving Brett away. When he wasn't punching holes in the walls, he was punching Gina. Time and again, concerned neighbors had summoned the local police to their home.

Reports of his violent behavior had begun to affect Dick's career. He had been counseled by his executive officer, his commanding officer and one of the base chaplains – none of whom, according to Dick, understood the pressure he was under.

This morning, the Admiral had discreetly asked about her home life, making it clear even he was aware of her marital strife. She was livid.

This is the icing on the cake, she thought.

She had planned to discuss this with Dick tonight, but he hadn't arrived home yet. Glancing at the clock, she realized he was two hours late.

Damn him! she thought, nervously tapping her foot, her anxiety growing along with her irritation.

She heard the garage door as it opened, stopped, closed and then began opening again. This happened frequently to Dick; somehow he hit the button on the opener twice – creating confusion for the garage door mechanism.

"Idiot," she whispered, "can't even operate a simple garage door."

She heard a loud yowl as he banged through the door and tripped over the cat, another of his "possessions" she took care of.

If the situation weren't so pitiful, it might be funny, she thought.

He apparently didn't see her waiting in the living room because he jumped when she spoke to him.

"Jesus, Gina, what the hell are you doing?"

"Waiting for you, Dick - for the last two hours!"

"Oh God, if I'm gonna get a lecture, let me at least grab a beer first," he said, rolling his eyes.

He sauntered in with a bottle of Coors and a hunk of cheddar cheese. She could almost hear the couch groan as he threw his 250 pounds down onto it.

Gina recapped her conversation with Admiral Miller while Dick fiddled with the remote control for the stereo.

She finally got his full attention when she yelled, "It is bad enough that you have so much trouble in your career Dick, but I will not allow you to ruin mine!"

Gina had recently been offered a two-year assignment supervising the University of Puerto Rico's Navy ROTC unit. She had planned to turn it down because Dick would be unable to join her. Now she informed him that she had changed her mind and was accepting the assignment.

"We need some time away from each other," she explained. "I hope this will help both of us decide what we want from this marriage."

Typically, Dick bowed his head and began to pout.

"Don't go babe, we can work it out better if you stay here with me where you belong. You know I really love you."

She had desperately wanted to believe Dick all those times he told her she was the only one he'd really loved, that she was different. But three years of raging, screaming fights, his physical and verbal abuse of her, and the recent series of drunken episodes, after which she had often driven him home and put him to bed, provided ample evidence that most of what he'd said was a lie. She felt the pain of that knowledge to her very core.

"It won't work this time, Dick," she countered, "I'm going, my decision is final. I leave next month."

Suddenly, he had her by the shoulders. She looked up into a face she did not recognize, it was so twisted with rage. His eyes flashed darkly, his mouth in a cruel grimace. He shook her roughly then lifted her to bring her face within an inch of his.

"You leave me, you fucking whore, and you will regret it for the rest of your life! You're no different than the rest of them. Cunt . . . Bitch . . . Whore! You probably already have some asshole you're fucking behind my back!"

He continued to shake her so hard her teeth rattled. For the first time in her life, Gina knew real fear.

Who is this monster? she cringed inwardly.

"Please Dick," she pleaded, "Put me down. Please!"

"You want me to put you down, whore?" Dick hissed as he threw her body across the dining room table, "I'll put you down where you belong and take what belongs to me, you fucking slut!"

He feverishly ripped her blouse and roughly pulled the front of her bra down. Gina tried to break away from him but he was more than twice her weight. He held her down with one hand while the other pulled at her waistband. The button of her slacks flew across the room.

"Please Dick, no!" she sobbed.

He savagely bit her right breast, his teeth ripping through her nipple as she struggled to get away. The pain was unbearable. Gina began to tremble and felt what little strength she had left begin to wane.

Suddenly, the oppression of his full weight was upon her, pinning her down as he continued his violent assault of her body. This man who was her husband continued to cruelly violate her. He had managed to pull one of her legs from her slacks; now his free hand yanked at her panties.

Tears streamed down her face. She was powerless to ward him off.

Gina heard herself scream as he penetrated her. Over and over he pummeled into her with his penis, the very instrument that had until now only provided her with pleasure.

"Whores, sluts, cunts, bitches, every one of you," he chanted as he fiercely battered her.

The very idea that this man, whom she had loved with all her heart and soul, was capable of so viciously assaulting her was completely unfathomable to Gina. She felt herself drift into a hazy, almost trance-like state, protecting her from the awful reality.

—⊷«◉»⊶—

Gina felt the cool wet cloth blotting her lips and opened a swollen eye. She recoiled and began to whimper when she saw Dick leaning over her.

"Shhhh babe, it's okay," he cooed. "I won't hurt you. I'm so sorry Gina. I just lost it when you said you were going away. I can't bear the thought of living without you."

She sat up and pulled a pillow between them.

"Get your filthy hands off me, you son of a bitch!" she snarled. "If you don't leave this house right now, I'll call the police and have them lock you up."

"Awww, babe . . ."

"Go now, Dick, I mean it!" she screamed.

"But, where will I sleep?"

"I don't care if you sleep in the gutter," she shrieked and pointed toward the door, "Just get out!"

—⊷«◉»⊶—

It had been three and a half weeks since Dick's assault. Picking up her carry-on bag, she winced with pain. Although most of her bruises had begun to heal, an occasional soreness flared up as a reminder.

While making her way toward the departure gate, she heard a familiar voice calling her name. Her whole body tensed.

Gina turned and saw him running toward her.

"Gina, wait," he called, "I just wanted to say goodbye."

Her mouth felt dry as she croaked, "Dick . . ."

He was suddenly standing before her.

"I requested leave for next month and I'm going to fly down to Puerto Rico to see you," he instantly related. "We need to spend some time together, away from the Navy, away from San Diego - just the two of us, talking and working this out."

She could no longer contain herself.

"Don't come one step closer to me," she screamed, oblivious to the scene she was creating as other passengers turned to stare.

"I swear, if you come near me, if I ever see you again, I will kill you – you son of a bitch!" she roared. "What do you think I am? Nobody treats Gina this way and gets away with it. Nobody! Now *leave me alone!*"

He turned red from his chest to the top of his head. That was her last view of him before she spun on her heels and hurried away.

"Revenge is an act of passion: vengeance of justice.
Injuries are revenged; crimes are avenged."

- Joseph Joubert

Chapter 10
San Diego, California;
July 23, 2003

Buchanan was leaning backward in his chair, his feet propped on the top of his desk, reviewing the autopsy report he'd just received from the Medical Examiner's office. Mike walked into the office waving a small stack of paper just as Ian took a large gulp of coffee.

With a scrunched-up nose and curled upper lip, Ian looked into his coffee mug and muttered, "You know, sometimes I wonder if the people who make this crap are actually terrorists trying to slowly kill us off . . . ."

Mike grinned from ear-to-ear and quipped, "Sounds like a case for Super Detective a.k.a. Ian Buchanan. . . . But in the meantime, maybe you'll settle for solving the *Case of Too Many Wives!*"

O'Reilly laughed hard at his own joke then dropped the stack of papers on the desk in front of Ian. "This just in," he cracked, "Li's report on the latent prints from the scene."

Ian's feet hit the floor with a bang as he sat up in his chair and reached for the report. "Anything good?"

"Only that they picked up two sets of prints from the door handle that didn't belong to the victim or Ms. Tripp – who, true to her word, came in and was fingerprinted yesterday. Li ran them through AFIS . . . no match. The prints from the wine glasses came from Tate."

"Okay . . ." said Buchanan, "we need to convince Gina and the other ex-wives to come in and get printed as well."

He then picked up the autopsy report and began to describe its contents. "I've only quickly perused this but I'll tell you what I got out of it so far. . ."

"I'm listening." Mike plopped down in the chair at his desk, which faced Ian's.

According to the report, Buchanan related, the first gunshot was from close contact with the abdomen. As Dr. Epstein had expressed at the crime scene, the second shot to the chest was from two to three feet away. The M.E. recovered both bullets from the body and sent them to Firearms Examination at the crime lab for further evaluation.

"From the 9 millimeter casings recovered at the scene, we already know the perp used an automatic hand gun. Once we get the Firearms report, we can hopefully narrow it down," Ian mused aloud.

"As we discussed, I'm gonna run this growing list of suspect names through the computer this afternoon to check for firearm registrations," Mike told him, "so hopefully we'll have that info when we get the report."

Buchanan nodded and then returned his focus to the autopsy report.

"She also found no evidence of recent vomit from Tate, which makes me feel more certain it came from the perp. If one of these ex-wives actually had the *cajones* to shoot the mother fucker, she may have had a little trouble stomaching it once she saw the results."

Mike looked thoughtful. "Yeah, it's looking more and more like one of these women did it. After talking to Gina yesterday and hearing her story, I'm leaning in her direction. She was definitely hiding something. I think she talked to him, I think she had dinner with him and I think she may very well have shot the bastard."

Ian nodded. "I hear ya. But think about what Mom said . . . Jordan and Meg were the *really* bad ones – so I want to talk to them as well."

"By the way," Ian quickly added, "the D.A. got the subpoena for Tate's phone records. I've got Cheryl working on those. It'll be interesting to see if he called our little prima donna."

Mike knew his partner was referring to Gina. The two had discussed her snooty attitude last night while driving home from the interview. Ian had also made the observation that she was not one of the women portrayed in the photos found at the victim's home.

"Well, we're gonna get the chance to talk to Meg – also known as wife # 2 – in about an hour," Mike reminded him. "As a matter of fact, we need to leave in half an hour if we want to get to her house in Poway by noon. When I set up the appointment, she mentioned she was taking the day off work."

"According to Miriam, Tate and Meg had a daughter together . . . I assume you requested her presence as well."

Mike nodded. "I did . . . but she was a little cagey with her answer. So, we'll see."

Buchanan's phone rang. It was Miriam Tate, calling to tell him a funeral service and then a graveside committal service would be held the day after tomorrow, Friday the twenty fifth. She also gave him directions to the Christian church in Chula Vista where she said "Dickie" had worshipped.

While headed north on I-15 toward Poway, they passed Marine Corps Air Station, Miramar, where Meg had told Mike she was employed.

The base at Miramar, formerly known as Miramar Naval Air Station, was turned over to the Marines in 1993. During the Vietnam War, the Navy had created a graduate-level training school for fighter air crews at Miramar, known as "Top Gun". The 23,000-acre Naval Air Station, once known as "Fightertown, USA," and its school, were the focus of the movie, *Top Gun.*

Meg had said she lived in a guest house on her parent's ranch, which was located at the rear of the property. Following her directions, they turned onto a driveway that led them past a large ranch-style house to a quaint cottage that sat about 250 yards beyond the main house.

When Buchanan climbed out of the car, a strong gardenia scent floated toward him. A tiny bed of flowers was planted under a greenhouse window to the left of the front door. Along with gardenia bushes, the well-manicured garden included pink and white candytuft, cosmos and geraniums.

O'Reilly, walking to Ian's left, suddenly scurried around to the other side of his partner. Ian crinkled his cheeks in puzzlement and asked, "What the hell is wrong with you?"

Mike looked away from Ian and toward the cottage's front

door, mumbling, "I hate fuckin' bees . . ."

Ian stole a quick glance at the flower bed and saw a swarm of bees busily fluttering in, out and around the plants and their blossoms.

He roared with laughter. He laughed so hard, his words were almost unintelligible when he babbled, "Do you want me to shoot them with my gun?"

Mike's face turned a deep crimson color as he cast a chagrined smile at his partner.

Just then, the front door swung open. An auburn-haired woman stood there, hands on hips and a wry smile. "Your demeanor tells me you're here because you're investigating a murder . . ."

Buchanan immediately recognized her as the redhead portrayed in the photos found in the victim's home office – the woman pictured with the young girl. He was mesmerized by her face. The idea that this stunning woman could have had a hand in murdering the man who had displayed her in such a hateful manner was sobering.

Ian had stopped laughing. He stood, open-mouthed, staring at her. Mike, clearly confused by his partner's apparent inability to speak, held up his badge with his left hand while offering his right hand.

"You must be Meg," he observed, "I'm Detective O'Reilly and this is . . ." his eyes rolled toward Ian, "my partner, Detective Buchanan."

A few seconds ticked by before Mike kicked Ian in the shin, nudging him from his dumbstruck state just as Meg reached out her hand to him.

Ian felt certain the expression on his face must appear sappy. He finally found his voice and said, "Very nice to meet you Meg.

And please allow me to apologize for our silliness out here. Investigating homicides can get to be so morose, sometimes we have to find the humor in life to get us back on an even keel..."

Meg smiled as she interrupted his rambling. "It's quite alright, Detective, I do understand. Won't you both come inside?"

Buchanan glanced in his partner's direction just long enough to catch a puzzled but amused look on his face. He ignored him and started through the front door.

Meg led them into her living room where the furnishings, Ian noted, were the complete opposite of Gina's. Rather than heavy, dark leather, this room was ultra-feminine — from the floral-patterned sofa to the lace curtained windows. Several Hummel figurines were delicately placed throughout the room and the walls were adorned with various prints depicting cherubs or women with parasols.

She motioned them toward the sofa, which Ian was almost afraid to sit on. Still feeling a bit awkward, he turned toward Mike, whose continued amusement was evident, as an indication he wanted him to do the talking.

Meg curled herself into a wing chair across from them and inquired, "So, do you have any suspects yet?"

O'Reilly cleared his throat. "Well, we're still in the preliminary stages of our investigation . . . but we're hoping what you tell us will be helpful on that front." Glancing toward the back of the house, he asked, "Is your daughter here?"

Meg squirmed in her chair and looked at her lap as she replied, simply, "No, she isn't."

"When will we be able to speak with her?"

Meg's jaw set. "Do you have kids?" she asked.

Mike shook his head.

"Then you probably won't understand, but I don't want my daughter subjected to harsh questioning," Meg explained. "After all, her father was just murdered. . . ."

She peered at Ian as if hoping he might better appreciate her feelings. "Isn't that traumatic enough?" she asked rhetorically.

"You didn't seem too concerned about the fact her father was murdered when I first told you about it on the phone . . ." remarked Mike insidiously.

Meg pursed her lips in a thoughtful frown and murmured, "I know, Detective, and that was very tacky on my part. You have to understand . . . my marriage to that man was horrific. My daughter has not spent much time with him over the past several years," quickly adding, "by her own choice."

"Well then, why would our questions be traumatic for her?"

"Because . . . when I told her about his death . . . before I even had the chance to tell her he had been murdered, she totally fell apart. It's complicated, Detective. She doesn't hate him – he's still her father."

"I understand," uttered Mike, "but in order to solve his murder we'll probably need to speak with her . . . eventually."

"We'll give her a few days to come to terms with this," Ian finally spoke up, "and if we can do this without her, we will. If we can't though, I hope we can count on your cooperation."

Meg was quiet for a moment then smiled uneasily and nodded her head.

O'Reilly broke the silence. "Why don't you tell us about your . . . self-described horrific marriage to Richard Tate."

Ian leaned forward in anticipation. He thought she was one of the most beautiful women he had ever seen. *If Dick Tate was as nasty as Gina had made him out to be, if he was sick enough to stalk this woman, along with the other woman he now assumed to be Jordan, how could she have become involved with him in the first place?*

"I will," she offered, "but I must tell you I'm doing so reluctantly. The very thought of him dredges up such horrible memories . . . I won't deny that I came to loath him."

Both detectives nodded in understanding and sat back to listen to her story.

~ MEG ~

"Sweet is revenge – especially to women."

Lord Byron
Don Juan I, 124

Chapter 11
San Diego, California;
Spring, 1982

"Come on Meg, let's go!" shouted Jackie. "You look just fine; quit fussing!

Meg spun away from the hallway mirror, grinned at Jackie and reached up to tousle her best friend's hair.

"Hey, watch the do, lady," Jackie chortled, then, "Okay, okay, we both fuss. Why? Because this might just be the night we meet our Prince Charming."

Meg grabbed her purse off the table next to the door and followed Jackie to her car.

"Oh yeah, how many years have we been waiting for that, Jack?" Meg laughed. "Yet, the minute we give up, that's when it will happen. And I, for one, don't want to be looking like the ugly stepsister when it does."

It was single's night at the Miramar Naval Air Station Officers Club. Meg and Jackie had missed only one of these weekly events in the past three years, and that was because Stuart was sick.

As they climbed into her car, Jackie asked, "How's Stuart

doing? Do our weekly outings bother him?

"Not only does he not seem to mind, he actually encourages me to go. Yeah, he's okay. I took him up to the big house after dinner."

As was their custom, Meg's parents watched her eight-year-old son while she enjoyed some time off from single motherhood. After her brief and disastrous marriage to Ruben, Stuart's father, Meg had moved into the guest house on the ranch in Poway where she had grown up. Her job checking groceries at the Miramar commissary barely covered their living expenses, so Meg was grateful to her parents for providing them a place to live, free of charge.

Meg did not receive any financial help from Ruben; in fact she had no idea where he was. He had walked out on them when Stuart was just six months old.

"Yeah, he's such a sweetheart. And yet he came home again the other day with more stories about kids bullying him at school. They call him such horrible names . . . I don't get it. The Hispanic community doesn't seem to accept him as one of their own and he's often the subject of racial slurs from others. Right here in Poway! The idea that so many in this town . . . where I've lived my whole life . . . are so close-minded is depressing."

"They're just a bunch of jealous idiots, Meg. I mean, look at Stuart. He's so handsome. How could they not be jealous of him?"

Meg smiled at her friend as she thought about her son's shiny black hair and beautiful olive complexion, resulting from the combination of her ultra white and Ruben's cocoa-hued skin tones.

"You're right. But it breaks my heart to see him hurt. He's my baby, ya know?"

Jackie nodded.

After a brief silence, Meg slapped her hand against her thigh, saying, "I didn't mean to be such a downer," as she reached for the radio dial. "Let's not talk about it anymore tonight!"

Meg and Jackie got in the right mood for the evening by singing along with the radio during their fifteen minute drive to the base. They bounced and wiggled in their seats as they bellowed along with Laura Branigan's intonation of *Gloria*.

The Marine guard at the front gate grinned and shook his head at them as he waved them through.

"Hey, cutie, you know we're looking for a few good men, too!" yelled Jackie as she eased her car through the gate.

Meg slapped her on the arm playfully while laughing uproariously.

"Ooh, I love those muscular ones," Jackie giggled.

"Um hmm, well it looks like there may be quite a few of that ilk here tonight," Meg pointed toward the O'Club parking lot, "judging by all those hot sports cars."

"Yeah, well it looks like we're gonna have to find a couple of hunks to walk us back to the car later tonight," Jackie winked. "You know how scared I am of the dark."

They could hear the music blaring as they approached the double glass doors at the front entrance. Inside, the crowd was so dense that not everyone could fit in the lounge where a disk jockey was playing the latest dance hits.

Meg saw a familiar group of F-14 pilots clustered in the lobby, several of them with women at their sides.

"Oh, man, Jack," Meg said, "the competition is stiff tonight. Look at 'em all!"

"You call that competition?" Jackie chortled, and then yelled toward the crowd, "Calm down guys, there's enough room on my dance card for all of you!"

Several obviously amused men turned in their direction.

They all know Jackie's bark is worse than her bite, Meg chuckled to herself.

"Uh-oh, here comes trouble," shouted one of them.

Meg and Jackie squeezed through the horde of bodies en route to join their friends.

"Wow," Meg exclaimed as they finally reached the group, "a few newbies here tonight, or what? I see a lot of new faces."

"Yeah, there are a few helicopter pukes from Coronado stinken' up the place," offered Terry.

Terry was an F-14 pilot and a close friend of Meg's. Jackie thought Terry was secretly in love with Meg and often teased her about that. Meg laughed it off but also tried to be careful she never did anything to lead him on, even going so far as to talk to him about her dates with or attraction to other men. Though she was very fond of Terry, she was not interested in a romantic relationship with him.

"So . . . no tables inside?"

"I don't know, just got here myself," Terry answered, "but it's pretty crowded so your chances don't look good. But tell you what," he ventured, "let's go check it out. Just hold onto me."

Meg motioned to Jackie to follow and grabbed on to the waistband of Terry's khaki slacks while he guided them through the throng of revelers.

All the tables were taken, so the three staked out a position near the bar with easy access to the dance floor. Meg barely had time to take a sip of her margarita when she felt Jackie tugging on her sleeve.

"Come on, girl; let's go put in our song requests!" Jackie urged as she pulled her toward the disk jockey's booth.

Meg and Jackie had a list of favorite dance songs they requested each week when they came to the club. Harvey, the disk jockey, was a retired World War II sailor who worked the San Diego military club circuit as a diversion. He was a gruff old guy who seemed to barely tolerate the two women.

"Oh, here they are," he remarked sardonically as he saw them approach, "my two social coordinators."

"Oh Harvey, admit it," Jackie joked, "we make you look good by helping you keep your music up-to-date. Everyone would stop coming if they were forced to listen to 'Don't Sit under the Apple Tree' one more time."

"Do tell," Harvey rolled his eyes, "You mean they would rather hear 'Man Eater' over and over and over again?"

"Exactly!" Jackie laughed, "You *are* a quick study, aren't you?"

"Okay you two, knock it off," Meg shook her head. "Jack, it sounds as though ol' Harvey has our request list memorized, so unless you have something new in mind, I'm going back to my spot before somebody steals it."

As she headed back toward the bar, Meg noticed a stranger in a flight suit talking to Terry. Just then Terry glanced in her direction, grinning like a Cheshire cat.

Uh-oh, what's he up to?

"Hey Meg," Terry reached up and placed his hand on her shoulder as she rejoined him, "Got a helicopter puke here who has a thing for redheads and wants to meet you."

The blonde-haired newcomer turned to face her and smiled, though his face was as red as a beet.

Wow, he's gorgeous! Meg thought, as butterflies fluttered across her abdomen and up through her chest.

"Dick Tate," he smiled as he reached out to take her hand, "And since I have just suffered utter humiliation at the hands of your friend here, I hope you'll dance with me and take me out of my misery."

"Yeah, he's famous for that," she replied, grimacing at Terry as she turned toward the dance floor. "I'd love to dance."

As they made their way to join the other writhing bodies, she heard Jackie chirp, "Go Meg!"

Dick, who was in front of her, glanced over his shoulder with an ear-to-ear grin.

"Okay, it's my turn to be embarrassed," she rolled her eyes.

Harvey had just rotated into one of his slower musical segments, for which Meg was grateful. She needed some time to recover and calm the butterflies.

Although Dick wasn't much of a dancer and kept stepping on her toes, she enjoyed being close to him. He was a good six feet tall and since Meg was all of 5'4" the top of her head hit just below his Adam's apple.

He kept up a constant chatter while they danced, which she attributed to nervousness. He explained that he was an SH-60 pilot at Coronado.

"Contrary to your friend's remarks, flying a helicopter is no easy feat," he asserted. "I get a little tired of these fighter jocks and their cracks about us. Since they've never flown a helicopter, they don't know what they're talking about."

"Oh, Terry was just kidding," she defended. "He's really a nice guy . . . just your typical fighter pilot. As with all of them, he has an ego that won't quit. But please don't take him seriously."

"Yeah, well, if you say so . . ."

Except for a brief interlude during which Meg introduced Dick to Jackie, they spent the entire evening with just one another. Meg was totally enthralled with his good looks, his broad shoulders, his soulful eyes and, she must admit, the way he filled out a flight suit.

He asked her if she had grown up in California. She explained that she was born and raised in Poway and that her grandparents had moved to California in the early 1920s.

"They were Okies," she laughed, "Probably drove out here with a mattress and chickens on top of the jalopy."

"My dad bought ranch land in Poway soon after my parents were married and they have been there ever since," she continued.

Poway, known as *The City in the Country*, covers about 39 square miles just east of the I-15 freeway. No more than 20 miles north of San Diego, the city's current population comprised fewer than 35,000 people.

"I love Poway," Meg declared. "It's close enough to the beach and to San Diego proper, but still has that small-town feel."

Just then she heard "The Last Dance" resonate through the large speakers on each side of the dance floor. This was Harvey's trademark last song, signaling to all that the evening was about to come to an abrupt end.

She glanced across the room to see Jackie flirting with one of the regulars and waved at her.

"Hey Meggie!" Jackie slurred as she walked toward them. "Wanna join the gang for breakfast? You can even bring your cute new friend."

"Uh, thanks," Dick muttered, "but I don't really think your

friends will want this helicopter puke tagging along."

He looked down at Meg with a look that started her butter-flies fluttering again.

"But, I would sure like to see you again Meg. Can I call you?"

"I look forward to it," she replied.

Meg beamed at him as she grabbed a cocktail napkin and jotted down her phone number. As she handed it to him, he held onto her hand, then leaned down and gently kissed the top of it.

"Oh, be still my beating heart!" Jackie teased.

Meg shook her head at her friend then looked back at Dick.

"Ignore her," she laughed, "she enjoys being a pain in the butt. Good night, Dick. I enjoyed meeting you."

"Ah, the pleasure was all mine, me lady" he chuckled, winking in Jackie's direction.

Chapter 12
Poway, California;
Spring, 1982

Meg heard the phone ring as she struggled down the path to the guest house, balancing a grocery bag on each hip.

"Stuart, honey, run and get the phone, will you?" she called.

As she reached her kitchen door, she heard her son say, "Just a minute, Mr. Tate, I'll get her."

Meg could not contain the instant smile that formed on her lips nor control the heat that rose to her face. She placed the groceries on her kitchen counter and reached for the phone.

"Hi, Dick," she said into the mouthpiece. She winked at Stuart as he raised his eyebrows in question.

Dick asked if he could take her to dinner on Friday or Saturday night.

Because of the negative reactions she had received from men in the past, Meg was usually hesitant to mention her circumstances too soon. For some reason, though, she thought Dick might be different and proceeded to explain about Stuart.

"It's difficult to get a babysitter and I hate to ask my parents too often. So, what would you think if I cooked dinner for you?"

Dick readily agreed and asked for directions to her home. When she explained that they lived in her parent's guest house, she sensed his hesitation. But after a brief pause, he told her he would see her around 5:00 on Saturday. As she placed the phone receiver back in the cradle she looked down at Stuart's anxious face and said, "Well, little guy, looks like Mommy has more shopping to do. What should I cook?"

"Mommy, do you have a *date?*" Stuart marveled.

"Well, yeah, is that so hard to believe?" she replied with a crooked grin.

"Make chili," he bounced up and down, "everybody likes your chili!"

Meg laughed. "Well, now that is a good suggestion. We wouldn't want him to think we're too formal, would we? Okay, hon, we'll give him the ultimate test. If he likes my chili – and you - he might just be a keeper!"

<hr />

"What do you think, hon?" Meg asked Stuart after giving him a taste from the batch of chili that had been slowly simmering in her crock-pot all day.

"Mmmm," he licked his lips, "Can I have some corn chips with it?"

"With dinner you *may,*" she laughed.

Meg moved the curtain aside and peeked out the window at the sound of a car approaching the guest house. A gray Toyota pick-up truck kicked up a cloud of dust as it sped down the dirt road toward the small patch of driveway her father had recently installed.

Ranching was only a part of John McAllister's lifestyle. He was fortunate to have a foreman and several other ranch workers who had been with him for over twenty years, leaving him time to run his business. The bulk of John's income came from his commercial development company, known throughout the state for its unique business park designs.

Having a driveway installed in front of the guest house, which was located on the back section of his property, was simply a matter of a phone call to one of his contractors.

"He's here Stuart, go wash your face," Meg instructed, removing her apron.

When Dick started toward the front door of the cottage, Meg called to him from her kitchen to come to the side.

"Well if it isn't Speedy Gonzalez," she laughed as he wiped his feet on the mat outside the door.

"Sorry, guess I have a bit of a lead foot sometimes," he chuckled. "Well, you certainly do live out in the boondocks, don't you?" he added, stepping into her kitchen.

"I told you it was like living in the country, didn't I? Why? Were you raised in the city and now feeling out of your element?"

"Not at all," he replied. "My parents live in Alameda now, but when I was a kid, we lived in the Napa Valley."

He explained that his father was a stock broker with E.F. Hutton, who had transferred to the Alameda office when Dick was a teenager.

"My dad makes a lot of money, but we didn't live in a big mansion like your family."

Meg laughed, but then the look on his face told her he was serious.

"Well," she stuttered, "my parent's ranch is very nice but I would hardly call it a mansion."

Meg turned as Stuart entered the kitchen, holding up his clean hands for her to inspect.

"Squeaky clean!" she chuckled. "Stuart, this is Dick Tate. He's the nice man who has come to sample Mommy's chili."

"Put her there, pal," Dick offered his hand.

As Stuart shook his hand, Meg was startled to see him flinch in pain. She glanced up to see Dick was laughing.

"Gotta have a good firm handshake if you're gonna hang with the men," Dick chided.

"Yes, sir," Stuart muttered, rubbing his hand.

Seeing the confusion on Stuart's face, Meg cleared her throat before leaning down to kiss the top of his head.

"Well, let's get this show on the road," she clapped her hands together. "How about a beer, Dick?"

While they enjoyed the chili, and Dick did truly seem to like it, she asked him more about his family life. Expecting to hear about his parents and any siblings, Meg was astonished to hear that Dick had been married before.

Dick told her his ex-wife and two sons lived in Sacramento.

"The divorce is almost final. Jordan is very resentful of me for leaving her. She has psychological problems and makes my life difficult on a regular basis. Of course, the only thing she really cares about is how much money she can get out of me."

What surprised her most was the fact that this man had two sons. She wondered what type of father he was and asked him to tell her more about his children.

"Carter just turned four," he explained, "and Brett is two years old. They're good kids, although I have a closer relationship with Carter. Brett was only a couple of weeks old when Jordan and I split. When it's all said and done, it will have taken almost two years to get all this court crap over with. But then you probably understand all about that . . . Did you make big demands for child support when you and Stuart's dad split?"

"On the contrary," she replied, "I don't receive child support. But, I'd really like to hear more about your kids."

Meg did not like to talk about her situation with Ruben. She rarely even discussed it with Jackie, who had been her best friend all her life. She certainly wasn't going to go into it with Dick, whom she barely knew.

Dick told her he was supposed to have his boys for two months every summer and at Christmas but that Jordan made it so difficult he ended up rarely seeing them.

"I really need to get into a more stable environment. Right now, I live in the Bachelor Officer Quarters on the base. That makes it really hard because there is no place for the boys to stay. But with all the money I give to Jordan each month, I don't have any money to get a place of my own, let alone to fly them both down here." He paused before adding, "My God, that woman is greedy."

Meg was beginning to feel uncomfortable with the direction this conversation was going. She sent Stuart in to take a bath and get ready for bed.

"Tell you what, Dick, while you help me with these dishes, you can give me advice on choosing a good wine. Since you grew up in Napa, I assume you know a thing or too about that?"

"Uh, yeah, I can make a few suggestions," he replied. Glancing at the pots and pans stacked in the kitchen sink, he asked, "Where's your dishwasher?"

Meg laughed, "Well, you're looking at it. With just the two of us, it has never seemed necessary to have an automatic dishwasher.

Come on, there are only a few dishes!"

"Oh, all right, Taskmaster," he chuckled.

While she washed and Dick dried the dishes, he described what it was like to grow up surrounded by vineyards. He told her about the times he and his brother ran and played in the fields near their home.

"My little sister didn't come along 'til I was twelve years old. I think my mom really wanted a daughter and just kept trying until she got one. But that meant she was stuck with all us rowdy boys," he remarked.

Meg explained that she had grown up with just one sister and had lived on this ranch her entire life, except for the year she lived in an apartment in Ocean Beach with Ruben.

It was apparent Dick wanted to know more about her relationship with Ruben; he continued to press for information. She explained that it was a very brief relationship and that she didn't know where Ruben was today.

"It's not something I like to talk about. But I will say, I have Stuart because of that relationship. For that, I am eternally grateful. He is the light of my life."

"Man, I wish my ex-wife thought like you do!" he laughed. "Maybe then I wouldn't be going into debt trying to pay for her highfalutin lifestyle."

Stuart came into the room, bathed and in his pajamas. Meg excused herself to go tuck him into bed.

"Goodnight, Mr. Tate," Stuart called from the hallway.

"You can call me Dick," he replied, "Goodnight, pal."

———⊶«◗»⊷———

While Meg was getting Stuart down for the night, Dick selected a Cabernet from the small wine rack in the corner of her kitchenette.

They sipped wine and shared stories the rest of the evening.

When Dick finally rose to leave, Meg was startled to see it was past midnight.

"Time flies when you're having fun," Dick laughed. "Of course, we could have even more fun if I just stay!"

"Uh, I think it is a bit soon for that, Dick" she promptly replied. "Plus I need to be careful around Stuart."

"I understand," Dick said half-heartedly.

Meg walked him to the door, where he leaned down and kissed her passionately. Meg responded with enthusiasm, then pulled back and looked up into his eyes.

"Keep that up and I might forget all about Stuart," she gasped.

Obviously pleased with himself, Dick started toward his truck. "That's precisely what I had in mind, Madam."

Dick started the engine and began to whistle a quiet tune. Meg chuckled to herself as she turned out the lights and prepared for bed.

Chapter 13
Summer, 1982

Although they had seen each other several times since the chili dinner, Dick was meeting Meg's parents for the first time today. They were going to the big house for a barbeque and a swim in her parents' pool.

Because he was the first man Meg had been involved with since Ruben, she was feeling a little anxious. Her mother was still angry with Ruben for leaving his wife and child to fend for themselves; her father had always been overly protective of both his daughters. She wondered how they would feel about Dick once they had met him.

Meg had chosen her outfit with care. Not wanting to dress up too much for a simple family barbecue, yet wanting to wow Dick, she had chosen pale yellow overall shorts that complimented her red hair.

Meg peered out her kitchen window at a clear blue sky and could almost feel the warmth of the sun as its rays reflected off the hood of her car. *At least it's a beautiful day for a barbecue - that's a good sign.*

She placed a cover over the peach pie she had baked for dessert and prepared to head up to her parents'. Stuart was already there, playing in the pool with his cousin, and Dick was supposed to meet her there a half hour from now.

She thought about Dick now and felt her skin tingle. It had only been a few weeks but she knew she was falling hard for him. He seemed to feel the same and had already hinted that he wanted to marry her as soon as his divorce was final. He had even brought up the possibility of moving in with her. Meg had told him that, although it was a nice idea, they might be moving a bit too fast.

"Don't you think you should at least meet my parents before we jump into something so serious?" she had asked with a wry smile.

That discussion had led to today's get-together.

When she had broached the subject with her parents, her mother said, "Well, I wondered when you were going to get around to introducing us. Stuart talks about him all the time and we've certainly been babysitting more than usual, so we knew this one was more than a casual friend!"

Her dad had been a little leery of the situation. "As you know, I was a sailor during World War II and I know what they're like. Makes me nervous to know my daughter is getting involved with one."

"Oh Daddy," she'd laughed, "Dick isn't really a sailor; he's a pilot. There *is* a difference."

To that, John McAllister had simply grunted and said, "Not much."

Meg now picked up her pie and muttered out loud, "Well, here goes nothin'," as she headed out the kitchen door toward the big house.

Meg could hear the kid's laughter and the splashing of the water as it slapped against the Mexican tile surrounding the pool.

"That was a good one!" she heard her sister Gwen shout.

As she rounded the back of the house, she realized that Gwen was congratulating Stuart on the large splash he made with his cannonball dive. Gwen's daughter Katy was standing on the edge of the pool, preparing to make what she hoped would be an even better cannonball splash.

"I see the competition has already begun," Meg laughed as she approached her sister who was standing just outside the sliding glass doors that led from the house to the pool area.

"Oh yeah," Gwen answered, glancing over her shoulder at the sound of tires crunching on the driveway.

"Hey, looks like your guy is here," she ventured.

"Oh, he's early!" Meg panicked. "Are Ma and Daddy ready?"

"Just!" she heard her mother's voice through the screen door.

Meg ran inside, placing the pie on the kitchen counter, and hurried toward the front door.

"Well, I guess we can't call him late for dinner," her father remarked from the hallway.

"Be nice, Daddy!" she scolded.

Her dad's deep chuckle harmonized with the doorbell's melodious chime.

"Hey babe!" he grinned as she opened the door. She eyed his blue-flowered bathing trunks and sandals.

Meg introduced him to her parents, trying to ignore her mother's raised eyebrows. She, along with her parents, was a bit taken aback by his attire. Meg had told Dick her parents were having a barbecue in his honor and had mentioned that he should bring a bathing suit so they could swim later. She hadn't expected him to show up as though he was only here for a dip in the pool.

After all the introductions were made, Meg went into the kitchen to help her mother. She could hear Dick talking to her father while he prepared the grill. He was telling John about his college swimming background.

"Yeah, I could line my walls with swimming medals if I wanted to," he bragged.

"You know," he went on, "I swam against Mark Spitz. I didn't beat him but sure came close a couple of times."

"That so?" she heard her dad respond as Dick continued to describe his athletic feats.

Meg cringed inwardly. She could tell by his manner that her father wasn't too impressed with Dick.

Her mother was harder to read, although later that evening while Meg and Gwen were doing the dishes, Mary McAllister professed, "Well, Dick is certainly an enthusiastic eater!"

Gwen laughed and winked at Meg, "Well, what would you expect, Ma? He's a big boy."

"I wasn't being critical, Gwen," Mary reproved, "just making an observation. He's a nice young man."

Meg breathed a sigh of relief.

Chapter 14
Winter, 1982

Dick's divorce would be final in a week.

He had moved in with Meg a month ago, during which he had described all of his woes with the courts and particularly with Jordan, his ex-wife.

Dick had told her that Jordan was seeking revenge on him for leaving and that she would do anything to get back at him.

"The judge ordered me to provide her with a phone number. But I don't want you to have to deal with her, Meg. If she calls here, don't talk to her. Hang up. She's a real bitch and won't hesitate to dig her claws into you the first chance she gets."

So when she answered the phone and the woman on the other end identified herself as "Dick's ex-wife," she had been mortified.

"His son misses him and would like to talk to him," Jordan had told her.

Meg had managed to mumble, "He's not here," before quickly hanging up the phone.

Now, she was pacing the length of her kitchen, waiting for

Dick to return from the store.

Her hand trembled as she swiped at her brow to catch the droplets of sweat slowly trickling into her eyes.

"Why is it so hot in here?" she fretted, "Is the air conditioning not working?"

"It's not hot, Mommy," Stuart answered. "Are you sick or somethin'?"

"No honey," she waved her hand at him, "I'm just anxious for Dick to get home I guess."

After what seemed an eternity, she saw Dick's truck headed down the drive. He casually leaned across the seat to grab the fishing pole he had just purchased. As he hopped down from the truck's cab, he looked up to see Meg standing in front of him and grinned.

His smile faded immediately, Meg's anxiety clearly written on her face.

"What's up, babe?" he asked.

She explained about the phone call and saw his concern turn to fury.

"Damn that bitch! I told you she would call," he erupted.

He scowled as he pondered the ground for a moment then looked at her and said, "You did the right thing, Meg. Don't worry - I'll take care of her . . . Fucking bitch!"

Meg felt Stuart's presence and spun around to see a look of terror on his face.

"Wh-what's the matter, Dick?" he stammered.

Meg went to Stuart. She wrapped her arms around him and stroked his hair

"Just grown-up stuff, honey," she soothed, "Dick is just upset. It'll be alright."

Shooting daggers at Dick with her eyes, she turned and walked Stuart back toward the house. She would discuss his cursing in front of Stuart later. Right now, she just wanted to calm Stuart, and herself.

A half hour later, while settling Stuart in front of the television set, Meg overheard Dick on the phone. Judging by his tone, it was apparent he was speaking to Jordan. She tensed at the anger in his voice.

"This is my girlfriend's house," he fumed. "Don't ever call here again! Got it?"

Seconds after she heard the phone receiver bang into its cradle, Dick walked into the room with a self-satisfied look on his face.

"I don't think you need to worry about her calling here again," he smirked.

"But she said one of your boys wanted to talk to you…"

Dick's face colored as he glared at her and blurted, "Well, if you had a fucking brain, you would know she just used that as an excuse to call here!"

Meg was stunned. She reached up and placed her hand on her cheek as if to salve a hornet's sting.

She struggled for a moment to regain her composure, mostly for Stuart's sake.

Then, eyes narrowed and speaking through gritted teeth, Meg hissed, "Get out of my house – now!"

It was Dick's turn to be stunned. He stared dully at her, slack-jawed, as though unable to comprehend her words. Slowly, his eyes began to display a sense of panic. He reached his hand out toward Meg.

Meg instinctively took a step backwards.

"Babe, I'm sorry. I'm just upset. I didn't mean to take it out on you. I love you, you know that. Please forgive me," he pleaded.

Gazing into his eyes, Meg sensed that he meant it. She told herself that Dick had just reacted poorly to an unpleasant situation. *I'd probably respond with anger in the same situation,* she thought. *I'm sure he didn't mean to be so hurtful.* She stepped into his open arms and wrapped her arms around his neck, melding her body to his.

"Shhhh, its okay, hon, I know, I know . . ." she whispered into his ear.

Meg glanced down at Stuart's questioning face then reached out her arm and pulled him up against her.

"Sometimes grown ups act very silly," she murmured.

Chapter 15
Winter, 1984-Spring, 1985

"Well, I guess I'm never going to have the chance to plan a real wedding," Mary grumbled. "You and Ruben eloped, Gwen never married the jerk who fathered her daughter and now you and Dick want a small, intimate wedding with immediate family only."

Meg chuckled, then leaned over and kissed her mother on the cheek.

"I'm sorry, Ma, I would like nothing better than for you to put on a big, lavish wedding celebration for me. But you must agree it would be somewhat inappropriate since Dick was recently divorced - not to mention the fact that both of us will be marrying for the second time."

Mary nodded grudgingly and said, "Yes, I have resigned myself to these facts. But don't expect me to be cheerful about it as well!"

We have all resigned ourselves to certain things, Meg reflected.

She had always dreamed of being married on Valentine's Day and had expressed that desire to Dick, but he'd insisted they wed by the end of the year, saying that otherwise she'd have to wait six months to get her military spouse benefits.

Now, Mary was helping Meg plan the small ceremony that would take place in mid-November. Since the guest list would only include Meg's immediate family and Dick's parents, they had decided to have a simple wedding dinner in the back room of a local steak house.

Although Meg was a practicing Catholic, Dick was unwilling to convert, which meant they could not be married in her Parish. As an old family friend, though, Father O'Connell had agreed to marry them under the arbor in the McAllister's backyard.

Explaining that he and his mother were born-again Christians, he'd told her, "My mother is none too pleased," then had laughed as he added, "But she said it was better that I marry a Catholic than another heathen like Jordan. I was raised as an Episcopalian, so I can relate to some of your beliefs."

The other issue they had compromised on was the honeymoon. Dick did not have any military leave accrued, so had promised Meg a honeymoon in Hawaii next year. "We could go to Maui for Valentine's Day if you want."

"Well at least you know you two can find the middle ground for those issues on which you don't agree – an important ingredient to a good marriage," Mary pointed out while discussing these plans with Meg. "At the same time," she observed, "it seems as if you're the one conceding the most."

Meg's head jerked up from the bridal magazine she had been perusing. The crease between her eyebrows deepened.

"Oh, Ma, I'm sure there will be plenty of things Dick will compromise on during our marriage. These things are just more important to him than to me. I don't mind, really!" she insisted.

"Well, I hope so. I just don't want the two of you to start off on the wrong track."

Her parents had insisted that Meg, Dick and Stuart continue to live in the guest house. But since they would now have Dick's income in addition to Meg's she felt it only fair that they pay rent.

Her father agreed because he said, "Dick needs to feel as though he's taking care of his family," but suggested an amount much lower than they would have to pay to lease an apartment or house elsewhere.

———⟨◉⟩———

Dick was depressed. Their wedding had gone off without a hitch; however his parents had told him they were getting a divorce. This came as a shock to Dick and he had been moping around the house for weeks.

When he wasn't brooding about his parents, he was complaining about Jordan.

Now, as he walked into the kitchen where Meg was preparing dinner, he was studying Jordan's expense statement.

"God, that bitch is greedy. How can she possibly need all this money to live on?" he scoffed. "Am I supposed to provide steak dinners for her and all her boyfriends? This is ridiculous!"

With their divorce filing, both Jordan and Dick were required to declare any income, along with their expenses. Jordan was a college student and not employed; her only income was derived from the GI bill payments she received.

"How can she possibly spend $300 for food each month?" he asked incredulously.

"Well, I don't know Dick. We spend more than that each month . . . and we shop at the Commissary."

"Whose side are you on, anyway?" he turned to glare at her.

"Oh Dick, stop it!" she cried, "You know perfectly well that I'm totally supportive of you."

She watched as his facial expression changed from irritation to a stunned, contemplative look and then a wide grin.

"You know what, babe? I think you may have hit on something!" he exclaimed. "Jordan is probably shopping in the commissary and she shouldn't be. She was supposed to return her ID card but said she lost it."

Chuckling, he added, "Well, we will just see about that! I'm going to report her to the Navy. And another thing," he continued, "you work in the Commissary . . . Let's put a list together of normal food items and then price them at both the Commissary and the local grocery store. That will tell us if she's lying about her monthly expenses."

Meg wasn't sure what to make of his idea.

"Dick, aren't you carrying this a bit too far? The judge has already established what you have to pay each month – why dwell on this? It's not going to change anything and it will just continue to make you unhappy."

"Because I have to know, okay?" he scowled at her.

Meg reluctantly agreed to help him. It seemed to make him feel better for reasons she could not understand. His spirits had seemed so low since their wedding, making life with him nearly unbearable. She would do anything to bring him out of his funk.

Dick attacked this new project with zeal. He grabbed a piece of paper and started making a mock grocery list. "Okay.

Mayonnaise, peanut butter . . . what else?"

Meg sat down next to him with a sigh. "Okay, let me see what you have so far . . ."

On Valentine's Day, Meg reminded Dick of his promise to take her to Maui for a honeymoon.

Dick scowled at her and said, "You never let anything go, do you?

This time, Meg responded with anger.

"You know what, Dick? I'm sick and tired of your moods. I'm tired of you being depressed and grouchy and taking it out on me all the time. You insisted we get married in November because you said I wouldn't be able to get military benefits for a year. Well, I happen to know that was a bald-faced lie. I talked to some of the other wives . . ."

Dick's hand jerked up as though he were going to slap her; Meg flinched, the palm of his hand stopped an inch away from her cheek.

"You're right," he growled, "I lied. I wanted the tax benefits, okay? I could claim you and Stuart on my taxes so long as we were married before the end of the year. So yeah, I made that up."

Meg was stunned. She felt as if he *had* followed through and slapped her.

"And we can't afford to go on any damn honeymoon! Don't you get it? Are you a total idiot? How the hell am I supposed to pay all that damn support to that whore ex-wife of mine and take you to Hawaii?" he spewed.

She just stood there, gaping at him, speechless.

Dick turned and crashed through the kitchen door, making Meg jump as it slammed with a bang behind him.

What have I done? she wondered. *My God, I've married a lunatic.*

. .

She turned to see Stuart standing in the hallway. The look on his face told her he had witnessed the entire scene.

Softening, she walked over and wrapped her arms around his head, pulling him up against her.

"I'm sorry you saw that, honey. It's going to be okay – you'll see. Dick just needs to go somewhere and calm down."

Chapter 16
Summer, 1985

Spring blossoms were fading as bright summer blooms in full spectrum began to appear in pots and gardens throughout the city.

Meg and Jackie were dining on the patio of Ricardo's, a Mexican café near the naval base. Ricardo's had been one of their regular hangouts before Meg had met Dick.

Meg had been thrilled when Jackie called her and suggested lunch. Because Dick made no bones about the fact he didn't like her best friend, the two had not spent much time together during the past year.

"Now I'm getting depressed, Jack," Meg complained to her friend, "Dick is so morose all the time and so pissed off at everybody, mostly his ex-wife. It's like an obsession with him.

"Last night for instance, we were lying in bed, my head on his shoulder, his arms wrapped around me and he's telling me how much he hates Jordan. I can't even have that time with him without her consuming his thoughts! I'm beginning to hate her too."

"Well, I don't blame you, hon. You guys are newlyweds and all he does is talk about his ex? You deserve better than that." Jackie retorted.

"Have you met this woman? Do her horns show or are they safely hidden under her hair?" she snickered.

Meg smiled.

"Yeah, I saw her once at the court house in Sacramento and another time when we went to mediation. Because I'm his wife and the boys come and stay with us during summer vacation and holidays, I had to go talk to the mediator too.

"Actually, she seems like a reasonable person, but according to Dick she's putting on an act for the benefit of judges and mediators. He said if they saw the real Jordan, they'd grant him custody of his kids without blinking."

Jackie placed the palm of her hand on top of Meg's, which was tightly wound around her water glass.

"I know you don't want to hear this, hon . . . He's your husband. You love him and you want to believe everything he tells you," Jackie said seriously. "But . . . well . . . you remember Joe Davis – the fighter jock?"

Med nodded.

"I saw him a few weeks ago and he asked about you. I told him about your marriage. As it turns out, he's a friend of Jordan's . . . He's known her for years – since before she met Dick – and apparently they've stayed in touch."

"Fancy that," Meg remarked sardonically.

Jackie frowned at her and then continued, "Anyway . . . his opinion was that Dick's just another guy suffering from a wounded ego. That he hasn't forgiven Jordan for leaving him."

Meg looked at Jackie with surprise, "Jack, she didn't leave him, he left her!"

Jackie shook her head.

"Au contraire, mon ami. Joe said Jordan kicked Dick out . . . that he was abusive toward her and the kids."

Meg stood up so abruptly her chair fell backwards and hit the floor with a bang, drawing the attention of other diners.

"Why are you doing this Jackie? Why are you discussing my husband with someone who's Jordan's friend?" she fumed. "And you do her dirty work for her by spreading these lies about him? You're supposed to be my best friend! I guess Dick was right about you, after all. You *are* jealous of my marriage!"

Meg turned on her heel and practically ran out of the restaurant.

Once in the car, Meg laid her head against the steering wheel and wept so hard she didn't see Jackie approach. The tapping on the window so startled her that she actually smiled with relief when she realized who it was.

Jackie took in Meg's tear-streaked face and puffy eyes and then reached down to open the car door.

"Oh, Meg, honey. I'm so sorry I hurt you. You've been my best friend since I can remember. I'd never do anything to intentionally cause you pain. Please forgive me," she cried.

Meg reached her arms toward Jackie, who leaned in for a hug.

"I'm sorry too, Jack," she sniffed, "I'm just so miserable right now. I feel like I made a terrible mistake to marry Dick and what you told me only made me feel worse. I'm sorry I doubted you."

Jackie walked around to the other side of the car and got in.

Meg studied her lap for a moment and then murmured, "You know, Jack, we were at a party a few weeks ago . . . a Navy thing, with people he works with. I was talking to the Executive Officer's wife and she said, 'Oh, Dick Tate is your husband? I'm sorry, but I think he is the most obnoxious man I've ever met.' Jack, I was stunned - stunned that she would actually say that to his wife. Then I realized she must dislike him so much she didn't care. But, can you imagine how I felt? I was fretting over my marriage even before that conversation. Now I feel as though people think I'm stupid as well!"

Jackie put her hand on Meg's shoulder and gave her a half-smile.

"Oh honey, you aren't stupid! That woman is the stupid one. I don't care what she thinks - she never should have said that to you. Nobody thinks you're stupid – at least nobody who matters. You loved him, you married him. Maybe he just needs to get this divorce well behind him and then he can concentrate on his current relationship."

Meg leaned over and hugged her. "Oh Jack, I'm so glad I have you in my life."

She turned her gaze to look out her window and murmured, "But that's something else I have to contend with. Dick doesn't like me to spend time with you - my mom either. Every day I feel more and more isolated from my friends and family. I live on the same property as my parents but hardly see them."

Meg looked back at Jackie. The pity she saw in her friend's eyes only added to her misery.

For the next few minutes both women were silent, seemingly lost in their own thoughts. Meg's mind was racing, as she mulled over the past year and a half of her marriage.

Suddenly, she turned to look at her best friend and said, "You know, Jack, you're probably right. Dick just needs to resolve his issues with his ex-wife. And I probably should be more supportive.

Maybe we need to take a short vacation, get away from it all for a few days and spend some time together, just the two of us. You know, work on *our* marriage instead of focusing on his last one."

Jackie seemed pensive for a few seconds but then smiled and with her best attempt at a British accent said, "By Jove, I think you've got it, luv!"

The two laughed then and for a few minutes Meg felt as carefree as she had before Dick, before her wedding – just laughing and joking with her oldest friend.

———— ⊃«⦿»⊂ ————

Meg was sitting in the living room, waiting for Dick to get home from work. A chicken casserole was baking in the oven and the table was set. She was excited about her vacation idea; she was even humming, something she hadn't done in months.

Stuart was in his bedroom doing homework.

He had noticed her improved mood when she arrived home and had remarked, "You've been kinda grouchy lately, Mama, I'm glad to see you being happy again."

Meg immediately experienced feelings of guilt.

She looked into her son's soulful eyes and said, "Oh honey, I'm so sorry. I have been a grouch, haven't I? I'm going to work on that - try to be my old self again."

Now, she could hear Dick's truck speeding down the driveway. Her heart began to pound and butterflies fluttered in her stomach. She jumped up and ran into the kitchen to greet him at the side door he always entered.

As he opened the door, she was surprised to see a wide grin on his face.

Wow, she thought, *how nice to see him smile again. Maybe it's contagious today!*

"Hey baby!" she cooed as he came into the kitchen.

His arms were around her in an instant. Lifting her up off the floor and pulling her toward him, he planted a big kiss on her mouth.

"Guess what!" he exclaimed.

Meg giggled, kicking her feet forward and back as they dangled beneath her.

"My lawyer called today. The boys are going to stay with us all summer! I have to fly to Sacramento on Friday to pick them up and then fly back here with them – and you're going with me! That means we'll have two whole months to get them out from under Jordan's spell. I can teach them to be men, instead of the fags she's turning them into."

Meg's face fell. She didn't know what to say. She had been so excited about her vacation plan and now realized it would not be possible.

But maybe having his kids here will improve his mood, she told herself.

She could already see this news was having a positive affect on him so forced a smile and said, "Oh Dick - that *is* great news. I'm sure Stuart will enjoy having them here to play with this summer as well."

"Yeah, he can play big brother full time!" he beamed. "Let's go give him the news."

—•⟩•—

Meg went with Dick to pick up the boys for their visit. They and Jordan were waiting for them near the gate where they would momentarily board a flight back to San Diego.

The boys seemed happy to see their father, but reluctant to leave their mother. Carter greeted Meg and Dick with a big smile but glanced over at Jordan repeatedly, as if to assure himself she was okay.

Meg realized that Jordan was not handling this well. Her puffy eyes were rimmed with red, making it obvious she'd been crying.

Now, as she said goodbye to the boys, she began to sob. Jordan's mother, who had accompanied them to the airport, embraced her while Dick, Meg and the kids began to board the airplane.

Then Meg looked up and saw a pleading, almost-pitiful look in Jordan's eyes. At that moment, she felt deeply sorry for her. She knew Jordan had never been away from the boys for longer than a weekend. As a mother, she understood the anguish this was causing her husband's former wife.

Meg winked at Jordan and mouthed, "Don't worry - I'll take good care of them."

Jordan's eyed widened and then, her face softening, murmured, "Thank you."

⸺◦⟨◉⟩◦⸺

Carter and Brett had been with them for two weeks, during which Dick had worked a lot, leaving Meg to take over the primary parental role. Although she liked the boys, she resented being put in this position.

Just last night, she had discussed the situation with Dick. He became angry with her, telling her that he treated Stuart as if he were his own, asking why she couldn't do the same with his kids.

"They need to spend time with you, Dick. They aren't here to be with me, they are here to be with their father."

Although he'd still been angry at bedtime, he'd promised to spend the entire weekend doing something with the boys – all three of them. That was two days from now and Meg was as excited as the boys were.

Although having the boys with them had substantially improved Dick's mood, Meg suspected that depriving Jordan of the kids was what was really behind his new cheerfulness.

Instead of doing something fun with the boys, such as taking them fishing as Dick had originally hinted, he had decided he was going to test and improve their intellectual abilities. He'd come home on Friday with math workbooks and flash cards.

"I don't think Jordan pays any attention to their schooling," he explained to Meg. "Carter doesn't seem like he's at the level he should be. So, I'm going to spend the rest of the summer getting him up to snuff."

Meg was flabbergasted but kept her thoughts to herself. She figured any time Dick spent with his kids would be beneficial.

While Carter had spent the weekend doing his "homework," Dick took a couple of hours between watching sports on television and dozing on the couch, to show Stuart and Brett how to shoot a BB gun.

When Meg protested, Dick had snapped, "First you want me to spend time with them . . . then when I do, you bite my head off. My father taught me how to shoot a BB gun. It's a male thing.

So get off my fucking back, Meg!"

Now, she stood at the window, watching in horror as Dick shot a Robin. Falling from the top of the fence where it had been perched moments before, the bird now lye on the grass. Meg could see the bird's tiny chest rise and fall as its heart beat rapidly, then watched in despair as it finally stilled. Stuart and Brett both looked as if they were going to be sick. She couldn't hear what Dick was saying to them, but by the expression on his face she could tell it wasn't pleasant.

Just then she was startled by a banging sound coming from another part of the house. She rushed into the family room to see Carter banging his head against the wall.

"Carter, honey!" she shouted.

She quickly walked over, leaned down and wrapped her arms around him.

"Whatever is the matter?" she asked in a soothing voice.

Carter looked up at her with an expression that broke her heart.

"I'm so stupid, Meg. I'm dumb. I can't think right. I don't know how to do this stuff. Dad said I should know this and to keep working on it until I did. But I don't understand. Why am I so stupid?"

Meg hugged him tighter, smoothing his hair with the palm of her hand.

"Shhhh, honey, don't talk that way," she whispered, "You aren't stupid. Don't ever think that. I'll talk to your dad and get him to understand that these lessons are too hard for you."

Carter looked at her in horror. "No, Meg, don't tell my dad I can't do it!" he pleaded, "He'll be really mad. He'll call me dumb and say bad things about my mom again."

Meg was dumbfounded. *How*, she wondered, *could Dick be so cruel and insensitive to his own son?*

"Okay I won't say that," she assured him, "but I will talk to him about all this school work he has you doing. Between you and me, I disagree with your having to spend your summer studying. Now, promise me you won't call yourself stupid anymore. You're very smart, Carter, you must believe that!"

He nodded, but she sensed he didn't really believe her words. Anger welled up inside of her. She was determined to make Dick understand how he was harming his child.

As she stood, she kissed Carter on the top of his head. "I think that's enough for one day, honey. Why don't you come in the kitchen with me while I prepare dinner?"

Carter glanced out the window at his father.

"Don't worry," she quickly added, 'I'll tell your dad I made you quit, okay?"

He slowly rose and followed her into the kitchen.

———

That night Dick and Meg had a loud argument that kept all three kids awake. Brett crawled into bed with Carter and they huddled up together trying to ignore the quarrelling.

"They're *my* kids!" Dick bellowed, "I'll decide what's best for them. Don't you *ever* countermand my instructions again!"

Meg was furious.

"And I'm their stepmother," she contended. "You've hardly been around the whole time they've been here. Just who do you think has been taking care of them?

"Dick, what you are doing to Carter is wrong. I can't just stand by and watch you abuse him this way and not say anything!"

She felt her head jerk backward as the back of his hand smashed across her face. In an attempt to calm the stinging pain, she placed her palm on her cheek and felt the wet stickiness of blood trickling from the side of her mouth.

Meg glared up at Dick, who turned, grabbed his car keys off the top of his dresser and headed for the door.

"Yes, that's right. Go! Get the hell out of my house!" she screamed after him. This time I mean it, you asshole!"

She flinched as the front door slammed.

It was then that she heard Brett crying. Meg raced down the hall to Stuart's bedroom where all three boys had been sleeping. Though Carter was trying to calm Brett, he continued to wail.

She smoothed Carter's hair from his forehead and then scooped Brett up into her arms.

"It's okay, guys, really!" she murmured. "Sometimes big people get mad at each other and fight, just like you guys do, ya know? We can be pretty dumb sometimes. But your dad will be back later when he's calmed down and everything will be okay again."

"I want my mommy," Brett sniffed.

"Oh be quiet, Brett," Carter whispered. "You know we can't see Mommy for a couple more months."

Carter glanced at Meg.

"He doesn't mean anything against you, Meg," he explained, "He's just a big baby sometimes."

Meg forced a smile.

"I know, honey, I'm not offended. I just want you both to know that I love you just like you were my own."

"Me too," Stuart said from the other bed, "you guys are my brothers."

Meg stayed with the boys until they were all asleep. When she went back to her own bedroom, she was startled to see Dick asleep in their bed. She considered sleeping on the couch but decided against it.

She carefully climbed into the bed so as not to wake him and then scooted as far away from him as she could. An inch further and she would have fallen off the bed.

She was too anxious to sleep, so spent the next few hours mulling over the problems with her marriage and with Dick.

———※◎※———

The next morning, Dick apologized to Meg for striking her.

Although Meg outwardly accepted his apology, she had made some decisions during the night between her fitful attempts at sleep. She planned to seek out the advice of an attorney as to how to handle potential divorce proceedings.

———※◎※———

Somehow they all survived the rest of summer. Brett had begun to wet his bed and Meg was stuck with cleaning him up and washing his sheets every day. Carter had continued to struggle with the summer schoolwork Dick had assigned, and it broke Meg's heart to see how miserable he was, and how much he feared his father.

One Saturday afternoon, all three boys had wandered down to a nearby creek to play, contrary to Dick's strict instructions that they were not to go anywhere without permission.

Dick was furious. He dragged Carter and Brett back to the

house, all the while berating Stuart for being a bad influence on them.

He sent the boys to their room, after informing Carter and Brett that, as their punishment, they would have only bread and water to eat for the next two days.

Meg tried once again to intervene, to no avail. But after Dick went to bed, she sneaked food in to them.

When it came time for the boys to go home, everyone was relieved.

Meg was relieved for the boys' sake, while Stuart was hoping that their not being there would ease the tension around the house. Dick, on the other hand, seemed happy to be rid of the responsibility of being a full time parent.

Having them back at home also enables his continuing harassment of Jordan, Meg thought with disgust. Lately, these types of disturbing thoughts plagued her on a regular basis.

Chapter 17
Fall, 1985

Meg was sitting on the edge of a lightly padded wooden chair, repeatedly twisting her hands. Her period was three weeks late.

Jackie, the only person to whom she had confided this information, had come with her to the Doctor's office. Now, without saying a word, Jackie placed one hand on top of Meg's to still them. The two continued to wait in silence for her long-time family doctor who would provide the results of an earlier pregnancy test.

After what seemed like hours, the nurse called her name. Meg flashed a timid smile at Jackie before following the nurse to the examination room.

The state of Meg's marriage was so miserable she was desperately hoping she was not pregnant, but when Peter Adams, her long-time family doctor, burst into the room wearing a huge grin, Meg knew her worst fears had been realized.

She burst into tears, startling the doctor.

"Why Meg, I thought you would be thrilled with the news," he said.

Meg swiped at her eyes, trying to stop crying. But it seemed as though the harder she tried to block the tears the harder she sobbed.

Dr. Adam's face was full of concern. He grabbed a tissue from the box on the counter and handed it to her.

"Do you want to talk about it?" he asked soothingly.

Meg blew her nose and then began to hiccup. "I – I always hiccup when I cry," she told him, "why is that?"

Before he could respond, she began to tell him about her troubled marriage. She explained that, although she had tried everything she could think of to make it work, she feared her relationship with Dick was doomed to fail.

"Dr. Adams, how can I bring a child into the world under these circumstances? Just a week ago, I was considering the idea of making an appointment with a friend's divorce attorney. Now this! Obviously having a baby complicates matters."

Dr. Adams tried his best to console her. He paused before saying, "I know your religious beliefs rule out abortion but I want you to know that the option is out there. The best thing you can do at this point is to take some time to yourself and mull all this over. It's not necessary to make a decision right away."

She nodded and grabbed a fresh tissue to dab her eyes. Noting the tiny pieces of white tissue clinging to her eyelashes, Dr. Adams suggested Meg stop in the restroom and wash her face with cool water.

"If there's anything I can do to help, Meg, please let me know," he murmured as she headed toward the nurses station.

⸺ ◉ ⸺

From the instant she'd seen Meg's red-rimmed eyes and gloomy expression, Jackie seemed to perceive Meg's despair. She suggested they go to Ricardo's for a bite to eat and Meg jumped at the idea.

"A Margarita sounds really good right now," Meg remarked, "but I guess I shouldn't because of the baby."

That's when it really hit her. She was pregnant with Dick's child.

The two women were silent for a few minutes, Meg lost in thought and Jackie allowing her the solace she needed.

"You know, Jack, I could never get rid of any child I created. It's not just because of the church, but also because of the miracle of life that's growing inside me. Somehow, I'll make this work. You never know, it might even bring Dick and me closer together. Maybe having a new child to think about will take his mind off the boys somewhat. Not that I want him to forget the children he already has, but maybe it will diminish his obsession with Jordan," she rambled.

Jackie seemed to recognize this soliloquy as Meg's way of working things out in her own mind. She'd also learned not to express any opinions one way or the other when it came to Meg's relationship with Dick. So she sat there quietly while Meg chattered on and on.

By the time they finished their meals, Meg had convinced herself that having Dick's child was just the thing to make her marriage succeed. So, with a lilt in her step, Meg followed Jackie out of the restaurant. Now she couldn't wait to get home to tell Dick the news.

Chapter 18
Late Spring, 1986

Placing a hand on her aching back, Meg stood back and admired her handiwork. She had spent every spare minute over the past several weeks wallpapering and preparing the tiny room that had previously served as her sewing room.

According to the ultrasound she had undergone two months ago, she was expecting to deliver her baby girl in three weeks. This knowledge prompted her to purchase pale pink wallpaper, decorated with dark pink bunnies. She had also dug out Stuart's crib and painted it white.

Dick had been thrilled with the news of her pregnancy and though he didn't share the work with her, supported Meg's efforts at preparing the nursery. Soon after he arrived home each evening, he would wander in to see that day's accomplishments.

Stuart's excitement was infectious. He somehow sensed that having a baby sister would be a unique experience – different from that of his role as big brother to Carter and Brett.

While Meg stood in the corner of the room smoothing out a bubble in the wallpaper, she heard the kitchen door slam. Dick had gone to the hardware store to buy some new pulls for the used dressing table Meg had picked up at a yard sale. At Meg's suggestion he had taken Stuart with him.

She waited expectantly for one or both of them to come into the nursery, but no one appeared. It was actually very quiet in the house and she began to wonder if she had imagined the sound of the door.

Suddenly, she heard tires screeching in the driveway. Her curiosity got the better of her; she ran over and peered out the living room window just in time to see Dick's car speeding toward the main road.

What on earth is going on? she wondered.

Just then, Meg heard a sniffling sound as though someone was crying and felt a chill tingling down her spine.

"Stuart?" she called out.

She received no response. She stood very still and listened. There! She heard that sniffling again. It sounded like it was coming from Stuart's room. She turned and ran in that direction.

As Meg approached his bedroom, the sniffling got louder. When she walked into the room, however, she saw no one. Totally baffled, she spun around, looking in every direction to determine where the sound was coming from.

It was then that she saw one of Stuart's feet sticking out from under his bed.

"Stuart, honey?" she coaxed, "What's wrong? Why are you under the bed?"

She reached beneath the box spring and placed her hand on his back. She was stunned to find he was trembling.

"Baby, what is it? What's happened?" she implored as she pulled him out from under the bed and embraced him.

For several minutes they sat in silence, Meg holding Stuart tightly against her. Finally, his shaking eased and she could feel his tension begin to subside.

His face was streaked with tears.

"Tell me what happened, sweetie. Please."

With one last shudder he murmured, "D-D-Dick said he would have to k-kill me."

Startled, Meg let out an audible gasp. "What?"

"I was asking him about the helicopter he flies. He was mean, Mommy. He yelled at me. He said I was too nosy for my own good and then he said, 'If I tell you I'll have to kill you.' Then he laughed at me in a scary way and said he'd decided he was going to tell me after all. I started to cry and he said I was a big baby and that I should act like a man. He was driving really fast and when we got home he told me to get out of his car. He said he didn't want to be around a whiny baby like me."

Inwardly Meg was furious but realized what Stuart needed most right now was reassurance. She held him tighter, rocking back and forth.

With a forced calm she said, "I'm so sorry Dick scared you, honey. He was wrong to say that to you. But he wasn't serious. Sometimes things seem funny to Dick that really aren't. I don't know how to explain it to you, but please trust me when I tell you that nobody's going to harm you in any way. "

Stuart didn't say anything but after several minutes she felt his body relax. Meg sat on the floor embracing her little boy for the next half hour, at which point his shallow breathing told her he'd fallen asleep. Slowly rising with Stuart in her arms, she placed him on his bed. Smoothing the hair away from his face, she leaned down and kissed his forehead.

"I love you, sweetie," she whispered before turning to leave the room.

＝＝＝((O))＝＝＝

When Dick walked through the door, Meg met him face on.

"How dare you?" she sputtered. "Does it make you feel like a big man to terrorize a little boy? What is wrong with you?"

She watched while first shock, then anger, then distress flashed across his face. Meg began to feel uneasy as he stood there quietly gaping at her.

Finally, he uttered, "I should have known he'd come running to Mama. You baby that boy," he charged. "How is he ever going to become a man if you always treat him like he's going to break?"

"You know what, Dick - I now understand why Carter and Brett fear you! You don't know how to treat children. My God! We are talking about *children* here!"

Now his expression turned to fury. He roughly shoved her up against the broom closet, holding her by the throat with one hand. She could feel the door trim digging into her back. Dick's face was within an inch of hers.

"You stupid, cunt!" he barked, "Don't say another word about my kids. And don't think for a minute that I'm gonna let you *or* that other bitch I married turn my kids into pansy asses like that whiny little sissy you molly-coddle on a regular basis."

She reached up to wipe away the spittle that sprayed her face as he spoke, but Dick grabbed her wrist with his free hand, raised it over her head and rammed it against the closet door.

His face was almost against hers, but far enough away that she could see the menacing look on his face.

"You brainless bitch!" he spat, "If you weren't carrying my child in that fat belly of yours . . . ."

Suddenly he stopped talking. He stood and looked at her for a minute, scrutinizing her face. Releasing her wrist, he wiped his spittle off Meg's cheek.

Stepping backward, his expression changed once again. His face crumpled and he began to sob.

Meg was so taken aback that she just stared at him, her mouth agape.

"I'm so sorry, baby," he wailed, "I don't know what came over me. It's like something takes over and I don't know who I am anymore. I don't want to hurt you. I don't want to hurt our baby. You're both precious to me."

Instinctively, she wrapped her arms around his neck, pulling his head toward her.

"Oh hon, please don't cry. It's okay . . ." she paused, "I know you don't mean to be so cruel. But, truly, Dick, I think we need to get some help if we're going to make this marriage work, if we're going to be good parents - not just to our little girl but the children each of us has already created."

Dick embraced her and leaned down to kiss her. Meg turned her face to give him her cheek.

"No, Dick." Meg pulled back. "I can't just forget everything that has happened. But I love you and I do want us to be a happy family. Father O'Connell will counsel us. Please promise me you'll go with me to see him."

Dick peered into her eyes for several minutes then his lips curled into a slight smirk.

"Well," he said, cracking a smile, "I don't know what the hell a priest knows about marriage but if that's what you want to do, I'll go."

———— ((◦)) ————

Meg had never seen Dick so nervous. He had not stopped fidgeting since they walked into the rectory.

They were sitting on wooden chairs, waiting for Father O'Connell to join them. While Dick stared at the large oil painting - a well-done copy of *The Last Supper* - hanging over an ornately carved mahogany desk, Meg eyed the door as if to coax Father O'Connell into the room.

"You know I don't have much time, Meg, I have to get back to work," Dick muttered.

Meg was still surprised that Dick had actually joined her for this counseling session. Just as she started to worry that he would change his mind and bolt out of the manse, Father O'Connell bounded into the room.

After exchanging pleasantries, the priest asked them each to describe their marriage and explain any problems. While Meg told him of the difficulties she was experiencing, Dick displayed his discomfort by constantly shifting his body in the chair. Meanwhile, Father O'Connell sat with his elbows on the desk, index fingers press together in front of his mouth, listening intently.

When she described Dick's frequent violent episodes, the priest looked in Dick's direction. Dick looked down, avoiding his eyes, as if to ward off the impending scrutiny, but his reaction seemed to prompt Father O'Connell to speak.

"Dick, I'd like to hear your explanation for resorting to such violent behavior toward your wife."

Dick shrugged.

Father O'Connell leaned forward and stared sternly into Dick's face, then said, "Young man, I assume you're here to try to resolve your marital difficulties. But in order to do that you must first acknowledge the problems and then take responsibility for your part in them. Sitting there slumped in your chair and answering my questions with a childish shrug only serves to waste your time and mine."

Startled, Dick shifted forward in his chair and uttered, "Um, I'm sorry, sir, I'll try to answer your question."

With that, Father O'Connell reverted back to his listening pose.

Dick began by recounting his childhood.

Meg leaned forward in her chair. Dick had never shared his childhood experiences with her and she was very interested in what he had to say.

He described growing up with an abusive father and related several painful incidents. As he continued to talk, he frequently glanced at the priest as if to gauge his reaction to these stories but Father O'Connell sat motionless, wearing a poker face. Meg wondered what he was thinking.

After about ten minutes, Dick stopped speaking and exhaled loudly. He sat back and peered intently at the priest. Meg thought the expression on Dick's face was that of a child desperately seeking approval from an adult and at that moment actually felt sorry for him.

Father O'Connell stunned both of them when he frowned at Dick and said, "Okay, so you had a rough childhood. It's time to grow up and get over it."

Dick beamed as he looked down at his baby daughter's face. "She is the most beautiful baby I've ever seen," he murmured. "Like an angel."

Though exhausted from eight hours of labor and a rough delivery, Meg managed a brief smile. She was thrilled that Dick was so infatuated with their new child, but she was even happier to see the large grin that had replaced the pout he had worn from the moment Father O'Connell berated him for what he termed as Dick's "poor excuse for bad behavior."

They had not gotten much further in the conversation when Meg felt a pop, and then a gush, as her water broke. Father O'Connell had helped Dick get her into the car. She hardly remembered the ride to the hospital but did recall Dick's quiet and sullen demeanor while she suffered through excruciating labor pains.

Now, her voice faint, she said, "Well, Daddy, while you and sweet Caitlin get acquainted, I'm going to take a little nap."

Dick seemed only aware of his daughter; he paid no attention to Meg as she drifted off to sleep.

Chapter 19
Summer, 1988

Two years later
The strain between Dick and Meg had grown increasingly worse.

Soon after Caitlin's birth, Dick had stopped the automatic child support payments to Jordan so she'd refused to let him see the boys. Dick ranted and raved for days, then began plotting his revenge.

He hired an expensive, hot-shot attorney in Sacramento and proceeded to do whatever he could to make Jordan's life miserable.

Meg observed this and knew what he was doing, but felt powerless in her attempts to get him to stop. She was particularly disturbed that he'd stopped paying child support at Christmas time. Dick had actually forbidden her to send any presents to the boys. Every time she tried to discuss it, he berated her.

Unbeknownst to Dick, Meg had received a phone call from Jordan one evening and the two had talked for several hours. Not wanting to betray her husband, Meg hadn't disclosed much information but had openly sympathized with Jordan. She came to realize that she actually liked and identified with Dick's first wife.

Over the past couple of years, Meg had grown fearful of Dick. Her whole body ached from the tension caused by the mere sound of his voice. She dreaded his arrival home each evening. The discord between them had gotten so bad that Meg had begun to sleep on a rollaway bed in Caitlin's room.

Now, Meg sat on the living room floor playing with Caitlin. Suddenly she heard the crunch of his tires out front and felt the familiar tightening of her neck muscles. As she reached up to massage them, she rose and walked into the kitchen.

It was a hot summer evening so she'd decided on a large salad for dinner. As she stood at the counter slicing an onion, Dick barreled through the door. The pain traveled upward and began to pulse in her head.

"Well, as expected, I got my orders today," he declared. "Looks like we're on our way to Iceland!"

Meg spun around and looked at him.

"As expected?" she cried, "As expected? What the hell are you talking about?"

"You know Meg, that's what I love about you – your shitty attitude about everything I say or do!" Dick snarled at her.

Turning back to her chopping, Meg retorted, "And that's what I love about you Dick – your communication skills. You never once mentioned you were expecting any orders. Do you really expect me to just pack up and leave everything I know and love because you snap your fingers?"

"Yes, I do. You're my wife and, as much as you'd like to forget it, Caitlin is my daughter. So, yeah, you go where I go. Besides," he continued peevishly, "I think it's high time you moved away from Daddy. I'm so fucking tired of him breathing down my neck. Then, of course there's your mother. Holy shit, does that woman ever shut up? Blah, blah, blah. . . . "

Meg hands began to tremble, her heart pounding so loudly she thought it would surely burst right through her chest.

"How dare you talk about my parents that way? They've welcomed you into our family and gone out of their way to help us time and time again. You're the most despicable man I've ever laid eyes on, Dick Tate! If you think I'm going anywhere with you, you're sadly mistaken."

Meg watched as the familiar darkness entered his eyes. Knowing his wrath was seconds away, she scurried to the other side of the kitchen.

As she quickly picked up the phone and started to dial, she shouted, "Don't come near me, Dick. I'm calling my dad . . . and if you lay one hand on me he'll be all over you in a heartbeat!"

His face twisted into what could only be described as subhuman. Now Meg's heart was pounding so loud she thought surely they could hear it at the big house.

"You fucking bitch!" he yelled. "Go ahead and hide behind Daddy! I don't want you to go to Iceland with me. I don't want anything to do with you or that sniveling brat of yours. But mark my word, Caitlin is mine and she's coming with me!"

She shook her head from side to side as he spoke.

"After all these years in courtrooms with Jordan, you think I don't know how to work the legal system?" he snarled. "I'll get custody of Caitlin, have no doubt about it."

Meg froze. Dick's words rendered her speechless.

She stood there staring at him intently for several minutes. Dick moved away as though her glare was a flame searing through him. He cast his eyes about the room, looking at everything but Meg.

In a low, robotic voice, she said, "If you don't leave this instant, I'll call my father to have you physically removed."

Dick slowly turned and gazed into her eyes.

Holding both palms up, he murmured, "Baby, I'm sorry. I didn't mean it. I just love you so much and the thought of going to Iceland without you is more than I can bear."

Meg continued to glower at him. Several seconds passed before she returned her attention to the phone and continued dialing.

"Have it your way, Dick," she said resolutely.

Just as her father answered the phone, she heard the kitchen door slam. Knowing that Dick had left, she didn't bother to turn around and look.

"Daddy, I need your help," she said into the phone. "Dick and I are through. He's threatened to take Caitlin. I need the best attorney I can find."

John McAllister had been secretly hoping to hear these words from his daughter for years. He'd come to despise Dick Tate, but for his daughter's sake had kept his feelings to himself.

"Not to worry, honey," he responded. "That sniveling coward hasn't a chance of gaining custody of Caitlin or any other child he's spawned."

Just then the dam broke. All the despair Meg had been holding inside bubbled up and spilled forth. She began to sob so hard she could hardly breathe.

"I'll be right there, honey."

She managed to stammer, "I-I'm okay, Daddy," just before hearing the click of the phone as he hung up.

Suddenly she felt Stuart's arms around her shoulders, hugging her tightly.

"Mom, what's the matter?" he asked haltingly.

Meg wiped her nose on her sleeve then turned and looked up into her teenaged son's anxiety-filled eyes.

"Oh, my sweet baby boy, I'm okay. Really! Dick and I will be getting a divorce. But these are not sad tears - rather they are tears of relief. This has been a long time coming."

Stuart smiled gingerly.

"Yes it has, Mom. I only hope you mean it this time."

Meg looked at him with surprise. "This time?"

"What, you think I haven't heard you two fighting over the years? I've heard you threaten to leave. I've heard you order him out of the house. Mom, I've even heard him hitting you. I did nothing because I was a little chicken. But that was when I was young. I waited to see if he would try that shit tonight, because tonight I would have beat the crap out of him myself!" he declared. "He knew it too. Why do you think he ran like a bat out of hell when I walked in the kitchen?"

Stuart's arms were still draped about her shoulders. Meg reached up and placed her hands on his forearms and smiled.

"Stuart, please watch your language."

He grinned and then began to laugh. Meg looked at him in surprise. Then suddenly, she felt a slow giggle start low in her throat that turned into a slightly louder snort and finally escaped as a guffaw.

That's how John and Mary McAllister found them as they rushed through the kitchen door.

The next day, Mary looked out her kitchen window to see Dick's car darting down the side road. She knew no one was at the cottage. Meg was at work and Stuart at school. As was usual, Mary was taking care of Caitlin, who at this moment napped peacefully in the spare room.

She immediately picked up the phone and called John at his office.

"Go down there and just keep an eye on him," John told her. "I'll be right home."

Mary walked quickly toward the cottage. As she approached, Dick walked out of the house with an armload of clothes.

"Hello Dick."

"I'm just here to get some of my stuff, so you can take your fat little face and go right back to your own house," he retorted.

Mary's back suddenly became very rigid. She gritted her teeth and stated, "This *is* my house . . . As a matter of fact," she declared while holding out her palm. "I want your key right now."

Dick spun around with a look that Mary later described as pure evil and spewed, "Fuck you – bitch!"

Mary staggered backward, the palm of her hand smacking her chest, her mouth agape in utter shock.

Suddenly, John's car was flying toward them.

"Oh, called out the cavalry did you?" Dick sneered, quickly getting into his car and starting the engine.

Though still trembling, Mary was emboldened by her husband's imminent presence.

"Your key?" she demanded, once again holding out her palm.

Dick began fumbling with his key ring, all the while glancing nervously at John's car. He threw the cottage door key at Mary just as John stepped out of his car.

Dick threw his car into reverse and raced backwards down the drive, his tires spinning wildly.

John looked at Mary and grinned.

"Gosh, Mary, what did you say to him? Looks like you scared the daylight out of him!"

"Hardly," she answered with disgust. "You're the one he's afraid of – the coward! He can be mean and abusive with women, but he'll run when any man comes around."

Mary then described the scene before his arrival, including the appalling words Dick had hurled at her. John's jaw set with determination.

"Well, now the sumbitch can deal with me! If he so much as sets his big toe on this property, call me immediately. I got Meg an appointment with the best divorce attorney in San Diego. Let's see how brave he is now!"

He glanced toward the house and with a slight smile said, "Since I'm here, how about some lunch . . . and, by the way, where's my sweet granddaughter?"

"Oh my goodness!" she said, hurrying toward the big house. "With all that ruckus I forgot about the baby."

Chapter 20
1988~1993

True to his word, Meg's father had hired the best divorce attorney around. And, though Dick had pulled every trick in the book, none of it worked. Meg had the advantage because she had personally witnessed most of his legal shenanigans with Jordan.

Although Dick was now living in Iceland, he managed to fly in for the court hearings. Meg figured he must have an outrageous phone bill from communicating with his San Diego-based attorney all the time, not to mention the harassing phone calls to her. She also felt fairly certain he was behind the frequent telephone hang-ups she had been receiving in the middle of the night.

Since the first court hearing, where Dick had tried to strike up a conversation, her father accompanied her to all legal proceedings. It was apparent he was afraid of John, whose penetrating looks seemed to turn Dick's knees to jelly. Meg regaled Jackie and her mom with descriptions of his reactions to her father's glowering.

California had passed new family support laws, one of which required child support payments to be automatically deducted by the employer of the person responsible for making them. Meg was thrilled with the new law because it meant Dick could not play the same games with Caitlin's child support that he had with his payments to Jordan.

Within a couple of months after tossing Dick out her life, Meg felt like her old self again. The sky seemed bluer and the sun brighter. Jackie had commented on the new bounce in her step.

"Oh, Jack, I can't believe I stayed with him as long as I did. The only good thing that came from my relationship with that asshole is Caitlin."

Jackie nodded in agreement.

"At the same time, it breaks my heart having to send my baby girl off to spend time with him," Meg lamented. "But my attorney says I must - at least until we have the visitation agreement finalized. Honestly, though, I feel as if I'm delivering my child into the hands of the devil himself."

Five years later . . .

Meg was putting the finishing touches on Caitlin's hair. Thanks to Gina, it was too short to do much with.

Caitlin had come home from her most recent visit with Dick, sporting a pixie cut. Meg was furious. When she'd questioned Dick about it, he told her he'd asked Gina to cut it because it was easier for Caitlin to do her own hair that way.

"Who the hell do you think you are – and who the hell is Gina – to cut her hair?" she had demanded to know.

"I'm her father, that's who!" he'd shot back.

Now, Jackie sat at the kitchen table watching and chatting

animatedly about her date Saturday night with the latest "love of her life".

"That's great, Jack," Meg murmured absentmindedly.

"Well, do try to hide your enthusiasm a little, pal!" Jackie retorted amicably.

Meg glanced at her friend and cracked a half-smile.

"I'm sorry," she said, "I'm still fuming about that stupid jerk ex-husband of mine and his loony wife cutting Caitlin's hair! How dare they?"

Caitlin reached up and patted her mother on the shoulder.

"It's okay, Mom, I don't mind. Don't be mad anymore, okay?"

Meg laughed and gave Caitlin a hug. "Always the cheerful one, aren't you? Okay, you run on up to the big house. Make sure your brother or somebody else is at the pool to watch you. If they aren't, you wait for me, understand?"

Caitlin yelled, "Yeah, Mama, I got it!" as she jogged out of the kitchen, slamming the door behind her.

Meg grinned at Jackie and cracked, "Thank God she inherited my sunny personality instead of her father's psychotic one!"

Jackie looked at Meg with apprehension.

"Meg, ever since that day we had lunch and you got so upset over what I told you, I've tried to keep my thoughts to myself. But for Caitlin's sake I feel compelled to break my own rule."

Meg's smile faded slightly as she looked into Jackie's emerald green eyes.

"I apologized for that Jack," she interrupted. "You must know that things are back to normal now - and that I value your opinion. Please, say whatever you want."

"Okay, I will." Jackie smiled. "I'm just a little concerned about

Caitlin. She's told me several times that she hates her daddy - that she doesn't want to go see him. Meg, that's not a good thing. Despite the fact that he's a bastard, he's still her father. I just hope you aren't responsible for encouraging those feelings."

Meg's face reddened as she looked at the floor. "I can't feign total innocence here. " I know I've said too much about him in front of Caitlin and I know I shouldn't. I appreciate your concern for Caitlin and I'll try to be more careful in the future."

She lifted her head and looked straight at Jackie. "But Jack, I swear it's not just me. Caitlin's told me that Dick is constantly telling her what a horrible person I am. At first I was really pissed off. I mean, how can I defend myself against that? But then I realized I didn't need to. Caitlin resents it and she tells him so."

Shaking her head in disgust, Meg continued, "She's also told me about what goes on at his house. She said Dick and Gina fight constantly and that he smacks Gina around. Nobody seems to care that Caitlin is watching all of this. A while back, Brett was living there – God knows why Jordan allowed that – and he protected Caitlin from some of it. But he's just a little boy himself. He shouldn't have to witness it either."

Jackie nodded in agreement.

"Speaking of Jordan," she probed, "have you talked to her lately?"

"Yeah, it looks like they're gonna subpoena me to talk to the judge. Hopefully I'll be able to help her prove what a wacko he is. After that, maybe she can help me. Caitlin hates visiting her dad. The man is a psycho! I mean, it really scares me sometimes to think what he might do. I hate having to force her to go."

Swirling her finger in a circle next to her temple, she continued, "And his wife is almost as cuckoo as he is. Caitlin told me that

Gina gives her the creeps because she's always fawning over her."

Jackie laughed. "So, what'll you do if Jordan doesn't win her case and you have to continue to send Caitlin to his house?" she asked.

Meg shook her head and in a low voice hissed, "Buy a gun."

"We've practiced loving long enough,
Let's come at last to hate."

Georg Herwegh
Lied von Hasse

Chapter 21
San Diego, California;
July 23, 2003

By the time Buchanan and O'Reilly finished their interview with Meg and got back to the office, it was nearly three thirty in the afternoon.

Cheryl greeted them with the news that Jordan had called.

"She said she and her husband are flying in tonight and that she could meet with you in the morning," Cheryl explained. "Knowing how anxious you are to meet with her, I scheduled a tentative appointment for 10:30 tomorrow morning. Is that okay?"

"Absolutely," replied Ian, "That's great!"

"And, the phone company faxed six months worth of Dick Tate's phone bills," she said, handing him a small stack of papers. "Here you go."

Ian cracked a half smile and said, "You're a gem, Cheryl. Thanks."

She turned to go back to her desk, throwing over her shoulder, "That's right. And don't you forget it!"

Ian quickly thumbed through the fax pages listing both local and long distance calls that had originated from Dick's home phone. His brow creased in concentration as he murmured, "This ought to be interesting . . ."

Mike slapped him on the back and declared, "Have fun, partner. I'm gonna go do some gun registration searches."

Ian nodded distractedly and sat down at his desk to go over the phone records.

***

Two hours later, Ian leaned back in his chair and rolled his head from side to side to get the kinks out of his neck and shoulders. His growling stomach prompted him to look at his watch, which read, 5:42. He looked toward the computer where O'Reilly had been working and saw an empty chair.

He was hungry, his muscles ached from sitting hunched over his desk for hours and he wanted to share what he'd learned with his partner. He pushed himself up from his chair and set off to find Mike.

He found him in the kitchen area, holding a cup of coffee and flirting with one of the dispatchers. "Your sweet voice makes me wish I was still a uniform driving 'round in a squad car so I could listen to you all day long . . ." Mike said as Ian approached.

The young woman's eyes twinkled as she smiled back at him and handed him a slip of paper. She murmured devilishly, "Here's my number . . . call me and I'll talk all you want, sugar."

O'Reilly watched as she sashayed out of the room then turned to grin at Ian, who asked, "Haven't you heard the expression 'don't dip your pen in company ink'?"

"Said by someone who couldn't get any . . ." replied Mike. "Glad to see you finally came up for air."

"Yeah, and I'm hungry. Let's go to my place, order a pizza and compare notes on our findings."

Mike smiled, exclaiming, "Throw in a couple beers and I'm there!"

<hr/>

The two detectives sat on opposite sides of Ian's coffee table, a cardboard box containing a large pepperoni pizza between them.

Mike took a long swig from his bottle of beer, wiped his chin with the back of his hand and said, "Talked to Li. He's pushing Firearms to get their report done quickly . . . says we should have something by tomorrow."

"That'll work," remarked Ian.

Mike nodded. "For all the good it does us . . . not one of the ex-wives has a gun registered to them. I checked Jordan's husband, Meg's parents . . . all of 'em. Nada."

"Well, that just means they didn't obtain a gun legally. Who's to say the killer didn't buy one off the street or borrow one from a friend?" reasoned Ian.

"I'm holding judgment until after we meet Jordan tomorrow," Ian continued, "but I'm with you - I'm leaning towards Gina. You know, she's got all those connections in the military . . . easy for her to get her hands on a gun."

Mike's head jerked up. He looked directly at Ian and asked, "Wait a minute, why are you so quick to rule out Meg? She's got just as much reason to kill him as Gina did – maybe more because of her daughter!"

Buchanan focused his eyes on the pizza.

"Just my detective's intuition. She doesn't seem the type."

"What the hell has gotten in to you?" Mike questioned loudly. "I've never known you to rule out any suspect based on your *feelings* before . . ."

Ian's eyes narrowed as he glared at his partner. "I'm not ruling her out!" he retorted. "I'm just expressing my opinion based on my experience. I don't think she did it. That doesn't mean I'm not gonna do my job. You know me better than that!"

"Calm down, Buchanan, I'm not questioning your integrity," Mike uttered, "But admit it, you're letting your dick think for you. You're obviously smitten with the woman."

"Fuck you!" Ian replied as he stood and stomped out of the room.

He went into his bedroom, muttering to himself, "Shit, how did I get stuck with this asshole for a partner?" He batted his fists against the punching bag that hung in the corner of the room.

Ten minutes later, Buchanan emerged from his bedroom and returned to his position in front of the coffee table, mumbling, "Sorry."

Mike waved off his apology. "Tell me what you found in the phone bills."

Ian's lips formed into a quasi-smile, his eyes communicating gratitude to his partner for once again forgiving his temper tantrum.

"For one thing, they provided more evidence that Tate was indeed obsessed with his ex-wives. There were several calls to Meg's number, most in the middle of the night and hundreds of calls to Jordan. All of them were recorded as one minute calls.

But since the phone company rounds up to the nearest minute, the calls could have been shorter. My guess is that they were what Nick Gallagher referred to – Tate called and then hung up when somebody answered. This guy was one weird-ass fucker!"

Mike laughed. "Well, we kinda knew that after seeing his photo collection."

"And . . ." Ian continued, "You were right - he did call Gina. There were ten calls to her number during the past month. Except for one call, they all lasted just one or two minutes. But the last one was five minutes long. She lied. She *has* talked to him."

O'Reilly slapped his hand against the coffee table and exclaimed, "I knew it!"

"This could be the probable cause to impel her to provide fingerprints . . . and possibly a hair sample for DNA testing." Ian said hopefully, "I'll call the ADA tomorrow."

"You know . . . ." Mike interjected, "even if you exclude that five minute call – or even suppose he left a long message on her answering machine . . . Why didn't Gina mention he'd called her? She could've told us about those calls during the interview and explained that she hadn't had a conversation with him . . . but she didn't do that. "

"Good point," replied Ian.

Mike chortled, "Gotcha, Gina!"

Ian grinned as he held both hands in the air and said, "Now, now, O'Reilly, let's not jump to conclusions . . ."

Chapter 22
July 24, 2003

Buchanan watched as the large hand on the wall clock bounced forward to land on the six, telling him it was exactly 10:30. Simultaneously, the phone rang, making him jump and his partner laugh.

He grabbed for the phone and after identifying himself in his usual gruff manner, heard the receptionist announce that Mr. and Mrs. Gallagher were here to see him.

"Be there in a sec," he barked.

Ian picked up his coffee cup, tossed down the last of the cold, muddy sludge and grimaced. He glanced in Mike's direction, announced, "Showtime!" and hurried out of the office.

"I'll meet you in the interview room," Mike called after him. Ian kept walking but threw a thumb into the air to indicate agreement.

This time when he descended the stairs into the front waiting area, he was greeted not by a relaxed and presumably grieving mother but by a very anxious couple. Ian instantly recognized her from the photos at the victim's home; she was pictured both in the framed photo found in the bedroom and in one of those hanging on the wall in the office area. The tall, slender woman was wringing her hands and pacing the floor. The man was talking softly to her in an obvious attempt to relieve her nervousness.

As he entered the room, the woman peered at him and asked, "Are you Detective Buchanan?" Stress was etched across her face; dark circles appeared under her eyes. Ian pondered that fact for a moment, wondering why she was so nervous.

"Yes," he answered, "and you must be Mrs. Gallagher. May I call you Jordan?"

Nodding her head as she shook his hand, she replied, "Oh, of course." She then placed her hand on the arm of the man standing beside her and said, "This is my husband, Nick."

The two men shook hands.

Buchanan led them up the stairs, showing the couple into the same tiny room in which they'd interviewed the victim's mother. Mike was there waiting for them. Ian made the introductions then motioned toward one of the chairs.

"Please . . . have a seat," he said, and in an attempt to lessen her anxiety, "I promise I won't bite, Jordan."

She smiled then and said, "I'm sorry. I'm sure you won't. This has just been . . . well, a little unnerving. Not only was the father of my children murdered but, well, to be quite honest, I've never had dealings with the police - except for an occasional traffic ticket . . ."

Ian returned her smile and said, "I understand."

Nick sat down next to Jordan on one side of the table, while Ian and Mike pulled up chairs across from them.

"So, what happened . . . I mean, how was Dick murdered?" Nick asked.

"He was shot," Buchanan replied, "but before we get into

that, I'd like to ask Jordan a few questions . . . just to clear a few things up."

Jordan nodded and said, "Okay," once again wringing her hands.

"Tell me what you were doing in San Diego last weekend," Ian began.

"I was here for my high school reunion," she explained.

"You went to high school in San Diego?"

She shook her head. "No, in Germany, actually. My father was in the military, so we traveled a lot. My high school was on the Air Force base – all the students were military dependents. Needless to say, getting a reunion together was quite an accomplishment. The people who organized it live in Southern California so chose to have it in San Diego."

"Oh . . . okay," he murmured, "What day did you arrive?" He already knew when she had left to go home.

"I got here on Thursday. My son Brett was with me. He spent most of the weekend with his dad." Her eyes suddenly filled with tears and she swiped at them.

She retrieved a tissue from the box Mike offered and said, "I'm sure you wonder why I'm so emotional . . . about the death of a man that I, frankly, detested. It's just that it breaks my heart to see the pain this has caused my sons. Despite how any of us feel about the man, he was still their father. That's all. I'm sorry."

Ian bowed his head. "We would like to talk to Brett . . . did he come back with you by any chance?"

"Yes, as a matter of fact he did. He – uh – both of my sons came down for the funeral tomorrow," she murmured. "Brett called around and found out when it was. Um, can you wait a few days to talk to them? They're pretty upset right now."

"I understand. But I'm sure they would like to see their father's murderer caught and punished . . . Maybe tomorrow after the funeral?"

Jordan was silent.

"Will you be attending the funeral?" Mike interjected.

Nick spoke up. "We talked about it but decided not to. Both of us thought it would be hypocritical to do so."

"Okay," Buchanan said in an attempt to get them back to the subject at hand, "Do you know when Brett last saw his dad? During this recent trip, I mean."

Dipping her head slightly, she responded, "Yes, it was Sunday morning. He had brunch with him . . . I'm not sure where . . . but afterward he came back to the hotel and had dinner with me. Most of my classmates left Sunday afternoon, so I was alone."

"So, it was just you and your son?" he questioned.

"Yes," she answered.

"And you were together the whole evening?"

Again, she replied, simply, "Yes."

"What restaurant did you eat at?"

"We went to Jack's Steak House."

Suddenly, she sat upright in her chair and through pursed lips asserted, "Tell you what, Detective, let me save you from asking my full whereabouts on the night of question . . . since it's obvious what you're getting at . . ."

Ian was taken aback by the abrupt change in Jordan's demeanor, which up until now had been rather quiet and demure.

"I stayed at the Radisson in La Jolla. Brett arrived back at the hotel a little after two o'clock. He went down to the lobby with me to say goodbye to some friends who were leaving for the airport to go home. Then we took a walk on the beach . . . just enjoyed the rest of the afternoon together."

"We went back to the room at about five thirty, then showered and changed for dinner. Our dinner reservations were for seven o'clock. It was such a beautiful evening we decided to walk to the restaurant, which was about a mile away. We left around six forty. It took about fifteen minutes to get there."

Ian glanced at Mike who was sitting back in his chair, his lips curved into a droll smile. He appeared to be struggling to hide his amusement.

"We had dinner . . . you don't need to know what we ate do you?" Jordan asked wryly before continuing. "That took about two hours. We walked back to the hotel, arriving at about nine thirty. We watched television for awhile then, knowing we had to get up early Monday morning to drive home, went to sleep."

She paused for a moment then with raised eyebrows asked, "Did I leave anything out?"

Buchanan chuckled softly and said, "Give me a minute . . ."

Ian was nonplussed when Nick leaned forward and draped his arm protectively around Jordan's shoulders. *Seems to me she does just fine all on her own,* he thought.

After a moment's pause, Ian said, "Actually, you can help us eliminate you as a suspect. Would you be willing to be fingerprinted . . . and maybe supply a saliva sample for DNA testing?"

Jordan cast a wary eye in Nick's direction who, after a moment's hesitation, answered for her, "I think maybe we should consult an attorney before we consent to that."

At Buchanan's cocked eyebrow, Nick continued, "My wife has nothing to hide, Detective. I just want to be sure her rights are protected."

"Okay," Ian replied, trying to keep the irritation out of his voice but not succeeding. "Maybe you can do that today. It will certainly be easier for everybody if we can accomplish this while you're in town."

Nick nodded and then declared, "I'll make some calls as soon as we're done here."

Ian sat back in his chair, arms crossed over his chest, as if resigned. He returned his gaze to Jordan and said, "We'd like to know more about your relationship with Richard Tate."

"What would you like to know?" Jordan asked hesitantly.

"Well... the circumstances of your marriage. For instance, when you met, how long you were together, about your children."

She frowned and looked up at the ceiling. In a voice just above a whisper, she said, "The day I received my last child support check, I actually celebrated. I thought it meant I would never have to think about that man again, never have to feel that hatred . . ."

A tear trickled down her cheek as she turned and looked directly into Ian's eyes. "I will tell you all about it, Detective, with the hope that maybe, finally, I will be able to put those bitter memories away and never think about him again."

Buchanan found himself actually sympathizing with her, this woman who could possibly turn out to be their prime suspect. "I hope so, too," he said softly as she began her story.

~ JORDAN ~

"Vengeance to God alone belongs;
But when I think of all my wrongs
My blood is liquid flame!"

Sir Walter Scott
Marmion VI, 7

Chapter 23
Fort Rucker, Alabama;
Fall, 1976

Jordan was looking forward to some time off from her military training. Until recently, the discipline had been intense and her time controlled, first by drill sergeants and then by instructors.

She started her six-week basic training at Fort McClellan, Alabama in July. Now stationed further south at Fort Rucker, she was two months into the Army's Air Traffic Control Tower Operator course.

Jordan could hardly believe that only four days before reporting for basic training she had celebrated the nation's Bicentennial with a group of Navy fighter pilots.

Shaking her head and grinning to herself she reflected upon the dramatic changes to her lifestyle since her enlistment. Jordan had taken so many things for granted - until they were no longer readily available. She recalled her utter joy when, upon her initial arrival at Ft. Rucker, she'd been told she could hang a poster above her bunk. The fact that there were very precise and specific instructions for the placement of that poster was beside the point.

Now, she and pals Candy and Brenda were preparing for what would be their first night off since arriving at Fort Rucker. After dinner at the only Mexican restaurant in town - *possibly in the entire state of Alabama* - thought Jordan, the girls had plans for an evening of drinks and dancing at the Enlisted Club.

In contrast to Jordan's tall, thin silhouette and long blonde hair, her roommate Candy was a short, pixyish towhead who hailed from Arizona; while Brenda, a brunette with a long face that hosted a fairly large nose, grew up in New Jersey. All three had been together since basic training and had immediately hit if off.

Jordan was applying a light raspberry lipstick while Candy wildly swung her hips to the music blaring from her radio when they heard Brenda call from the doorway, "Ready gang?"

Since Brenda was one of the few trainees who had a car with her, she was always the designated driver. She'd flown home for a week after basic training primarily to pick up the canary-yellow Volkswagen she'd dubbed *Oscar*.

Jordan swung her head in her roommate's direction and with a laugh said, "I don't know, Candy seems a little down in the dumps!"

"Yeah," Brenda chuckled, "I can see that."

Candy twirled around in a circle, snapped her fingers and said, "Hey, I was born ready! Let's hit it."

———※———

The women were a little disappointed to find fewer than twenty people in the Enlisted Club bar. There was a band playing behind a large dance floor, but no one dancing.

After making themselves comfortable at a table, they glanced around to find they were the only females in the room.

"Well, the pickin's are slim," Candy quipped, "but so is the competition!"

Jordan laughed. "Yeah, and apparently we don't have a cocktail waitress either. I'll make the first bar run. What do you guys want to drink?"

Jordan had imbibed in a couple of Alabama-style margaritas at dinner. They weren't exactly the best she'd ever tasted but, considering how long it had been since she'd had one at all, she'd enjoyed every sip.

The tequila had given her a mellow, relaxed feeling and was probably responsible for the way she was flirting with the cute bartender right now. While she made small talk, he poured their drinks, regarding her with an occasional smile.

Suddenly a voice to her right said, "I hope you aren't planning to drink those all by yourself."

Jordan lifted her eyes to see a blonde-haired, blue-eyed Adonis smiling brightly at her. She was momentarily so flustered all she could do was gape at him.

Then, realizing she must look quite the fool, stammered, "Uh, well, no. The others are for my friends."

She pointed toward the table where Candy and Brenda sat, both of whom were smiling broadly.

The stranger chuckled, then reached out to take two of the drinks and said, "Why don't you let me help you with those . . . I'm Dick, by the way."

Jordan smiled and let him take the drinks. She picked up the other one, winked at the bartender and headed back to the table. Dick followed.

As they approached, Jordan noticed that both her friends were grinning ear-to-ear. She made the introductions and then invited Dick to join them. He mentioned he was with a friend and asked if it would be alright if he called him over.

"The more the merrier . . . come one, come all . . . especially if he looks anything like you!" Candy chimed in, waggling her eyebrows up and down a couple of times.

Jordan kicked Candy under the table. Candy grabbed her shin and glared at Jordan, whose smile was reminiscent of Mona Lisa.

Dick returned and introduced his friend simply as, "Jeff." Later, while Dick and Jordan danced, Jeff kept Candy and Brenda entertained. They were the only couple on the floor, but that was fine with Jordan. Her love of dance made her comfortable on any dance floor, no matter the circumstances.

Raising his voice above the music, Dick said, "You look like a California girl – are you?"

She nodded and shouted back, "Yeah, Southern California".

He told her he was also from California and began to ask for specifics about where she grew up.

Jordan was a little embarrassed. Although she claimed Southern California as home, and it was in fact where her parents were currently living, she'd not actually grown up there and didn't know a lot about the area. As a military brat, she had lived all over the world, moving every couple of years. She'd always found it simpler to just tell people she was from California. But now she was talking to someone who was more familiar with that neck of the woods than she. If she kept going, he'd figure her for a liar. She didn't want him to get the wrong impression; so flashing her most charming smile, she explained the situation to him.

"But my father grew up in Southern California," she added, "so does that still make me a California girl?"

"Well, in my book it does!" he answered.

Dick told her he was in training to be a helicopter pilot. He'd enlisted in a special pilot candidate program which allowed the Army to recruit young people who didn't have a college degree. He told her he'd attended San Jose State University on a swimming scholarship but had only completed two years because he thought this opportunity to become a pilot was too good to pass up.

Jordan was familiar with the flight program; the barracks for the pilot candidates were right behind hers. Although they had a much stricter regimen, the candidates shared the mess hall with Jordan and her classmates.

"So, will you get into trouble for fraternizing with us lowly enlisted persons?" she inquired.

He laughed. "Well, I guess that's a risk I'm willing to take."

Jordan blushed, as butterflies danced in her stomach. Not only was this man gorgeous, but in a few months he would be a full-fledged pilot. Having grown up the daughter of a military officer, she was troubled with the notion of dating enlisted men. She realized those thoughts might appear snobbish to others so had never mentioned it aloud. But inwardly she viewed a potential relationship with someone like Dick as a perfect fit. She was delighted when he invited her to dinner and a movie on Saturday night.

At the end of the evening, he walked her to Brenda's car and lightly kissed her goodbye. As she crawled into the back seat of the little yellow bug, her friends teased her lightheartedly.

"Ah, you guys are just jealous," she said with a giggle.

"Yeah, you're right. Jeff was quite the comedian and kept us laughing, but I don't think I'm quite ready to bed him," Candy joked.

⸻ ❦ ⸻

They'd arranged for Dick to pick her up at 6:00 that evening. Jordan took the stairs down to the barracks lobby at 5:45 only to find he was already there.

"Wow," she exclaimed, "You're early! I like a man who's punctual."

He grinned and replied. "Well good, because punctuality is my middle name."

Dick escorted her to a silver Camaro that appeared to be brand new. He further impressed her by opening her door for her. She rewarded him with a beguiling smile.

He took her to a fast food restaurant that specialized in seafood, which didn't impress her much and the movie he'd chosen wasn't much better. It was a graphic story about a little boy who drilled a hole in his bedroom wall so he could spy on his mother and her lover.

Dick seemed ill-at-ease. "I'm sorry. I didn't know what the film was about when I picked it."

Also embarrassed, Jordan didn't know quite what to say so she just nodded.

It was only 10:00 p.m. when they exited the theater and neither of them wanted to end the date, so they drove around trying to figure out what to do. Jordan suggested they find a place with music so they could dance some more.

"How about a motel?" Dick smiled suggestively.

Jordan stole a glance at him, trying to gauge if he was serious or just teasing her. She decided it was the latter. Dick had his eyes on the road so she used the opportunity to appraise him. She'd often said her dream man would have blonde hair, blue eyes and an athletic build. Dick's physical appearance epitomized that ideal. She smiled. Although she had only recently broken off her three-year engagement to Ernie and was somewhat on the rebound, the idea of a long-term relationship with this man gave her goose bumps.

Dick peered over at her with a raised eyebrow as if seeking an answer to his proposal.

She laughed shyly and said, "I hear The Organization, has a great band playing right now."

He grinned back at her, said, "Okay, let's give it a shot," and turned the car in the direction of the nightclub.

⚫

They stood in front of the door to her barracks, the glow from the streetlight illuminating her face as she smiled up at him. He leaned in and lightly kissed her lips.

Jordan had truly enjoyed the evening with Dick. The Organization had been very crowded but that was okay with her because it forced her body into close proximity to his. They had danced a little and then headed back to the base because it was nearly midnight and Dick still had a curfew.

She said goodnight, then floated up the stairs to her room.

Candy's sleepy voice came at her from the darkness. "How did it go?"

Jordan hugged herself and smiled brightly. "It was wonderful," she replied, "and so is he!"

With that, she climbed up onto the top bunk and, with visions of Dick fluttering through her mind, quickly fell asleep.

———⊳《◉》⊲———

For the next two months, Jordan spent every spare minute with Dick and their relationship grew more serious.

She had only one week of school left and was expecting her orders for her permanent duty station any day. Jordan would be graduating as the top student in the class, which had led two of her teachers to suggest she consider staying at Fort Rucker as an instructor. To their disappointment she'd declined, explaining that she didn't think she could teach anyone how to be an air traffic controller without actually having the work experience. Although flattered, it had irritated her when Sgt. Kellogg insinuated he would recommend her for an instructor position anyway.

Much to her dismay, everyone else in her class had already received their orders. She was afraid Sgt Kellogg had followed through with his threat and that was why she didn't yet have her assignment.

She discussed her concerns with Dick but, since he still had three months of schooling left, he was delighted at the thought of her staying there. They were sitting in his car down by Mott Lake. She explained her reasons for not wanting to do so but couldn't get him to agree with her, which prompted her to broach the subject of women in the work force. Jordan was a staunch feminist. Dick listened to what she had to say and then declared that he wholeheartedly agreed with her.

"I guess I'm just being a little selfish," he rationalized, "because

I love you and want you with me as long as possible."

Jordan was stunned. This was the first time Dick had uttered those words. She turned and looked at his profile, barely outlined by the glow of a full moon. She could tell he was a bit flustered by what he had said because he wasn't looking at her. Instead he stared out through the windshield.

"You do?" she asked.

He glanced sideways at her, then reached out and pulled her into his arms.

"Yes, Jordan, I do. Very much," he whispered.

She returned his embrace, then softly said, "I love you too Dick . . . and I want to spend more time with you, but I'm also anxious to get out there and start putting my training to use. Can you understand that?"

"Yes, I can. But what about us?" he asked. "I don't want to lose you."

Tears formed in the corners of her eyes. *Do I love him?* Jordan pondered. *If so, shouldn't he take priority in my life?*

She held him tighter and murmured, "You aren't going to lose me, Dick."

She was totally bowled over when he asked, "Will you marry me, Jordan?"

She pulled away and peered into his deep blue eyes, at his handsome face, then without further thought answered him, "Yes, Dick, I'll marry you!"

His eyes grew wide; unmitigated joy written all over his face.

"Did you say yes?" he asked incredulously.

Jordan smiled softly and nodded.

Dick pounded his fists on the steering wheel and yelped, "Yee haw!" Jordan burst into laughter.

Two days later, Jordan received her orders. She was assigned to Fort Carson, Colorado near Colorado Springs. Knowing that many of her classmates were on their way to Army bases surrounded by muddy swamps or located in the middle of a desert, she considered hers to be a choice assignment.

She couldn't wait to tell Dick. *Oh, if only he could get orders for Colorado as well*, she thought. She planned on seeing him at the mess hall later and would share her news with him then.

Christmas was three weeks away. They had already arranged to drive across the country in Dick's car with two other pilot candidates; one headed to El Paso, Texas and the other to Phoenix, Arizona. Jordan was going to spend Christmas with her parents in Long Beach, while Dick traveled on to Alameda.

She was looking forward to spending all that time with Dick, and to showing him off to her parents. Her mother and father had both expressed concern about the hastiness of their decision to marry but she was sure that once they met him they would come around.

Besides, her parents had known each other for less than a month when they were married. Jordan knew the circumstances were similar to hers, in that the Air Force had transferred her dad from Southern California to a base in South Carolina. They had wed quickly in order to be together. *So how could they not understand?* she wondered.

Chapter 24
Christmas, 1976

Bob and Pat Campbell met Jordan and Dick at the door, both hugging their daughter exuberantly. Grinning from ear to ear, Jordan proudly introduced them to her new fiancé.

Dick planned to stay for dinner and then continue north to his parent's home.

Later, while Jordan helped her mother clean up after dinner, Bob entertained Dick with war stories. Bob had served as an Air Force fighter pilot for over thirty years. He recounted his initial days of flying the P-51 Mustang in the Pacific during WWII, then went on to describe the thrill of maneuvering the F-86 Sabre Jet at mach speed in Korea and of leading young pilots through dangerous night flights in the F-4 Phantom during the Viet Nam war.

Jordan peeked through the kitchen door at them and then laughingly told her mother that Dick appeared to be hanging on Bob's every word, exclaiming, "I'm so glad to see them getting along!"

"Yeah well, your dad likes anybody who will listen to him

talk," Pat said wryly.

Jordan chuckled and then peered at her mother.

"Soooo, what do you think of him?" she asked.

Pat finished drying a pan and kneeled down to put it into the cupboard, saying, "Well he likes to eat, that's for sure. It's always nice to cook for someone who appreciates it."

Jordan wrinkled her nose. "Mom, you know what I mean," she complained. I want to know what you think of him as my future husband."

Pat gave her daughter a half smile and said, "He seems nice enough, honey, but you know I'm concerned that you're plunging headlong into this marriage. You're young. You have time. What's the rush?"

"Mom, if anybody should understand it's you. After all, we've already known each other longer than you and Dad did when you got married."

Pat chuckled. "Well then, maybe you should learn from my experience. I wish now that your dad and I had waited. Besides, things are so different for you kids nowadays. It's easier for you to see each other. Air travel is cheaper and long distance is a whole lot less."

Jordan somberly gazed back at her mother and then down at the floor, lost in thought.

A moment later, she lifted her head. Her voice broke as she sighed, "I'm so afraid I'll lose him if I wait, Mom. This is right, I just know it. I love him."

Placing her arm around Jordan's shoulders, she murmured, "Just spend some time getting to know him first, honey. If he is truly the one you are meant to spend the rest of your life with, he'll wait."

Saying goodbye to Dick brought tears to Jordan's eyes, for which her father teased her unmercifully. Inwardly, she admitted it was a bit silly since she would be seeing him in just a few days. He was planning to come back after Christmas, spend a couple days and then take Jordan up to Alameda to meet his parents.

⸻))(◊)((⸻

Jordan had been prattling on and on about anything and everything. For reasons she didn't understand, it unnerved her to ride in a car in total silence. So she did her best to fill the void.

Dick had told her about his family during the first couple of hours on the road but for the past hour had been fairly quiet. It would take them another seven hours to reach the Tate home in Alameda.

Suddenly, Dick turned to her and asked, "Jordan, have you accepted Jesus Christ into your heart?"

"Wh-what?" she stammered.

Glancing back and forth from the road in front of them to Jordan, he stated, "You heard me. Are you a true Christian?"

"Where did *that* come from?" she asked. "Talk about out of the blue. I-I'm not sure how to answer your question."

Dick frowned. "Gee, Jordan, what is so difficult about the question? Are you or are you not a Christian? This is important. You are about to meet my mother who, like me, is a born-again Christian. I want to be able to tell her I'm preparing to marry a believer."

She gazed out the window for a moment, inhaling deeply. She suddenly felt very uncomfortable. They'd never discussed religion in any form and now, without warning, he was asking her to define her beliefs. She thought Dick had put her on the spot and that irritated her.

Without looking at him, her voice resolute, Jordan slowly said, "I don't quite know how to define my religious beliefs, Dick. I have never been a church-goer, was not raised that way. So, I guess my answer to your question is no. But I have to ask - if this is something that is important to you, why have you not brought it up before?"

His jaw set as he looked straight ahead. Then, glancing sideways at her, he answered, "I guess I just put it off. Maybe I was afraid what your answer would be. But this seems as good a time as any to discuss this. I don't want to tell my mom you aren't a Christian, though. I want her to like you and she won't if she thinks you're a non-believer."

Jordan wasn't sure how to deal with the feelings that came over her. On one hand, she felt anger but on the other she realized this was an important discussion for two people who planned to marry and raise children. She felt a chill rush from her neck to her feet, and then numb all over. For several minutes, she said nothing.

"Have you read the *Bible*?" Dick inquired.

She took a moment before answering quietly, "No, I haven't."

"If I give you one, will you read it?" he asked. "I mean, don't make up your mind that you don't accept Jesus Christ as your savior before you really know him."

Jordan peered thoughtfully at Dick. *He has a point*, she thought. *How do I really know what I believe when I've never been exposed to any particular doctrine? Maybe I should at least read the Bible before I make up my mind.*

"Okay, I'll give it a shot." she whispered.

He grinned broadly and said, "I'll help you Jordan. I'll guide you every step of the way."

She nodded her head then turned once more to gaze out the window. Now she welcomed the quietness that settled between them. They rode that way for the next half hour. Dick finally broke the silence by suggesting they stop for lunch. Though their subsequent conversations were diverse, the subject of religion was not brought up again.

To Jordan's surprise Dick pulled into the driveway of a fairly modest home and stopped.

"Well, here it is," he said with pride, "home sweet home!"

Jordan didn't know what to say. Dick had told her his father was a very successful stock broker, leading her to believe his parents were fairly well-to-do. So she wasn't prepared for this humble abode.

She realized she had not appropriately responded to his enthusiasm and scolded herself. *Shame on you*, she thought, *you're acting like a snob.*

Pat Campbell had praised her daughter's dramatic abilities for years, to the point of suggesting she consider acting as a career. She would have been proud to see the wide grin Jordan affected now as she peered over the top of the car at Dick.

The stairs leading to the front door were in disrepair and, thought Jordan, *a little dangerous.* But she managed to keep a smile plastered on her face.

They walked through the front door and Dick called for his

mother. To the left of the tiny entry was a small living room, crammed with unmatched furniture.

From an easy chair with sagging upholstery, a gruff male voice called out, "She's in the goddamned bedroom Dick, so stop yelling. Either go get her or shut the hell up!"

Jordan was so astonished she almost laughed aloud. Ever since Dick had described his mother as a good Christian, she had been apprehensive about meeting her. The last thing she expected was to hear foul language spewing forth from his father.

Dick's face flushed with embarrassment. He glanced at Jordan and shrugged, as if to say *there's nothing I can do about him.*

In an effort to put him at ease, she smiled her understanding.

Just then, a tall, thin woman with graying brown hair walked into the living room and said, "Dinner's almost ready, Dickie, what took you so long? You said you'd be here a couple of hours ago."

"Well, we got a late start," Dick maintained with a wry smile.

Reaching out to pull Jordan closer, he said, "Mom, this is Jordan."

"Well, yeah, I assumed as much, Dickie, unless you're like your dad and you're stepping out on your fiancé," she retorted.

Now Jordan was blushing. She glanced over her shoulder to gauge his father's reaction to that remark but saw none.

Miriam Tate turned to Jordan and said, "It's nice to meet you, Dear."

Jordan smiled and said, "You too, Mrs. Tate."

"Och, call me Miriam," she scoffed as she turned and headed for the kitchen.

Her abrupt departure left Jordan feeling a little rebuffed but she decided she was the one who needed to make an effort.

After all, this woman would soon be her mother-in-law. So she followed the older woman into the kitchen and offered her help. Miriam said she didn't have anything for her to do but that she was welcome to keep her company while she finalized the meal, which eased Jordan's discomfort somewhat.

Dick's sister Emily came home just in time to eat. Although up until now Richard Tate, Sr. had not spoken two words to Jordan, he became rather chatty at the dinner table. The conversation revolved around swimming. Dick, Sr. was the coach of Emily's swim team and the two would be attending practice after dinner.

Everyone helped themselves to large portions of the food being passed around. Jordan was a little taken aback by what appeared to be a family ritual. Her dismay increased when she realized all the meat was gone before she'd had the chance to get any.

Dick was seated to her right. As she lifted her eyes, she saw him grinning at her. Sticking his fork into one of the pork chops on his plate, he lifted it and put it on hers. She smiled her thanks.

"Gotta move fast if you wanna eat in this house," Dick, Sr. quipped before shoveling a forkful of food into his mouth. Everyone laughed.

"Unless it's oatmeal," Emily blurted out with a chuckle.

Her comment was met with hilarity all around, Jordan being the exception.

"I guess you had to be there," Jordan said uncertainly, glancing around the table.

So, with a few interjections from Dick, Emily and Miriam recounted the story for her.

One morning, Miriam served oatmeal for breakfast. It was a well-known fact that Dick, who was in high school at the time, hated oatmeal. When he refused to eat it, Miriam told him he would just have to go without breakfast that morning. Dick left for school without touching the oatmeal.

Because the school was only a couple blocks from their home, the Tate kids regularly walked home for lunch. When Dick came in that day, he found the now-cold, thick and gloppy oatmeal from breakfast waiting for him at the table. In what Miriam described as his adolescent rebellion, Dick once again refused to eat the oatmeal and once again went without.

As expected, the bowl of oatmeal was yet again at Dick's place at the table for dinner. This time Dick got angry and shouted that he hated oatmeal and he was never going to eat it.

Suddenly, Dick, Sr. had one hand around Dick's neck. Saying, 'You wanna bet?' he forcefully smashed Dick's face into the bowl of oatmeal and held it there. Dick started waving his hands around in a panic. He had oatmeal in his eyes and deep in his nostrils and couldn't breathe.

At that point, his father decided he had made his point and released Dick's neck. Dick lifted his head, wiped his face with a napkin and with tears streaming down his face, slowly began to eat the oatmeal.

By now, Dick's family was nearly in hysterics. Jordan was appalled. *What did these people find funny about that story?* To her it was abuse, pure and simple. Baffled, she looked at Dick and was almost relieved to see the anguish behind his smile. She felt desperately sorry for him. Reaching under the table, she gently squeezed his thigh. He placed his hand on top of hers and smiled tenderly.

Later that evening, Dick took Jordan on a brief tour of his home town. She was totally enamored with the Victorian homes that graced the tree-lined streets.

So-named by popular vote in 1853, Alameda means *grove of poplar trees* in Spanish. Located in San Francisco Bay, the 12.4 square-mile island was created when completion of a tidal canal severed the peninsula from Oakland.

Dick drove down to the Alameda State Beach and parked. The air was too chilly for a walk on the beach, but they enjoyed a splendid view of the Bay Bridge and the eastern San Francisco skyline.

As he cut the engine, Dick turned in his seat, peering into her eyes. He cleared his throat and began, "Jordan, I have something I need to tell you."

Sensing the seriousness in his voice, Jordan shifted her body to face his and raised an eyebrow in inquiry.

Dick pulled his wallet from his back pocket, reached in and retrieved a photo and then handed it to her. Jordan peered at the smiling face of a blonde girl who looked to be two or three years old.

She shifted her eyes upward and as they locked with Dick's he uttered, "I think she's the most beautiful little girl in the whole world."

When Jordan said nothing, he looked out the window. In a barely audible voice, Dick explained that she was his daughter. He described a brief relationship with her mother while both were students at San Jose State University. Her name was *Colleen*, he told her. She had also attended college on a swimming schol-arship but had been forced to quit the swim team during her fourth month of pregnancy.

"I offered to marry her," he said, "but she told me to get the hell out of her life."

Jordan was still in a state of shock, but felt some relief at these words. She explained that her immediate thought when he'd handed her the picture was that he was married, or had been married.

"Do you see her often?"

Dick shook his head. "Colleen's dad won't let me."

"How do you feel about that?"

He stared at his lap for a moment and when he raised his head, Jordan looked into eyes brimmed with tears. She reached up and dabbed at the tears before folding him into her arms. She held him like that for nearly an hour, both of them quietly gazing at the soft waves as they hit the shore of the moonlit beach.

⸻ «(◦)» ⸻

The next day, Dick drove Jordan back to her parents' house. He was returning to Fort Rucker; she had a flight to Colorado Springs in two days.

Jordan tearfully said goodbye. She promised to write every day, he promised to call. As Dick climbed into the car, he grinned and promised, "I'll send a modern version of the *Bible* for you to read. Then we can talk about it on the phone when I call."

Jordan nodded and blew him a kiss.

Chapter 25
Fort Carson, Colorado;
Spring, 1977

True to his word, Dick sent Jordan a copy of *The Way*, a modernized version of the *Bible*. She read it cover to cover. Although they discussed some of the verses over the phone, Jordan did a lot of self-study.

Her analytical mind made it difficult for her to fully accept truth in the words she read. On the other hand, she absorbed the symbolism portrayed and accepted the morals and values preached within the Book.

More than anything, she wanted to please Dick, to make him proud to have her as his wife. So she told him she was ready to accept Christ into her heart and worship as a Christian.

During her spare time, she worked over the phone with her mother to plan her wedding. Her mother had finally given up on her attempts to persuade Jordan and Dick to wait and had dedicated every spare minute into organizing a beautiful ceremony for her only daughter.

Jordan went to Fort Rucker for Dick's graduation. The couple then drove to Long Beach, arriving a week before the wedding ceremony so as to finalize the plans.

Dick had received permanent duty orders to Fort Bragg, North Carolina. As soon as they were legally wed, Jordan planned to submit her request for a "domestic transfer" to Fort Bragg.

She had worked hard to get into the FAA's Air Traffic Control certification program. Because of that, and because she'd grown fond of Colorado Springs, she'd suggested that Dick attempt a reassignment to Fort Carson. Dick refused, stating that because he was an officer and she only enlisted, she should follow him to his assignment rather than the other way around. She'd expressed her disappointment but was determined that it would not get in the way of her happiness. She was so looking forward to her wedding day.

The day after they arrived at the Campbell home, Pat took the couple to a local mall that housed several gift and greeting card shops. They were seeking inspirational words they could use to write their own wedding vows.

While Jordan and her mother thumbed through various books of verse, Dick repeatedly came to her with biblical scripture. Finally, Jordan explained that what she had in mind were poetic verses depicting the love between a man and a woman.

Dick exploded. His eyes grew black as thunder as he glowered at Jordan. He accused her of lying to him about her newfound Christianity.

"If you truly believed," he raged, "you'd understand that our union needs the Lord's blessing – in fact you'd insist on it!"

Jordan was stunned. She felt a room full of eyes staring at them; her sense of humiliation quickly followed.

"D-Dick," she started, pleading with her eyes, "I think you're overreacting."

"I'm overreacting?" he snarled, "No, you and your mother want to do *everything*, even down to writing our vows. So, tell you what, I don't wanna write any fucking vows. I'm outta here."

He turned and stomped out of the store. When Jordan glimpsed pity in the sales clerk's eyes, she felt the heat rise up her neck to her face. She reached up to wipe away the tears welling in her eyes.

She felt Pat's hand on her arm and looked up to see a face etched with indignation. Her mother led her out of the store to an outside bench.

"Jordan, you just got a warning signal that you need to listen to. It's not too late to cancel this wedding," her mother declared.

Jordan was horror-stricken. "No, Mom . . . I can't do that. He's just under a lot of tension, from the wedding and everything . . . It'll be alright," she answered with little conviction.

Pat placed one hand on each of Jordan's shoulders and peered into her face. "What tension, Jordan?" she asked bitterly. "You're the one under stress here! This is supposed to be the happiest time of your life and this is how he acts? He's behaving like a petulant child . . . and his language! A gentleman doesn't speak that way in front of a lady. He obviously has no respect for either one of us. You deserve better!"

Jordan felt as if she were being pulled in a hundred different directions. Although she knew her mother had some valid points, she told herself that she was in love with Dick and that, though unpleasant, his behavior was not bad enough to call off the whole thing.

Besides, she thought, *people are coming from all over to attend the wedding, the room has been booked, food catered, flowers ordered. I can't imagine inconveniencing so many people over this petty disagreement.*

Jordan stood up and, for the first time in her life, went against her mother's advice.

"I'm not calling off the wedding, Mom. I love him. His religious beliefs are important to him. I can certainly concede on this issue."

Pat shook her head, her disappointment obvious.

"That's not the point," she started.

Jordan held up her hand, said, "I don't want to discuss it anymore, Mom," then turned and headed in the direction of the parking lot. Pat quietly followed.

As they approached, Jordan was surprised to see Dick leaning against the rear bumper of the car. Without a word or even a glance at Dick, Pat opened the driver's side door and climbed in.

Jordan walked over, threw her arms around his neck.

"Let's forget about writing our vows," she softly suggested, "and just stick with the traditional ones."

Dick wrapped his arms around her, lifting her so high her feet dangled. "I think that's a good idea."

The car ride home was plagued with an oppressive silence.

———⊰⊱———

Jordan's orders to Fort Bragg came through five months into their marriage. She was a little disappointed with the timing because she was only a month from obtaining her FAA certification. Yet she was excited to finally be joining her husband.

Jordan also realized that living with Dick would be better for them financially. Because Dick had rented the apartment, bought furniture on installment and had monthly car payments, Jordan had been sending him money each month to help out. This was something she struggled with in her mind. On one hand, she felt it was right for her to contribute financially to the marriage; on the other hand, she resented the blatant differences in their lifestyles. But she'd decided her feelings were not important enough to chance an argument with Dick so had kept them to herself.

With mixed feelings, Jordan prepared for her move to North Carolina.

Chapter 26
Fort Bragg, North Carolina;
Winter, 1977

Jordan arrived at the Fayetteville airport on a crisp November day. As Dick drove to their apartment, she gazed with pleasure at a landscape prolific with Maple, Gum and Magnolia trees and marveled at their splendid display of rust, gold and burgundy leaves.

"This is absolutely beautiful!" she exclaimed.

"Yeah, it's certainly different from what I'm used to," Dick said with a chuckle. "I mean, I love California's rolling hills of gold, but I have to admit I kinda like all the trees here."

"I like the weather, too," she declared, noting that the temperature was hovering at sixty degrees. "It's pretty cold in Colorado already."

He laughed. "Well don't get too used to it. The summer was a bear and I hear the winters can get pretty damn cold as well."

Fayetteville, which was the first capital of North Carolina, is located in the south-central portion of the state, about 60 miles south of Raleigh, the current state capital. The city was named after the Marquis de Lafayette, the well-known Frenchman who commanded troops during the American Revolutionary War.

Fayetteville is home to both Fort Bragg and Pope Air Force Base, which together comprise one of the largest military complexes in the world.

The Tate's apartment was situated about 15 minutes from Fort Bragg, where both of them were now stationed. Known as the "home of the airborne," Fort Bragg is the headquarters of the 82nd Airborne Division.

⸺⸱⟨⟨⊙⟩⟩⸱⸺

On Monday, Jordan reported to her new unit to find she'd been assigned to the base motor pool.

She was not happy about this turn of events and inwardly groused, *Prior to my reassignment here, I was only a month away from being FAA certified as an Air Traffic Control Tower Operator, and I gave that up for this? Washing and painting a fleet of "deuce and a halfs"?*

That evening she voiced her concerns to Dick.

"Oh well," he responded flippantly, "I guess you'll have to pay your dues."

"I paid my dues at Fort Carson, Dick!" she snapped.

His eyes narrowed as he growled back at her, "Well, now you are here - with your husband where you belong. You need to start thinking more like a wife and less like a soldier, Jordan. Consider my career for a change," he continued angrily. "After all, I'm the real breadwinner in the family!"

Jordan stared at him with incredulity for several long minutes.

Finally she said, "I can't believe my ears. Did you lie when you told me you believed women were intellectually equal to men?"

Dick gazed at the wall for a moment. He stood suddenly and, using his hands for emphasis, boomed, "The *Bible* clearly states, *Wives, submit yourselves unto your own husbands, as unto the Lord. For the husband is the head of the wife, even as Christ is the head of the church.* Ephesians five twenty two and five twenty three."

His words set off an alarm in Jordan's head. She felt as if someone had poured ice cold water over her head and it was now slowly trickling down to her toes. *What have I done? I have managed to tie myself to a man who is not only a bible-thumping chauvinist but a liar to boot!*

Dick eyed her inquisitively. "What are you thinking?" he probed.

Jordan peered at him momentarily before answering, "I'm thinking that I don't know you very well, Dick."

Rising from the couch she said, "I'm tired, I'm going to bed."

About an hour later, Jordan awoke to find Dick's hands moving over her body.

Seeing her eyes open, Dick uttered, "You know they say married people should never go to bed angry."

But she *was* angry, livid to be exact. Scooting toward the edge of the mattress, she turned her back to him. She nodded off again, this time with sounds of Dick muttering to himself behind her.

———◄(()►———

Jordan hadn't been feeling well so was visiting the aviation clinic during her lunch hour.

She was seated on a metal chair in a small waiting area down the hall from the exam room where she'd consulted with the medic on duty. Her impatience grew. She restlessly bounced her left leg across her right knee. Just as she'd decided to give up on hearing the results any time soon and was ready to head back to work, she looked up to see the medic walking toward her.

Handing her a slip of paper, he crowed, "Congratulations, Specialist Tate!"

Confused, she glanced down at the word "positive" written across the paper containing her lab results and then back at the medic.

"You're gonna have a baby!" he exclaimed, grinning widely.

The feelings that came over her at that moment were nothing less than surreal. Unable to contain herself, she laughed out loud and broke protocol by throwing her arms around his neck.

She spun on the heels of her combat boots and shouted over her shoulder, "I have to go tell my husband!" As she bounded out the clinic door, she heard the medic chuckling behind her.

The clinic was next door to the aircraft hanger that housed Dick's office so she didn't have far to go. Jordan practically flew up the narrow staircase in her excitement. Dick was seated behind his desk and looked up in surprise as Jordan darted through the door of the office he shared with two other officers.

With a huge grin on her face, she quickly walked toward him and, without saying a word, slapped the lab sheet down on his desk. He looked at it then back up at her and then down again. When his head came up again, he was grinning widely and his eyes were as big as saucers. He let out a loud whoop, which drew the immediate attention of his office mates.

Seeing the curious looks on their faces, Dick gleefully shouted, "I'm gonna be a dad!"

Chapter 27
Early Spring, 1978

Jordan began wearing civilian maternity clothes once she could no longer button her fatigue pants.

She'd recently been reassigned to Range Control where she was responsible for guiding air traffic safely through "hot" areas – or restricted areas where artillery and infantry units practiced their combat skills with live ammunition and explosives. Even though she wasn't manning the airfield tower, and despite Dick's grumbling over her assignment to the late night shift, she enjoyed her job.

Both Dick and his commanding officer had begun to pressure Jordan to apply for a pregnancy discharge from the Army, pointing out potential problems stemming from her enlisted status.

They had also been notified of their selection for military housing, another issue affecting her decision to get out of the Army. Dick told her they would not be able to move into officer's housing as long as she was enlisted. Ultimately, Jordan requested a discharge.

———«(0)»———

Six months into her pregnancy and after serving two years as a soldier, Jordan received an honorable discharge. She had mixed feelings about what she considered to be a capitulation on her part. On one hand, she regretted giving up her military career but on the other hand she looked forward to being a full-time mom. One month later, the couple moved into a three bedroom house on Fort Bragg.

———«(0)»———

Soon after her Army discharge, Jordan had enrolled in college correspondence courses which took up a lot of her spare time. Dick was also taking classes to complete his degree but claimed his job kept him from having enough time to study, so Jordan found herself doing his homework along with her own.

She was sitting at the dining room table finishing a recent assignment when she heard Dick pull up in the car. She stood and began putting her books away. Suddenly, he slammed through the screen door leading into the kitchen from the carport.

"Hey babe!" he called.

Jordan scurried into the kitchen to greet him and was pleased to see he was in an unusually chipper mood.

"What are you so happy about?" she asked with a smile.

He explained that he had met some people who bred boxer dogs and that they had a new litter of puppies.

"You know how much I love boxers," he exclaimed, "I want to get one!"

"You mean now?" Jordan asked haltingly. "I mean . . . we're going to have a baby in two months. Don't you think that'll be enough to deal with?"

Dick's smile quickly turned into a frown.

"Yes, Jordan, I mean now!" he shouted, making her jump.

Though Dick's moods seemed as changeable as a chameleon of late, Jordan never failed to be astonished with his abrupt transformations. She'd been subjected to his anger more and more frequently of late. So, not wanting to incur his wrath, she acquiesced, "Okay, Dick, if it's that important to you."

"That's my girl."

Although she was pleased to see the smile return to his face, it suddenly occurred to her that he'd known she would give in if he threw a temper tantrum. She bit back the resentment that began to brew deep within her.

They chose a female and named her Brandy. Dick had promised he would be responsible for the puppy; however Jordan found herself cleaning up the inevitable messes Brandy made – a task that was increasingly more difficult as her delivery date drew closer.

Moments ago, Brandy had squatted on the kitchen rug. Jordan grabbed the rolled-up newspaper she'd been using to housetrain the puppy but didn't reach her in time.

Now, as she grasped the edge of the kitchen counter and pulled herself up from her knees, she groaned. But when she looked down at Brandy whose tail was thumping against the floor next to her, she couldn't help but smile.

"It's a good thing you're so cute," she muttered.

Waddling over to the sink to wash her hands, she continued her conversation with the puppy.

"You know, Brandy, I should probably be glad for the swelling in my feet because it lets me know they're still there," she quipped. "It seems like years since I've seen them!"

Brandy cocked her head to one side, her tail thumping wildly.

Jordan laughed and then mumbled to herself. "Now you're conversing with a dog!"

<hr />

Although Dick frequently cited *Bible* verses to Jordan, the couple had only been to church for Easter and Christmas services. Jordan thought it odd that Dick professed himself a devoted Christian yet was not a member of any local church. But, because she was not anxious for a repeat of the religious discussion they'd had a couple of years ago, she avoided the subject.

She was also disturbed by Dick's proclivity for lying. It seemed to her that he fabricated or embellished most everything, even when no purpose would be served by doing so. It particularly bothered her that he did this in front of her, knowing she knew the truth. Once, after an evening with friends during which Dick had told one of *her* life stories as if it were *his*, she questioned his motives.

He'd shrugged and mumbled, "I don't know why I do that."

<hr />

Jordan met her mother at the Fayetteville Airport. Pat was planning to stay through the birth of her grandchild and Jordan was grateful for the help.

Soon after arriving home, Jordan led Pat down the hallway to the spare bedroom, Brandy at their heels.

"I'm sorry, we don't have another bed but Dick rented this air mattress for you to sleep on while you're here," Jordan explained.

"I'm sure it'll be fine," Pat said distractedly. She was kneeling in front of Brandy, crooning and scratching behind her ears.

Jordan smiled. Her mother loved all animals, *sometimes more than people*, she thought.

Come on, let me show you the baby's room!" she said excitedly.

———

Jordan was tossing and turning in her bed. Dick was snoring beside her but she couldn't sleep. She kept replaying the evening in her mind.

It was obvious her mother and Dick didn't like each other and she was caught in the middle. Dinner had been a disaster. Her mother had given Dick unsolicited advice on barbecuing and, to Jordan's horror, he'd snarled in response. Later, when Pat asked Dick to blow up the air mattress she was to sleep on, he told her to blow it up herself.

At that, Jordan had exploded, "Not only is she my mother, but she's a guest in our home!"

Pure hatred had emanated from his face as he slashed his hand against a bowl of nuts sitting on the table beside him. The bowl crashed to the floor breaking into a hundred tiny pieces. Nuts rolled everywhere. Pat and Jordan were both so astounded they just stared at each other, mouths agape, as he stomped out of the room.

An hour later, Jordan was still angry. She looked over at him now. The slow rise and fall of his chest indicated he was enjoying a peaceful sleep. *I could pinch his nose off,* she mused. She rolled over on her side, aiming her back at him.

Suddenly, a sharp pain shot like a bullet from her abdomen to her lower back. She gasped and reached down to cradle her extended belly, as if to calm the fragile life inside her. Then the pain faded.

Just when she'd decided her discomfort was caused by rolling over too quickly, another pain stabbed through her. She sat up in the bed, wide-eyed and then slapped Dick on his chest. He came awake with a start.

"Wh-wha?" he mumbled sleepily.

"Dick, wake up!" she ordered. "I think I'm in labor."

Chapter 28
Early Spring, 1979

Carter Tate was born twelve hours after Jordan and Dick arrived at the hospital. Jordan loved him with her very being. And because her marriage was on a slippery slope, he became the sole focus of her life.

Though he'd never voiced it, she could sense Dick's resentment of her devotion to Carter. She didn't care. Every day she found herself disliking the man more. She dreaded the very sound of his footsteps each night when he arrived home from work.

Dick's temper grew more violent each day and Jordan had begun to fear him. Consequently, she found herself giving in to his every whim to keep the peace. *I've become the obedient and submissive wife he wanted me to be, and yet it's impossible to please him*, she lamented.

He repeatedly told her how stupid she was. On one occasion he'd actually inspected their home with a white glove and then blew his top when he found week-old leftovers in the refrigerator.

Ever since Carter's birth she'd become a little forgetful, something that only added to Dick's fodder. Last week, she'd been horrified to find her military ID card missing from her purse.

Not only couldn't she shop at the commissary without it, but she also needed the card to use the military clinic - and Carter had an appointment for his six-month checkup the next day.

She'd frantically searched everywhere.

When she told Dick it was missing, he'd rebuked her. "You're so stupid, you can't even hold on to a something as simple as an ID card. Well, I'm not going to sign the papers to authorize a new one until you prove you're responsible enough to handle it!"

Jordan couldn't believe her ears.

"I'm not a child who just lost a new toy," she'd sputtered. "I need the ID card so I can take Carter to see the doctor!"

He shook his head and laughed scornfully. "I guess you should have thought of that before!"

Three days later, Jordan went to the coat closet to get the vacuum cleaner. She glanced down to see her ID card lying conspicuously on the floor. She racked her brain to figure out how that was possible. She'd checked there. How could she possibly have missed it? Numbness slowly engulfed her, smothering her like a blanket placed over her head. She knew. Dick had placed it there. But where had he found it?

Soon after he arrived home from work, Jordan walked toward the closet, Carter balanced on one hip, to show Dick where she'd found the card. She watched his face for a sign he was behind the mysterious reappearance, but he made no attempt to conceal his part in it.

He laughed diabolically, then leaned down and with his face an inch from hers asked mockingly, "Did you learn your lesson?"

She backed away and yelled, "What the hell is wrong with you? I can't believe you'd actually let me cancel our son's doctor appointment so you could teach me a goddamn lesson!"

Suddenly, Dick's hand was around her throat. He slammed her head against the closet door and held her there.

"Don't blame me, you bitch!" he snarled. "If you weren't so fucking stupid, there wouldn't be a problem in the first place."

Carter began to wail.

Jordan looked into Dick's eyes and in a barely audible voice implored, "Please, Dick, you're scaring him. Please let me go." Her eyes overflowed with tears as Carter continued to howl.

Dick abruptly took his hand from her throat. "And another thing," he spat, "Don't ever let me hear you use the Lord's name in vain again!"

He turned and stomped out of the house, slamming the door behind him. She heard the car roar away seconds later.

———⚬———

It had taken nearly an hour to calm Carter. Now he was sleeping in his crib. Jordan was lying on her bed, her whole body trembling as she sobbed, "I deserve better than this! If things are this bad now, what will they be like after twenty years?"

She lifted her head to peer at the clock and then realized Dick had been gone for nearly two hours. She was sure he would be home soon. This had become a pattern. He'd get angry and ver-bally abusive with her and then leave for a few hours. When he returned he was always apologetic - and wanting sex. She moaned aloud at the very thought of it.

For the past several months, she'd dreaded his touch – to the point of having severe stomach aches every night when he came to bed. She was fairly certain the pain was psychosomatic. Sometimes she'd suffered through the sex act; at other times she'd informed him of her stomach problems. Dick had reacted by shouting obscenities and calling her frigid.

Her stomach clutched now as she heard the back door close and Brandy's low woof. She rolled over and feigned sleep.

She winced when she felt him lie down beside her. He pulled her into his arms and uttered apologies. She began to tremble. Knowing there was no point in trying to resist him, she closed her eyes and willed her mind to another place.

———————

"Open the hanger door," Jordan sang, "here comes the airplane!"

Carter clamped his lips together and turned his head away from the spoon, full of the dreaded green beans.

"Come on sweetie . . ." she cajoled as he continued to swing his head from side to side, "You need to eat something other than apple sauce!"

Jordan jumped at the sound of Dick's voice.

"What's the matter?" he asked as he walked into the dining room.

Jordan shrugged and said, "Oh, I can never get him to eat anything but fruit. He hates meat, he hates vegetables. It's frustrating sometimes."

Reaching for the spoon, Dick motioned for her to get up from her chair.

"Here, I'll get him to eat," he boasted.

Jordan handed him the spoon with trepidation. Dick usually left Carter's care to her. He'd never even changed a diaper. So now, a little over a year since his birth, she was a bit unnerved by his sudden desire to help.

Dick sat down in her chair and offered the spoonful of green beans to Carter. Once again, Carter turned his mouth away. Dick pulled his hand back and slapped him with a brutal force. Carter's shriek and instant tears indicated more than physical pain alone.

Jordan screamed, "Dick, no!" and started toward him.

Dick shoved her away and pushed the spoon toward Carter who again turned his face, and again Dick's hand cracked across his tiny face.

Carter began to bawl, his small body heaving with each sob.

Jordan felt as if her heart was breaking into a million pieces. She sank to her knees in front of Dick and reached for his hands.

"Please, Dick!" she sobbed, "I'm begging you to stop!"

Dick jerked away from her and then abruptly threw both the spoon and bowl at the wall. Green beans rained down on them. He stood and, as he slammed out of the room, yelled over his shoulder, "You wonder why he's a fucking whiny spoiled brat? It's because you make him that way! First you ask for my help but then you get pissed when I don't do it the way you want. If your way was working so well then what were you yammering about in the first place?"

Jordan pulled Carter from his high chair and held his trembling body close to hers, stroking his hair and rocking him.

That does it, she thought, *he's not gonna start on Carter now.*

"Oh my sweet baby, I'm so sorry," she murmured over and over again.

———◆———

The next day while Dick was at work, she called her mother

in Sacramento, where she had moved a year before. Jordan felt so helpless and isolated from her family that when she heard her mother's voice on the phone she began to sob uncontrollably.

"Jordan, honey, what is it?" Pat's voice was frantic.

Every time Jordan tried to speak, her throat tightened up. She felt as if she was choking.

"Breathe, Jordan" Pat commanded. "You need to calm down and tell me what's happened. Is Carter okay?"

After several minutes, Jordan quieted enough to relate the green bean story, along with several other violent episodes.

When she finished, her mother quietly said, "Jordan, I've felt for a long time that you've completely lost your individuality. You're like a robot with no personality. You can't let that happen. I think it's time to come home – don't you?"

<hr />

Jordan waited for what she thought was the right moment to tell Dick she was planning to leave. She didn't want to talk to him when he was angry and those times seemed to be few and far between. But tonight he'd come home in a fairly decent mood.

He was lying on the couch watching TV when she approached him. She told him she didn't think either of them was happy, that maybe they needed a trial separation to figure things out.

Dick glared at her as he slowly sat up. He raised one eyebrow, his lips forming a sardonic grin.

"You aren't leaving me, Jordan," he said slowly, "because, if you try, I'll get custody of Carter."

Feelings of sheer panic coursed through her.

"You wouldn't!" she breathed.

But the mocking look in his eyes and the smirk on his face told her he was serious.

"I'm his mother – no one would grant you custody!" she sputtered.

"Yeah Jordan, they would. Not only will you have no money to live on, but you've got no fucking skills. So, you wouldn't even be able to get a decent job. Believe it, Jordan. I'll get custody of him!"

A feeling of utter despair settled heavily in her chest. She leaned her head against the arm of the couch and wondered, *What the hell am I going to do, now?*

A moment later, she was startled from her trance-like state when Dick smacked her on the back and asked, "What's for dinner?"

—◦《◉》◦—

Jordan's period was nearly two months late and she had just taken one of those new home pregnancy tests. She'd heard the tests were not 100 percent accurate, but when she saw the positive result she was sure she was pregnant. She scolded herself for frequently forgetting to take her birth control pills.

Now she felt even more trapped in a bad marriage with a man she despised. At the same time, she liked the idea of another baby. She thought Carter needed a sibling and knew she had enough love for plenty more children, so she made an appointment with her doctor and convinced herself it would all work out fine.

Dick was thrilled when he found out.

Probably because he knows I won't leave now, she thought, *although why he wants a wife who hates him is beyond me.*

Jordan was awakened by Dick's shouts.

"You stupid fucking dog!" he hollered.

"What's wrong?" Jordan asked sleepily as she rolled over on her side and used both hands to sit up. Her large belly made it difficult to rise from a prone position.

The odor that suddenly reached Jordan's nose made it apparent that Brandy had adorned their bedroom floor with diarrhea.

"Get up Jordan," Dick commanded "we have to clean up this damn dog's mess!"

She bristled at the knowledge that by, "we," Dick meant *her.* These days, it was a strain just to rise from a seated position and now he expected her to get up and down from a kneeling position to clean up a mess created by the dog *he'd* insisted upon having.

"I can't do it," she boldly asserted, "I'm seven months pregnant and, in case you hadn't noticed, not very agile. No, Dick, this time you'll have to handle it."

Brandy was lying on the floor at the end of their bed. Her chest rose and fell rapidly, her eyes red and teary. Jordan realized Brandy was sick. Suddenly, and to her horror, Dick pulled his foot back and kicked Brandy in the stomach with all his might. Brandy yelped loudly.

It was Jordan's turn to feel sick. "Dick! Stop!" she yelled, "Can't you see she's not feeling well? Do you think she meant to have diarrhea for God's sake?"

She then heard Carter's cry and heaved herself from the bed to go to him.

Jordan carried Carter back to their bedroom and, to her surprise, found Dick on his knees cleaning up the dog mess.

Chapter 29
Summer, 1980

Dick's tour with the Army was almost over and he'd decided to transfer to the Navy. He was required to receive a full discharge from the Army before actually being accepted into the Naval Officer Candidate School.

Although Dick assured her everything would be fine, she felt tremendous anxiety. She was about to have another baby and her husband would soon be unemployed.

They planned to drive cross-country to California, a trip that would take more than a week. The Volkswagen bus they'd bought after Carter's birth had broken down several times in recent months. Jordan expressed concern about whether the bus could make such a long trip, but Dick insisted she was worrying over nothing.

To top it off, Jordan's mother had been diagnosed with ovarian cancer and was to have surgery within a week of their arrival in Sacramento.

During a recent phone conversation, her father had cautioned her that too much stress could be harmful to the baby. She tried to keep that in mind but found it difficult to remain calm.

———•《O》•———

George and Sally Wallace had recently moved into the house across the street and had quickly become the Tate's good friends. Jordan didn't like George much because he was verbally abusive with Sally and their kids, but hid her feelings from Sally, whom she considered a kindred spirit.

Tonight they were barbecuing at the Wallace's house. Dick was outside by the grill, enjoying a beer with George. Jordan was explaining their plans after Dick's discharge to Sally when she suddenly felt a pop and then a gush between her legs. Her eyes grew wide and her face reddened as she looked at her friend.

Sally's brow creased with concern. "What's wrong?" she asked.

"I—I think my w-water broke," Jordan stuttered.

Sally glanced down and noticed a small puddle forming at Jordan's feet and, pointing at the floor, wryly said, "Yeah I'd say so!"

"Dick!" Sally turned and yelled toward the back door. "You better get in here, your wife's in labor!"

A few minutes later, Sally helped her into the Volkswagen bus while Dick watched from the driver's seat, jiggling his knee impatiently. Sally wished them well, and then gently closed the passenger door behind Jordan.

Dick pressed on the accelerator and sped away. But before they reached the end of the street they heard a loud snapping sound and the van eased to a stop.

Jordan looked at Dick with surprise and asked, "What happened?"

"I don't know. It just stopped running . . . I'll have to borrow a car."

He got out and ran to the Wallace's. Jordan threw her head back against the seat and murmured, "Swell . . . just swell!"

Within minutes, he was back with Sally's car. The passenger-side door had been broken for months, so Jordan had to climb over the driver's seat to get to hers.

Once they were finally on their way to the hospital, she sighed, "I suppose someday we'll laugh about this," then bent over as her abdomen clenched in pain.

<hr />

Jordan gave birth to their second son shortly after arriving at the hospital. Because she had carried this baby so much differently than Carter, she'd been convinced she was having a girl. So, although they'd considered several female names, they'd only discussed one for a boy. They named him Brett, after her mother's brother.

Dick had left the hospital shortly after Brett's birth and had not returned, leaving Jordan feeling a bit neglected. It was late afternoon the following day when Sally showed up for a visit. Her friend had been taking care of Carter since they had left for the hospital the day before.

"Your husband has been under the car all day, trying to fix it," Sally explained. "I finally told him if he wasn't coming to see you, I was. I left Carter with him. Who knows when Dick will finish with that damn car," she shrugged, "So I won't stay too long. I need to fix dinner for my family . . . and I also want to be sure Carter gets something to eat."

Jordan could sense Sally's disgust with Dick and was embarrassed.

"Thanks so much for all your help," Jordan told her. "I don't know what I'd do without you! My mom was here when Carter was born but this time it's strange all the way around. I mean, we're supposed to leave in four days to drive across the country. Not only do we have a new baby, but our car is in bad shape. I have to tell you, I'm very nervous about this whole thing."

Sally reached over and patted her hand. "I'll do whatever I can to help. You just worry about getting some rest before your big journey," she said, then smiled encouragingly.

⸻ ◆ ⸻

Jordan's doctor expressed concern about her riding in a car for long periods of time so soon after childbirth. He made Dick promise to stop the car at least every couple of hours so she could get out and walk around. He told Jordan to take a pillow to sit on, suggesting her stitches might make her uncomfortable during the long trip.

Neither Jordan nor Dick mentioned their lodging plans for the upcoming expedition. Although they would receive compensation from the Army for their travel to California, Dick decided they would save money by camping out rather than staying in motels. A few days before Brett's birth, he'd spent a large portion of the travel pay on state-of-the-art camping gear. When Jordan had balked, Dick stoically reminded her he was the decision maker in their family.

Chapter 30
The Trip; Summer, 1980

The Tate family left Fort Bragg at 8:00 on Saturday morning. Other than a brief stop for gas and lunch, they drove 560 miles straight, arriving at Tennessee's Natchez Trace State Park at 6:00 that evening.

Jordan felt a desperate need to stretch her legs so, taking Carter by the hand and nestling Brett to her left side, she walked over to the information center where Dick was checking on a campsite. As she squeezed through the door, she saw him talking to a woman who looked to be in her late fifties. She was pointing at a large layout of the park posted on the wall.

"In this area you can see the third largest pecan tree in the world," the woman drawled. "And the story 'round these parts is that it grew from a pecan given to Sukey Morris by one of Andrew Jackson's men, who was on his way home from the Battle of New Orleans."

She presented Dick with a small map of the grounds, indicating with a red X the area where they could pitch their tent.

She then glanced over at Jordan and, with a look of disapproval, said, "My, that's an awful young baby to be camping with!"

Jordan's face felt hot as she studied the floor. Dick gave the woman a dirty look, snatched the map from her hands and motioned for his family to follow him out the door.

—————⊙—————

An hour later, Dick had unloaded the van and assembled the campsite. Jordan was boiling water on the portable stove to warm Brett's formula. While it heated, she jiggled the baby softly to calm him. Shortly after they'd arrived at the park, he had noisily made his hunger apparent.

She walked over and peered inside the pup tent where the four of them would sleep that night. She eyed the hard ground where she would later lie in her sleeping bag and could almost feel the hard rocks jabbing into her back.

"How did I end up here?" she muttered.

"What?" Dick asked, coming up beside her.

"Nothing," she replied evenly, "Just talking to myself."

Dick stretched and then groaned loudly. Placing his hands on the small of his back and leaning backward, he said, "Is this beautiful out here, or what?"

Jordan grimaced inwardly then motioned toward Carter and said, "Why don't you take him for a walk. Maybe the two of you can enjoy the scenery. I have to feed Brett."

Dick nodded. "Okay, but his diaper's wet, you better change it first."

Through gritted teeth, Jordan said, "Maybe it's time you learned how to change a diaper, Dick!"

Dick's bottom lip turned downward, giving him the look

of a pouting child.

"I thought once you had that baby, you'd stop being such a bitch," he countered.

Jordan stood her ground. "I don't know how this trip could possibly get any worse," she grumbled. "I ache all over, I have to cook dinner out here in the virtual wilderness and all I have to look forward to is sleeping on a pile of rocks. The least you can do is help by changing a diaper!"

She wasn't sure whether it was shock or anger that persuaded him but decided not to look a gift horse in the mouth; she kept quiet as Dick grabbed a disposable diaper and headed toward Carter.

———— ◆◆◆ ————

The next morning Jordan was painfully conscious of every muscle in her body, including some she wasn't aware existed before now. Brett had slept fitfully so she hadn't gotten much sleep either.

They left the park a little after sunrise and drove to Jackson, stopping at a coffee shop for breakfast. Jordan sighed gratefully as she sank into the booth's cushioned bench.

Glancing at Dick, she inquired softly, "Do you think there's any chance of our staying in a motel tonight?"

He shook his head. "Nope, can't afford to. Besides, we need to take advantage of our new camping gear – and Carter is having the time of his life running around in the woods."

She looked at Carter, who was nestled up against his dad's side, and inwardly acknowledged that they were forging a closer relationship. Because that pleased her and because she knew Dick wouldn't give in on the issue anyway, she accepted this as her lot for the next several days. She wasn't happy, though, and spoke only when necessary from that point forward.

The van's air conditioning had cut out shortly after entering Tennessee the day before. The scorching heat only added to her suffering. She tried to recall a time in her life when she had felt nearly this miserable but none came to mind.

They got back on the road a little after 9:00 a.m. and drove non-stop to Ft. Smith, Arkansas, where they gassed up and had lunch.

Walking toward the diner with Brett in her arms, Jordan spoke for the first time since breakfast.

"I'm really sore and uncomfortable, Dick," she lamented. "Did you forget your promise to the doctor? You were supposed to let me get out and walk around every couple of hours . . ."

"Oh, quit your bitchin'," he interrupted. "You've done nothing but complain through the whole damn trip. Stop being such a baby!"

Tears stung her eyes. Her lips trembled and her voice wavered as she responded, "I gave birth six days ago! I shouldn't even be on this trip." She swiped at her eyes furiously but the more she tried to stop crying, the harder the tears fell.

He grabbed her by the shoulders and gave her a hard shake. A man and woman walking toward their car stopped and stared at them. When Dick realized they were being observed, he released her from his grip and turned to walk into the diner. Taking Carter by the hand, Jordan slowly followed.

⎯⎯⎯•((◊))•⎯⎯⎯

Shortly after crossing the Oklahoma border, Dick pointed at a sign directing them to the Fountainhead State Park in Checotah. Not waiting for a response from Jordan, he turned the van in that direction. Jordan peeked at her watch and was surprised to see it wasn't quite 5:00. She looked over at Dick, one eyebrow lifted in inquiry. Dick glanced at her and, noting the expression on her face, quickly turned his eyes back to the road ahead.

"I'm tired from driving for two straight days and I have to put the tent up so I think we'll call it a day," he explained.

Jordan hid her disgust. When she'd complained about her discomfort he'd reprimanded her, but now that *he* was tired they were stopping. *At this point, I don't care what reason he gives,* she thought, *I'll just be happy to get out of this vehicle.*

It was the third day of their trip. They were sitting in a coffee shop waiting for the waitress to bring their breakfast when he laid out his plans for the day. Dick's brother, Allen, lived in New Mexico and he was anxious to see him. He told her he thought they could make it as far as Santa Rosa that day, that it would take a little over nine hours.

Just as Jordan opened her mouth to protest, he held up a hand and said, "I think we'll stay in a motel tonight. I'm tired of having to pitch a tent every night, especially after driving hours on end."

Her astonishment was quickly replaced with feelings of relief. A smile crept onto her lips at the thought of sleeping on a mattress, in an air conditioned room.

A heat wave had recently struck the entire southwest so the

air had been unusually stifling, even for summer. These extreme temperatures and the lack of air conditioning in the bus had resulted in long hours of a smothering heat that zapped what little energy they had.

Jordan was particularly concerned for Brett. *He's so little,* she reflected, *he doesn't know how to express his discomfort other than to cry . . . and he's certainly been doing plenty of that.*

———◉———

Although the pillow Jordan brought to sit on helped ease the discomfort of her stitches, it caused her to sit higher in the seat. This made her seatbelt cut into her shoulder so she'd stopped wearing it the first day.

They were headed west on I-40 just outside Oklahoma City when Dick suddenly asked Jordan why she didn't have her seatbelt buckled.

As she started to explain, he began to yell at her. "You are the mother of two little kids. What if something should happen to you . . . what the hell would they do without a mother?"

"But, Dick . . ."

"You don't give a shit about your kids, do you?" he hollered. "What the hell kind of mother are you? Put your seatbelt on right now!"

Jordan glared at him defiantly and yelled back, "No! It hurts me and I'm not going to wear it - and you know I love my kids dearly so don't you dare say otherwise!"

Suddenly he pulled the car over, stopped on the freeway shoulder and got out. Before she knew it, he had opened her door and was pulling her out of the van. She instinctively grabbed at the rim of the door to hold herself in, but he easily overpowered her.

He pushed the lock down on the passenger door, slammed it, walked around and climbed back up onto his seat. Jordan began to panic. She looked back and saw Carter peering out the window anxiously, his expression indicating he was on the verge of tears.

"Dick, let me back in the car! Please!" she yelled.

He started the engine and started to pull away. Jordan began to sob, the anguish weighing her down as if a ton of bricks had been placed on her shoulders. She ran beside the car, pounding her fists against the passenger side window.

"Please . . . don't do this . . . please let me back in," she pleaded.

He screeched to a halt, which startled her and caused her to lose her footing. She fell onto her knees. Dick got out and walked to the front of the van. "Will you wear your seatbelt for the rest of the trip?" he demanded with a smirk.

She stood up and brushed the dirt off her knees. She'd scraped them both and flinched at the sting. Tears streamed down her face as she answered softly, "Yes."

He unlocked her door and she climbed in. After waiting to be sure her seatbelt was buckled, he accelerated back onto the freeway.

Jordan glowered at him and stated matter-of-factly, "Get me to Sacramento and then I never want to see you again."

She saw his jaw harden but he said nothing.

———— ◆ ————

When they arrived at Allen's house the next afternoon, Jordan was a nervous wreck. For the past three hours, the van's engine had been idling too fast and they'd heard a loud rumbling sound under the hood. In her mind, she'd pictured them having to lift the car and run like Fred and Barney in the *Flintstones* cartoon.

Allen's wife Debbie was all smiles when she greeted them at the door, but her face fell as soon as she saw Jordan.

"Oh, you look so tired – come in and sit down!" she exclaimed.

Jordan was carrying a sleeping Brett in his bassinet, which she set down on the floor before wearily sinking into the couch cushions. Debbie took Carter into the kitchen for oatmeal cookies and milk. She returned a moment later and motioned Jordan into the bedroom, encouraging her to take a nap claiming she'd care for the children. Jordan gratefully accepted.

She woke from her nap about an hour later to the sounds of Dick and Allen arguing.

Allen loudly inquired, "Why didn't you just put her and the kids on an airplane?"

"Mind your own fucking business, Allen! I'll deal with my family as I see fit."

As Jordan rose from the bed with a heavy sigh, she heard Debbie shush the two men, reminding them that she was sleeping. She walked into the living room to find both her babies sleeping soundly and looking more content than they had in a week.

When Debbie looked up and saw her, she stood, then walked over and gave her a hug, saying, "Your mother called while you were sleeping and said the date of her surgery has been moved up. She'll be admitted to the hospital three days from now and really wants to see you and the kids beforehand."

Glancing in Dick's direction, Debbie continued, "So, you guys need to cut your visit short and get going tomorrow."

Jordan didn't have to look at Dick to sense his anger, but when she did, she saw his furiously creased brow and pouting mouth that had become all too familiar.

The sense of desperation that had consumed her for days overwhelmed her at that moment. She bit back the tears. She wanted badly to see her mother before the surgery, but right now all she could think about was getting far away from Dick. Still, she was cautious about expressing her feelings too blatantly for fear of becoming the victim of his wrath once again.

<hr>

They got back on the road the next morning. Dick was in a particularly bad mood and had spent the morning grousing about the shortened visit with his brother. Jordan inwardly marveled at this because it seemed as if Allen didn't particularly care. In fact, his attitude toward Dick bordered on antipathy.

They were two hours into their trip, traveling down I-10 just east of Lordsburg, when suddenly the van began to shake. The turbulence was similar to that of an airplane flying into an air pocket. Jordan's knuckles whitened as she grabbed onto the arm rest. She looked at Dick, who was cursing and furiously clutching the steering wheel, and then back at Carter who had begun to whimper.

"What's happening?" asked Jordan.

Suddenly the engine began to sputter. Dick steered toward the highway shoulder as the van eased to a stop.

Jordan's ears pounded with the rapid throbbing of her heart. The sound, like the beating of a drum, was all she could hear. She turned to check on the boys. Carter sat in his car seat moaning fearfully. Brett seemed unaware of any problems.

She flinched when Dick suddenly shouted, "Shit!"

He opened his door and jumped out.

"Stay here," he ordered. "I'm gonna walk to the gas station for help. I may be awhile, so lock the doors."

Before she could respond, he slammed the door and walked away. She watched as he trudged down the side of the freeway and noted the lack of traffic. The few cars in the area were traveling at such speeds it would be difficult for them to stop. She spied a nearby sign that indicated an exit was not too far down the road.

The heat was oppressive. Jordan figured it to be at least 110 degrees.

"I have to open the windows," she muttered aloud as she stood and walked toward the backseat. "It's dangerous, but otherwise we'll all roast to death."

Droplets of sweat had already formed on her forehead and she could feel the onset of a headache. Brett began to cry and Jordan turned to see his face was bright red. She dug in the cooler for a bottle of juice. *He needs water*, she thought, *but this is the best I can do for now.*

A half hour later, a pickup truck pulled in front of them. Dick hopped out of the passenger side and walked back to the car.

Leaning through Jordan's open window, he said, "This guy's gonna tow us to the gas station down the road a bit. I called Allen and he's coming to get us.

━━━◦《◦》◦━━━

They'd waited in the gas station parking lot for nearly two

hours. Jordan had spent the time running back and forth from the restroom to the van. She'd taken towels, soaked them in water and placed them over the kids' heads to keep them cool but the intense heat warmed the towels so quickly she had to re-wet them about every ten minutes.

She was drenched in sweat, her head was pounding, she was hungry and she was worried about her children. Brett had been crying non-stop for the past hour.

She sat in the passenger seat, staring out the window and pondering their current predicament. At this moment, she truly hated Dick. She rued the day she'd met him. *Why did I let him talk me into this trip?* she wondered. *Allen was right, I should have taken the boys and flown home. We would be safe and sound at Mom and Dad's house by now.*

Just then a car pulled in beside them, but she felt too weak to even lift her head to look at it.

She heard Debbie ask, "Where is she?" and then she was opening the car door. Relief spread through Jordan, giving her the necessary energy to move. She practically fell into Debbie's arms.

"Get Brett, please, he needs cool air, "Jordan urged. "My poor baby, he's going to be sick. Oh, Debbie!"

Debbie pushed her toward the car. "You get in and cool off, I'll get the kids."

As she climbed into the back seat of their car, she heard Dick explaining the situation to his brother. Allen climbed up onto the driver's seat and turned the key. The engine sputtered for a minute and then started.

"Well it looks like maybe you overheated and it's okay now," Allen suggested.

Dick nodded. "Yeah, I added some oil because when I checked it was empty. I think it has a leak. So, I better have it looked at before we get back on the road."

They decided that Dick and Allen would drive the van back to their house, while Debbie, Jordan and the kids followed in the car. At this, Jordan smiled for the first time that day. She rested her head against the seat and heaved a heavy sigh.

———◦(◦)◦———

Two days later, they were still at Allen and Debbie's. Dick and Allen had driven the van directly to a Volkswagen repair shop, where the mechanic had estimated $900 to fix the problem.

In the meantime, Dick had suggested they consider buying a new Volkswagen Vanagon and had even visited a couple of dealerships.

"How on earth do you plan to pay for a new car," Jordan had asked, "considering you're not currently employed?"

He'd hemmed and hawed, then suggested his unemployment check would cover the payments until he was in the Navy, at which time they would have plenty of money. Jordan had rolled her eyes at this, which in turn angered Dick. They'd barely spoken during the past couple of days.

Debbie had picked up on this and had asked Jordan if everything was okay with her marriage. Considering she was technically Dick's family, Jordan didn't want to burden her with the truth so claimed everything was fine.

Debbie frowned. "You know what? I think Dick is stalling your departure. If I were you I'd be furious that he isn't trying harder to get to Sacramento so you can see your mom."

Privately, Jordan was fit to be tied over the whole situation. But her main goal at this point was to get away from Dick altogether. She was afraid if Dick suspected what she was feeling he'd stall even longer, so she kept quiet.

At that moment, Dick and Allen came through the door. They'd been playing basketball with some of Allen's friends. Debbie asked Dick if he'd checked on the van lately.

"No, Deb, I have not," he growled, "but since you're so anxious to be rid of us, I'll do that first thing in the morning. They closed a half hour ago."

Debbie shook her head and then turned and walked out of the room.

———⟞⟨◑⟩⟝———

The next morning Dick called the repair shop only to find the van had been ready the afternoon before. Allen drove him to pick it up and two hours later the family was back on the road.

Later that day, as they crossed the Arizona border, she realized she'd been holding her breath, anticipating another breakdown. But that hadn't happened, and after nearly nine hours on the road they pulled into a Motel 6 in Yuma.

It took them two more days to reach Sacramento.

Her dad met them at the door and immediately assured her Pat was fine. "Come in," he urged, "get something to eat, relax a bit and then I'll take you to see her."

"Will they let me bring the boys in?"

"Well no, but they can stay here with Dick while we're gone," he said, nodding in his direction.

She glanced at Dick nervously. "Will that be okay? I'll change them and get them down for naps before I leave."

"Sure!" answered Dick, flashing a big smile in their direction.

Jordan was flabbergasted. Never in a million years did she expect that reaction. *What's come over him?* she wondered. As soon as that thought crossed her mind, she realized he was putting on an act for her father's benefit. She had an uneasy feeling. He'd never taken care of the children on his own before.

"Well, we won't be gone long."

She smiled at her dad to mask her anxiety, but Bob's expression suggested her effort had been fruitless.

<hr />

On the way to the hospital, Jordan felt compelled to tell her father about the incident in Oklahoma City. Once the story began to roll out, she couldn't stop the flow; she went on to describe the state of her marriage. Her father listened, without saying much.

They spent the next hour visiting Pat. It had been two days since her surgery and Jordan was relieved to see her mother doing so well.

Pat again expressed her desire to see her grandchildren then with a chuckle, said, "I guess I can wait for two days 'til I get home, but it'll be hard."

As Jordan got out of the car upon their arrival home, she heard a loud, anguished cry from inside the house. After a brief glance at Bob, she ran to the house and through the door. Dick and Carter were standing in the family room just inside the front door.

Dick was practically foaming at the mouth, his rage contorting his face hideously. "Do something to shut that kid up!" he thundered.

Jordan flew down the hallway to the guest bedroom where Brett had been sleeping soundly when she left. As she reached down to pick him up, his sopping diaper fell off into the bassinet; then she saw the red, weeping skin where the diaper had been seconds ago. She fought back tears as she carried him into the bathroom.

Meanwhile, she could hear Bob's shouts down the hall as he laid into Dick with a fury of which she'd not thought him capable. Her father's usual demeanor was calm and composed; she had never seen him angry enough to yell at anyone before. But her father's rage was not nearly as shocking as what she heard next – Dick meekly apologizing.

She had just finished running warm water in the sink when Carter slowly walked into the room. He toddled over and hugged Jordan's knees. The pain in her heart was so intense at that moment she thought it would surely burst.

One week later, Dick left to go to his parents' house. Jordan walked him to the van and, as he climbed in, told him not to come back.

He scoffed as he put the van in reverse to back it out of the driveway. "If nothing else, I'll be back for my kids," he shouted out his window.

Chapter 31
Sacramento, California;
1980 ~ 1992

Dick did come back, but not for the kids. He presented Jordan with tickets for a marriage retreat. She responded by telling him their marriage was over and nothing could revive it. After he left, she grieved over the death of her marriage and yet was ecstatic to be liberated from it. It was as though she'd been a hostage, released by her captors after years of imprisonment.

———— ((●)) ————

In order to file for divorce, Jordan had to reestablish her California residency. That meant she had to live in the state for at least three months. During that period, Dick entered the Navy and moved to San Diego.

Once she did initiate the divorce, her attorney's attempts to serve Dick with the legal papers failed. Her suspicion that he was purposely avoiding the process server was proven when one week later he had her served with divorce papers.

His reasons for filing himself became clear when she realized she'd have to go to San Diego for court hearings, forcing her to make the long drive from Sacramento. This was particularly difficult since he had left her without a car. Not only did she have to borrow her mother's car, she had to borrow money for gas.

Her attorney assured her Dick would never get custody of the boys.

"I had a client once whose ex-wife was a cocaine addict and exposing the kids to that type of lifestyle - and he couldn't get custody." he told her. "You'll have no problem."

All told, it took nearly two years to finalize the divorce, during which she and the boys lived with her parents.

Dick provided no monetary support whatsoever. He'd made the situation worse by closing their credit card accounts, leaving her no way to buy clothes for two growing children. Fortunately, her parents had been willing to support the tiny family while Jordan endured long months of waiting, courtroom battles and continuous phone calls from Dick threatening to take the children.

She repeatedly asked her attorney about the possibility of a temporary order for child support until the divorce was finalized. Each time he put her off, telling her the divorce agreement would be settled soon – probably sooner than the time it would take to get the court to order temporary child support.

Jordan often remarked aloud that if she didn't have a family, she and her children would be on the streets with no food.

"I think it's criminal the way women are mistreated in this country, simply for having the audacity to leave an abusive husband," she asserted, "and apparently no one cares about the children either."

When at last she walked into the courtroom to finalize the

divorce order, she was disappointed to hear the pittance in child support recommended by Dick's attorney, not to mention his claim that she was not entitled to alimony. But what really galled her was when, through his attorney, Dick suggested she was a trained air traffic controller who could easily get a job in that capacity. He knew full well that wasn't true because she hadn't been FAA certified.

Her spirits lifted, however, when the judge commended her for her plans to make a better life for herself and her children by pursuing a college degree. And when he reproved Dick for what he referred to as his "reckless attitude toward the welfare of his children," she'd covered her mouth to hide the smile that appeared on her lips. Dick's jaw tightened as he studied the table before him.

"Based on the ages of the children, you are hereby ordered to pay child support and alimony in the amounts requested by the petitioner," stated the judge.

She was afraid to look in Dick's direction but her mother later told her he'd looked furious.

They'd already agreed to split the furniture between them. With her attorney's encouragement, she'd consented to pay half of the bills accumulated during the marriage.

⸻ ◉ ⸻

Jordan enrolled for the fall semester at Sacramento State, only to find her GI Bill benefits barely covered her childcare expenses, which meant there was little money left for books or tuition. She'd learned very quickly how to budget the few dollars she received each month.

Shortly after the support payments began, Jordan moved from her parents' house. Knowing she couldn't afford much on her own, she'd been pleased when two schoolmates, both divorced women, asked if she and the boys wanted to share a house with them.

For the first time since she had married Dick, Jordan felt positive about her future. She got a part time job in the veterans' office at the college and treated school as she would a full-time job. She selected early morning classes, leaving her afternoons free for studying. This allowed her to pick up the boys from their childcare center by 5:00 and spend her evenings with them.

Over time she slowly emerged from the protective shell formed during her marriage to Dick. One day it occurred to her that she was no longer intimidated by him, that he could no longer hurt her emotionally.

During one of Dick's frequent calls that were ostensibly for the purpose of speaking to the children, but actually a medium he used to verbally berate her and call her ugly names, she'd declared, "This is the beauty of divorce, Dick, I no longer have to listen to you," and slammed the phone down in its cradle.

After that, the number of times he called lessened, but when he did call he attempted to chat with her as if they were old pals. She'd grit her teeth and quickly tell him she would get the boys on the phone.

During one call he said he needed to discuss visitation plans with her so she'd stayed on the phone long enough to hear him say, "You'd love being a Navy wife, Jordan. If you ever want to reconcile, just say the word." His words had astounded her for several reasons, but mainly because he'd expressed them during the first year of his marriage to Meg.

Dick had met Meg while he and Jordan were in the midst of their divorce. When Jordan had heard he was planning to remarry, she felt a mixed sense of relief and curiosity about his soon-to-be wife. But mostly she felt pity for her.

Dick and Meg had been married for several months before Jordan had the opportunity to meet her. She eventually grew to like Meg, whose presence alleviated some of her anxiety over sending her young children to spend time with Dick.

On the whole, his visits with the boys were rare. He frequently told the boys he would have them for the summer or a holiday, only to disappoint them by not showing up. Sometimes he called Jordan to tell her he wasn't coming, leaving her to explain to the children.

Dick's support payments were equally erratic. She never knew from one month to the next if he would send a check and if he did how much it would be. At one point, when he had missed two months worth of support payments, her mother suggested she write to his commanding officer. A couple weeks later she was astonished by the commander's reply, reprimanding her for adding stress to the life of one of his young pilots.

<hr />

Not quite three years had passed since their original court appearance when Dick filed legal papers requesting a decrease in the child support payments. This would be the first of many such requests.

Contrary to the advice of her attorney and her parents, Jordan suggested her alimony payments should end when she graduated from college. She felt strongly about freeing herself from any dependence on Dick as quickly as possible.

"Once I've graduated, I can get a good job and I won't need his support anymore," she rationalized.

Although the court denied Dick's request to lower the child support, the judge did grant his request to ban Jordan from contacting his superiors in the future. He also issued a termination order for the spousal support payments. They were to end the month following her graduation.

Dick continued to pay his child support intermittently. It wasn't until Jordan's father wrote him an angry letter that she began to receive regular support payments.

———◉———

It was Christmas time, three years after their divorce, when Jordan's bank notified her of several bounced checks.

"How can that be?" she'd questioned, "My Navy allotment should have been deposited last week."

Although the support payments were sporadic during the first couple of years, Dick had finally set up an allotment through the Navy. The payments were automatically wired to her checking account each month.

After nearly a year of positive responses, she'd decided she no longer needed to call the bank to verify each deposit to her account. Now she realized that assumption had been wrong. After several phone calls, including one to the Navy Finance Office in Cleveland, she learned that Dick had completely stopped the allotment.

This meant not only that the boys would have no Christmas, but the checks she'd written to pay her rent and utilities had bounced so she owed the bank $150 in overdraft charges.

Jordan was beside herself. She didn't know how she would ever cover the bounced checks, let alone the bank fees that continued to accumulate.

A deep depression settled over her like a fog-filled valley. She was practically out of food and had no money to buy more. *How can I feed my kids?* she worried.

A few weeks later, a representative from the utility company showed up at her door to shut off the water because of the unpaid bill. Jordan was at her wits end. She pleaded with him to allow her another chance to pay the bill, explaining she had small children in the house. He gave her two days to come up with the money.

Because her roommates had already paid their share of the bills and her veteran's check had already been spent on child care, she didn't know where to turn. Totally devastated, she slid to the floor in a puddle of tears. After several minutes of self-pitying hysterics, she reluctantly went to the phone and called her parents.

Within hours her mother wired her bank enough money to cover her overdraft charges and pay her outstanding bills.

A little while later, her mother showed up at her door with bags of groceries. When Pat wrapped her arms around her, Jordan fell apart. Mother and daughter embraced for several minutes until, through gritted teeth, Jordan seethed, "I hate that man with a vengeance. I have never before felt anything close to the loathing I do right now. I wish he were dead!"

Ultimately, Jordan was forced to take a year off from her college studies so she could work full time. She and the boys again moved in with her parents. It took nearly two years to begin receiving support payments again and to recoup the back child support, most of which she used to pay her attorney.

Jordan re-enrolled in college.

In the summer of 1986, she attained her Bachelors degree and began a full time job. Although her salary was modest, the simple knowledge of it lessened her worries about any future stunts on Dick's part.

⇒⊲(●)⊳⇐

During the summer of 1990, Carter and Brett participated in Dick's wedding to Gina, his third wife, with plans to fly home two days later. Three months prior, Jordan and the kids had moved into a house with Nick Gallagher, whom she intended to marry.

When the boys told Dick about their new living arrangements, he phoned Jordan, ranting and raving that she was a whore and saying he would not allow her to expose the children to her evil ways. He then told her he wasn't going to return the boys as planned.

"I won't have them raised in that environment and watch their mother behave like the slut she is," he'd yelled before quickly hanging up.

Jordan panicked. When she explained the situation to Nick, he'd insisted there was no way Dick could follow through on his threats. "You have court-ordered custody of those boys, Jordan. He's just trying to pull your chain."

She shook her head. "You don't know him or what he's capable of. He doesn't care how much he hurts the boys, so long as he can make me miserable,"

Jordan and Nick went to the airport to meet the boys' flight, only to find they were not on the airplane. Jordan was beside herself. Nick tried to comfort her and, although she was calmer by the time they got home, she was unable to sleep that night.

The next day she hired a San Diego attorney, who obtained an emergency court order to retrieve her children. That evening the attorney put them on a flight home.

———⊃«(●)»⊂———

This time Jordan took Dick to court, asking the judge to order a psychological evaluation of Dick. She also asked for any future visits with the boys to be supervised.

She'd had several conversations with Meg over the past few years, which convinced her even more that Dick's treatment of the boys had been and would continue to be detrimental. Jordan recalled his verbal and physical abuse during their marriage and was determined to keep him from mistreating the children.

The court's response was to order Dick and Jordan, along with their spouses, to meet with a mediator and for both of them to undergo psychological evaluations.

Jordan's efforts to protect the children were discouraging throughout. Her attorney made several legal errors, causing the judge to throw out most of their evidence against Dick. The process continued for two more years. Along with her frustration, her legal bills mounted. Feeling as if she had no choice, Jordan finally settled the case. Because of the settlement, she was not allowed access to the results of the psychological examinations, leaving her to wonder what they indicated about Dick's proclivity for violent behavior.

———— ⇒‹‹◉››⇐ ————

At first she was consoled by the fact the boys had reached the age at which they could decide for themselves, but when Brett told her he wanted to go live with his father for a year, she was devastated.

"I want the chance to get to know my father," he'd said.

Jordan knew that Dick had been working on him during their phone conversations - that these were Dick's words, not Brett's. But she also worried her son might someday resent her if she refused. So, though she felt as if her heart would break, she relented.

Six months later, Brett informed her he was ready to come home.

Several months passed before he described the situation while living with his father. He told Jordan that his father drank heavily and was physically abusive with Gina. On one occasion, Caitlin, Dick's seven-year-old daughter from his marriage to Meg, had been visiting. Brett described a horrendous fight between Dick and Gina, culminating with Dick punching his wife. Brett had taken Caitlin into the bedroom to try to calm her throughout the incident.

Brett also related how Dick frequently left him alone to fend for himself and had even refused to buy him clothes, forcing him to wear one of Gina's jackets to school on cold days.

Jordan became furious when Brett described the verbal abuse his father had meted out and wept when her little boy reassured her that he was fine, that it was just the drinking that made his dad behave that way.

Inwardly, she vowed to never again expose either of her children to prolonged visits with their father. As it turned out, she didn't need to. Neither of them expressed any subsequent desire to spend time with him.

"I've never hated anyone in my life, until now," Jordan told Nick after repeating Brett's stories, "I wish there was a way to make him disappear from our lives forever."

"Because of its tremendous solemnity,
Death is the light in which great passions, both good and bad,
Become transparent, no longer limited by outward
appearances."

Soren Kierkegaard

Chapter 32
San Diego, California;
July 25, 2003

Buchanan and O'Reilly found a seat in the last pew, closest to the front doors. A few curious heads turned to look at them. This only compounded Ian's discomfort with sitting in the back of a practically empty church. He counted about twenty people in attendance, which included several children.

Mike leaned toward him and whispered in his ear, "Popular guy, huh?" Ian elbowed him.

Other than Maryanne Tripp, seated in the fourth row, and Miriam Tate, who waved at them from the front pew, he didn't know anyone. He intended to, though, as soon as the services were over. Ian figured Miriam was his best bet – she was undoubtedly familiar with most, if not all, the mourners.

Ian thought it noteworthy that none of the victim's ex-wives were present. He studied the faces of those who were in the church, wondering how they might be related to Dick Tate. Two young men sat on Miriam's left, one of whom looked so much like Jordan he was sure they were her sons.

A petite, white-haired woman sat at a small organ to the left of the front pew, playing solemn renditions of various hymns. Ian found himself slipping into a particularly somber mood as *Ave Maria* gently stirred the floral-scented air.

At center stage sat a mahogany coffin, draped with a white funeral pall.

Five minutes passed. Ian was just beginning to squirm on the hard wooden seat when the minister appeared. A man of medium height and slight build approached Miriam. He took her hands in his and bowed his head as he spoke to her briefly, then turned and walked up to the pulpit.

"Let us pray," murmured the minister.

As a Homicide detective Ian often found himself at churches, synagogues or mosques, but it had been years since he'd attended the Catholic Church in which he'd been baptized. During his teen years, he'd begun to question his faith and to this day felt conflicted about religion in general. He lowered his head respectfully but his mind was racing, thinking about the case he was trying to solve.

While others prayed, he pondered the evidence and the subtle clues he had to date. He made a mental list of things to do. Still curious about the vomit found at the scene, he reminded himself to call Jim Ritter to check the status of the DNA analysis. He also realized the importance of obtaining saliva samples from the victim's former wives so their DNA could be compared with the results. Afraid that, like Jordan, Meg and Gina would consult attorneys who would more than likely advise them against volunteering anything, he realized the need to contact them soon.

Ian's thoughts were interrupted by a low rumbling as the whole congregation rose to its feet, including Mike. He looked up to see his partner frowning at him and quickly stood. Voices rose to the accompaniment of the organ playing an unfamiliar hymn. He listened momentarily as they sang.

And He walks with me, and He talks with me,
And He tells me I am His own;
And the joy we share as we tarry there,
None other has ever known.

Once again Ian's mind began to wander. He thought about the vast differences between the victim's three wives. Gina had dark hair, olive skin and an athletic build, whereas Meg was a petite, light-skinned redhead. Jordan, on the other hand, was a tall, slender blonde. He found that odd. Judging by past experience, people's tastes tended to remain the same when it came to the opposite sex.

But it was more than just their physical features. Ian also saw a disparity in their personalities. He sensed in Gina a strong-willed, assertive personality - someone who felt a great need to be in control of every situation and whose main concern was herself. Jordan, who was quiet and genteel, seemed almost embarrassed by her anger toward and hatred of the victim, while Meg was outgoing, vivacious and straightforward about her hostility toward Dick.

Ian became aware the music had stopped; the funeral goers once again were taking their seats. This time he joined them with no nudging from Mike.

The minister began, "We are gathered here today in this service to pay our respects to Richard Tate. Today, for the comfort and hope we need, let us turn our thoughts to the love of God . . ."

Before he knew it, the service was over and the audience

slowly began to file out. He watched as the two young men who had been sitting with Miriam, along with four others, carefully carried the casket down the long aisle, past where Ian was standing and through the door to the waiting hearse.

Miriam suddenly appeared at his side and handed him a flyer containing the directions to the cemetery.

"Dickie's father insisted upon a military funeral, but I knew he would have wanted a proper Christian service . . . so we compromised. The Marines will conduct the graveside service," she explained. "You're welcome to join us."

"I think we will . . . and if you would be so kind as to introduce us to everybody, I would really appreciate it . . ."

Miriam glanced around uncomfortably. "Well, Detective, I can do that but most of these people are family. They, uh . . . you aren't going to interrogate them are you?"

"Oh, no Ma'am. It would just help us to know who they are and how they're related. For instance, I assume the two young men who were sitting next to you," he glanced toward the front door, "and were pall bearers, are Jordan's sons. Am I right?"

Miriam's jaw set, her voice rigid as she responded, "They are *Dickie's* sons, yes."

"Oh, okay," Ian murmured, picking up on her obvious sensitivity to the issue.

"I need to go," she said abruptly, "my family is waiting for me."

Peering over her shoulder at a small group of people huddled together at the front of the church, she said, "That tall, bald man is Richard Tate, Sr. - my ex-husband. You can talk to him all you want." She turned and walked out the front door.

From behind him, Mike said, "Man, if I was ever so inclined

to consider getting married, just thinking about these people - this family - would knock the idea right out of my head."

Ian glanced at his partner. "You can say that again."

Buchanan turned and studied the man Miriam identified as Dick's father. Along with his entourage, Richard Tate, Sr. began walking toward them. Out of the side of his mouth, Ian said to his partner, "What say we go have a chat with dear old Dad?"

Not waiting for Mike's response, he stepped out into the aisle and effectively blocked the man's path. A bemused expression came over Tate's face as he peered down at Ian.

Buchanan had to bend his neck backward to look up at the man he figured to be well over six feet tall. Offering his right hand, he said, "Mr. Tate, my name is Ian Buchanan. I'm investigating your son's murder."

Richard, Sr. shook Ian's hand firmly, and as his eyes turned in Mike's direction, Ian quickly introduced his partner. The two men shook hands and then Tate's gaze returned to Ian.

"So, do you have any ideas who did this?"

"We have several suspects we're looking at. No one has been arrested, if that's what you're asking. We're still gathering evidence . . . which should help us narrow the list."

The smirk that formed on the man's lips startled Ian.

"I told Dick all his God-damned marriages would come back to bite him someday. He married one bitch after another," he said disparagingly. "But did that shithead ever listen to me? Hell no. I assume those three blood suckers are high on your suspect list."

Good God, no wonder Dick was such a nutcase, thought Ian. *I thought his mother was a piece of work but this guy is something else.*

Before Ian could respond, one of Tate's male companions interjected, "Dad, this is a church . . ." then turned toward Ian and said, "I'm Allen Tate, Dick's older brother and," he placed his arm around the woman standing next to him, "this is my wife Debbie. If there's anything we can do to help, just let us know."

"I appreciate that, Allen. Maybe we could get together after the service." He returned his gaze to the victim's father. "And I would very much like to continue our discussion as well, Mr. Tate."

"Yeah, okay."

A woman to Richard Sr.'s right quietly said, "Dear, we should get going . . ."

Tate rolled his eyes and growled, "I'm coming . . . don't nag Blanche," as he turned and walked away.

Allen reddened and said, "We really do need to go, Detective. My wife and I look forward to talking to you later." He flashed a brief smile then turned to follow his father out of the church.

———=»((◉))«=———

The detectives stood a short distance from the group of people crowded around the coffin that was now draped with an American flag.

Three marines stood at attention while the minister recited, "*I am the resurrection, and I am the life,* says the Lord. *Those who believe in me, even though they die, will live, and everyone who lives and believes in me will never die.*"

As bowed heads were lifted, Ian perused their faces. Two women, who appeared to be mother and daughter, stood apart from the main group. The older woman had gray-streaked blonde hair and looked to be in her late forties or early fifties.

Buchanan subtly pointed them out to his partner. "They don't appear to be part of the family . . . or if they are, they've been ostracized."

Mike whispered, "Yeah, no doubt someone we should talk to."

"Umm hmm," murmured Ian.

The Minister stood back and Ian watched as the Marine Guard stepped forward, aimed their rifles into the air and fired seven shots for a twenty-one gun salute. A tingle ran down his spine. Buchanan had witnessed this ritual at the burials of several police officers over the years. The thought that his loved ones might someday observe this practice at his gravesite was an ominous one.

You could hear a pin drop as the soldiers marched to the coffin, lifted the American flag and began to fold it in symbolic fashion. One of the Marines turned and ceremoniously offered the folded flag to Miriam, saying, "Please accept this flag on behalf of a grateful nation."

Another Marine raised a bugle to his lips and began to play *Taps*. The low, plaintive dirge elicited a deep and pervasive sense of melancholy. Sounds of a soft, woeful and obviously feminine cry arose from the mourners and tugged at Ian's heart.

No one moved for several minutes after the conclusion of the bugler's performance, nor did they speak. Ian and Mike waited respectfully, but when they heard a hushed murmuring and the small cluster began to stir, they quickly walked over to Miriam.

Ian once again expressed his sorrow at her loss and then promptly asked if she knew the identity of the two women who were now headed in the direction of the parking lot.

Miriam glanced in their direction and said abstractedly, "Oh, yeah, she was Dickie's girlfriend in college." She waved her hand in the woman's direction as if to say she was insignificant.

Ian wasn't swayed. "Oh? Did Dick go to college here in San Diego?"

"Och, no," she replied hastily, "he went to San Jose State College."

"I see. So, this girlfriend . . . by the way, what's her name?"

"Colleen."

"So, Colleen lives in San Diego now?"

Miriam sighed audibly. Exasperation crept into her voice as she uttered, "No, Detective, she was in the area, visiting someone. She said she was shocked to see Dickie's obituary in the newspaper and, since she was in town, decided to come and show her respect."

Buchanan glanced over his shoulder to see Colleen and her companion rapidly approaching the parking lot.

"Please excuse me," he shot out as he took off in a jog to catch up with them. The clumping sounds behind him suggested Mike was in close pursuit.

As soon as he was within earshot, Buchanan shouted, "Colleen!"

The older woman stopped and turned around. Her eyes curiously scanned his face and as Ian came to a stop in front of her, she tentatively replied, "Yes?"

Once again, he explained who he was and introduced his partner.

Her bewilderment was evident as she asked, "How can I help you, Detective?"

"I'm hoping you can provide some background information on Mr. Tate."

Colleen nervously shifted from one foot to the other and answered, "I'm afraid I can't tell you much. I knew Dick a very long time ago. I haven't seen him in nearly thirty years."

Ian nodded. "Well, what brings you here today?"

"Pure accident, I assure you," she replied, "I just happened to be in town and read of his death in the paper. Because I was here and I could, I decided to attend his funeral."

"Is there some reason why you *just happened* to read the obituaries?"

Colleen's voice took on an irritated tone as she answered, "No, Detective. As a matter of fact, I didn't read about it in the obituary section. There was a local news article about his murder. And then, I only saw that because the newspaper was open to that page."

"My mistake," he remarked. "So, what brings you to our lovely city?"

Her eyes shifted to the woman on her left as she answered, "I'm visiting my daughter."

"Oh . . . and this is your daughter?"

He gazed at the tall young female. She had a fairly muscular build, short-cropped hair and a face that was a younger version of her mother's. A light went on in Ian's head. *Could this be Dick's daughter, the girl in the photo he'd shown to Jordan all those years ago?*

"Yes. Please forgive my rudeness . . . this is my daughter, Heather Monroe."

Heather acknowledged him with a slight smile.

Ian suddenly remembered Mike was there when he heard him exclaim, "You're Dick Tate's daughter, aren't you?"

Colleen's eyes grew with trepidation; her head jerked in Heather's direction. Ian thought she looked as though she might jump right out of her skin.

"Of course not," replied Heather matter-of-factly. "Jake

Monroe was my father. Why would you assume such a thing?"

Heather did not appear to share her mother's anxiety over Mike's question. *Could it be,* thought Ian, *this young woman is Dick's daughter but doesn't know?*

Colleen abruptly turned back to face the detectives. Her voice cracked as she murmured, "I'll be happy to discuss this with you later, but please don't involve my daughter . . . She has nothing to do with Dick Tate. She doesn't know him. Heather accompanied me here today at my request."

"Okay . . . can you come to the station this afternoon?" Buchanan asked.

Colleen still looked flustered as she nodded and took the business card Ian offered. She placed her arm on her daughter's back, gently pushing her in the direction of the parking lot.

Ian looked at his watch. "It's ten minutes to one. Can you be there at three o'clock?"

"Fine," replied Colleen over her shoulder as she hurried Heather toward their car.

Buchanan turned to see his partner looking at him expectantly. "So . . . what are you thinking?"

Ian shrugged. "I'm not sure. She . . . I can't put my finger on it but I just have the feeling she's not being totally honest with us."

"You think Heather is really his daughter?"

"Yes, I do," declared Ian. "But I also think Heather hasn't been told. That's why Colleen was in such a hurry to get her away from us."

Buchanan heard the drone of conversation from the rest of the funeral-goers who were now headed to their cars. Both detectives turned in their direction. They were walking in two groups; one headed up by Richard Tate, Sr., the other by Miriam.

Ian shook his head as he realized this family was split by loyalties to one parent or the other.

He was brought out of his reverie by Richard, Sr.'s bellowing, "What the hell did that little tramp say to you?"

Ian groaned. His brow creased in an angry scowl as he turned to the victim's father and snarled, "You know, I've had just about enough of you and your derogatory comments about women!"

Tate's jaw dropped. His expression fluctuated between anger and puzzlement, finally settling into a look of shocked indignation.

"Just who the fuck do you think you are . . . talking to me like that? Goddamned son of a bitch!" he blared.

Out of the corner of his eye, Buchanan could see that the other group had come to a halt a short distance away. Ian had to work at containing himself. If Dick Tate was anything like his father he could almost understand why a woman would want to kill him. At the same time, he wondered why any woman would want to have anything to do with him in the first place.

He felt Mike's hand on his shoulder.

In a strangled voice, he rasped, "I'm the son of a bitch who's trying to solve your son's murder. . . ." Ian eyed the man angrily as he whispered harshly, "And you don't intimidate me one bit Mr. Tate."

Buchanan turned his back on him, instead laying his eyes on the group of mourners surrounding Miriam. He spied the two young men who were the offspring of Dick, Jr. and Jordan and walked toward them.

His tone was much calmer as he inquired, "Which one of you is Brett?"

A tall and muscled twenty-something man stepped forward

and proclaimed, "That would be me."

He felt, more than saw, Richard, Sr. and his entourage continue on toward the parking lot. As they walked away, Ian heard the older man bark, "Move your fat ass, Blanche," and gritted his teeth.

Buchanan focused his attention on Brett. He raised his hand to block the sun from his eyes as he looked up at a chiseled face adorned by a gleaming smile. He couldn't help but grin back.

"I understand you were visiting with your father last weekend. I'd like to talk to you about that . . ." he began.

"Oh sure, do you want to do that now?" Brett asked, then added, "My brother too?"

Ian's eyes followed as Brett motioned toward the assembly of people behind him. The other son, the one who looked so much like Jordan, stood to one side of the group. As Ian peered at him, the young man rolled his blue eyes and cracked a smile out of one corner of his mouth.

"C'mere Carter," Brett waved to his brother, then leaned in to the detective and murmured, "He's kinda shy sometimes."

Carter walked over and reached out his hand as he uttered drolly, "I'm Carter Tate. Ignore my brother, he's a dweeb." Ian couldn't help but laugh as he shook Carter's hand. The sound of Mike chuckling next to him reminded him to introduce his partner.

He raised his arm to get a better look at his watch. It was now 1:00.

"We'd like to talk to both of you . . . If you could go down to the station with us now that would be great," Ian proposed. "We'd also like to get your fingerprints so we can remove them from the suspect list."

"We can do that," affirmed Brett. He swung his head around and peered inquiringly at Miriam then continued, "Grandma was gonna take us to lunch . . . I've never been known to turn down a free meal," he grinned and patted his flat stomach, "or any meal for that matter!"

Mike stepped forward and lightly slapping Brett on the back, quipped. "A man after my own heart. I'll bet Detective Buchanan would be happy to spring for a meal . . . "

Ian laughed and said, "Happy to," then, winking at Carter, declared, "Ignore my partner . . . he's a dweeb!"

Chapter 33
July 25, 2003

Brett and Carter rode in the backseat of Buchanan's car on the way to the Sheriff's station. Brett kept up a constant chatter, bantering back and forth with Mike, who was sitting in the front passenger seat. Carter sat quietly, occasionally shaking his head and grinning at his brother.

Glancing into the rearview mirror, Ian broached, "So, Carter, when was the last time you were at your dad's place?"

Carter's smile vanished. Averting his eyes, he muttered, "I haven't been to this house. I . . . haven't seen my dad in about five years."

Ian wasn't sure how to respond to that, so simply said, "Oh, I see."

"Yeah, I'm the only one who stayed in touch with him. He and Carter didn't see eye to eye . . ." remarked Brett.

Carter's eyes narrowed as he turned and looked at his brother in the seat next to him. "Shut up Brett," he whispered.

Crossing his arms and sitting back against the seat, Brett was quiet for the first time since meeting the detectives. An awkward silence ensued. Much to Ian's relief, they reached the station a few minutes later.

———※《◎》※———

Since Carter claimed he hadn't been in his father's home, and Ian believed him, the detective didn't think they needed to fingerprint him. But because he thought Brett might speak freer without his brother present, he and his partner agreed that Mike would take Carter to be printed and then interview him separately. Buchanan escorted Brett into the same cramped room he'd used to interview Jordan the day before.

"So, where do you want me to begin?" Brett asked as he lowered himself onto the gray vinyl seat.

Ian smiled at him. "How about telling me about your trip down here last week . . . what day did you arrive in San Diego?"

"Okay . . ." started Brett, "My mom and I drove all day Thursday - we got to San Diego around seven o'clock. It's a really long drive," he explained. "I talked to my dad earlier in the week and we'd made plans for me to go to his house on Friday. So, about eleven that morning, I borrowed Mom's car and went over there."

"And you spent the rest of the day together?"

"Yeah, Mom was busy with her friends from high school so Dad and I just hung out. We went to the Wild Animal Park."

"Did you spend the night at his house?"

Brett shook his head. "No, I would have had to sleep on his couch and I didn't want to. In case you hadn't noticed, I'm kinda tall. Couches aren't exactly the most comfortable place to sleep. Mom had two king sized beds in her room so I stayed with her."

TIFFANY CRAIG BROWN

"Gotcha," remarked Ian with a smile. "So, what time did you get back to the hotel that night?"

"Oh, not 'til about midnight," he answered. "I knew Mom would be out late . . . plus I'd had a couple beers," he flashed a toothy grin at Ian, "so didn't want to be out on the road. I waited until the alcohol wore off."

Ian nodded.

"Was your mom in the hotel room when you got back?"

"Oh yeah," he nodded. "She told me earlier that I shouldn't expect her until around two the next morning." Brett snickered as he added, "But I guess when you get old you can't stay out that late."

"Yeah, poor woman's ravaged with age" said Ian drolly.

Brett grinned. "My mom would like you."

"So . . . where were we?" Buchanan prompted. "Tell me about the rest of your weekend."

Brett sat up in his chair and said, "Yeah, okay . . . I, um, had breakfast with my mom and some of her friends, then went back to Dad's around noon. We spent the rest of the day at the beach, then went back to his house and barbecued some ribs." He licked his lips and said, "My favorite!"

"I'm getting the impression you like to eat," quipped Ian. "Go on."

"I got back to the hotel about eleven thirty or so. Mom wasn't back yet, so I just got in bed and watched a little tube."

"What time did your mom get in?"

Brett shrugged. "I'm not sure . . . I fell asleep. Mom must have turned the TV off cuz the next thing I knew it was morning. She was taking a shower. That was about nine o'clock. At about ten thirty, I went to have brunch with my dad – at some Mexican restaurant. It was really good . . . Ever had Mexican breakfast?" He smacked his lips.

Ian laughed out loud.

"So . . . where was I? Oh yeah . . ." murmured Brett, "I went back to the hotel and spent the rest of the day with my mom. Went to the beach . . . just hung out. Then we went to this really nice restaurant for dinner . . . that's about it. Mom wanted to go to bed early cuz we had to leave about six o'clock the next morning."

"And you're sure your mom was there the whole night?"

Brett opened his mouth but no words came out. He stared at Ian a moment, first with seeming confusion then annoyance. He leaned forward and sternly remarked, "Now I just know you don't think my mom killed my dad."

"I – uh – well, you must understand that I have to ask. I mean, I wouldn't be doing my job if I didn't cover all the angles . . . I'm just trying to find out who did this."

Brett grimaced. "I understand . . . but I can also guarantee my mom had nothing to do with it. She's the gentlest person I know. Besides, she doesn't even talk about my dad anymore. She's gotten over it . . . I mean, ya know it was just divorce stuff. That's been over a long time now."

Ian smiled slightly and asked, "Divorce stuff? What kind of divorce stuff?"

"Oh you know, like the child support – my dad didn't always send it - and um, other things like custody and visitation. She used to get really mad at him." Brett shrugged "But my dad wasn't *that* bad. I mean sometimes he got drunk and yelled and stuff but mostly he was an okay guy. And he was my father, so I loved him."

Ian dipped his head and then prodded, "But Carter doesn't feel the same way?"

"He loved him too. He's just more sensitive, ya know? He takes things to heart more. I tried to get him to be more forgiving but he's stubborn."

"Forgiving of what?"

"I don't know," he shrugged, "whatever it is that made him stop talking to Dad. He won't talk about it."

Ian sat back in his chair and stared at the ceiling a minute, then asked cautiously, "Do you think Carter had enough animosity toward your dad that he'd want to hurt him?"

Brett's eyes widened. He shook his head fiercely from side to side. "No way," he stated matter-of-factly, "He didn't *hate* him. He just didn't want to spend time with him, that's all. Besides, there's no way he could have done it. He was in Sacramento all weekend."

He paused, then continued, "He works weekends . . . I'm sure you can verify he was there . . . call his work . . ."

"We'll do that," Ian said calmly, adding, "I'm sure you're right."

Brett scowled and asked heatedly, "Man, is there anybody you *don't* think did this?"

Ian said nothing.

After a moment's silence, Brett said through clenched teeth, "Have you talked to Meg . . . his second wife? Dad told me she hated him so much she poisoned my half-sister against him. I mean Meg wouldn't let Caitlin see any of us – even me. Dad said Meg is really evil."

Buchanan's brow puckered as he responded, "Yeah, Brett, we've talked to all your dad's wives. Seems to me your dad thought they were all evil – including your mom."

Brett's eyes darted around the room finally resting on the table in front of him. His voice was barely above a whisper as he said, "I guess he did."

"Did you get along with Meg?"

Brett nodded. "Yeah. She was actually pretty nice to me. Carter liked her too."

"How about Gina?"

"Gina is . . . she was okay. I think she kinda resented us. I don't know why I think that but I do. But my dad liked her. I think he still does. He told me the other day he thought they might get back together. They were supposed to have dinner . . ." Brett's eyes closed and he paused briefly before continuing, "I thought he said Sunday night – you know, the night he was murdered . . . but I'm not sure."

Ian cocked an eyebrow. Brett pursed his lips and then shook his head, as if to ward off the thoughts passing through his mind.

A sudden knock caused both men to jump. Ian glanced up to see Mike peek his head around the door and say, "I have sandwiches . . ."

Brett grinned.

Ian chuckled and said, "Well, come on in . . . before this young man starves to death."

Mike walked in and set several brown bags down on the table. Carter was close behind with a cardboard tray that held four paper cups containing their drinks.

It was nearly 3:00 when Mike drove the two young men to their hotel.

"I'll check with Jordan to see if they've conferred with their attorney yet about the prints and DNA sample," Mike mentioned on his way out the door.

"Hurry back – you'll probably want to hear what Colleen has to say!" Ian called at Mike's back.

Mike peered up at the wall clock and replied, "Yeah, I do. Okay, I'm outta here."

Buchanan picked up the phone and dialed. His heart skipped a beat when he heard Meg's voice on the other end, and after he identified himself and she cheerfully responded, "Hi Ian, it's nice to hear from you," he grinned from ear to ear.

He quickly glanced around the room and was relieved to see no one was watching him. *Man, I'm glad Mike isn't here right now – I'd never hear the end of it,* he mused.

"Hi Meg," he started timidly, "I'm calling because I forgot to ask you the other day . . . I, uh, wanted to see if you would mind coming down here so we can get your fingerprints?"

Meg hesitated.

"I guess so . . . what do you need them for?" she asked warily.

"Well, I assume you haven't been in his house lately?" he stated in the form of a question.

"Hardly," she replied derisively.

Buchanan cleared his throat and continued, "I just need to be sure yours aren't a match with those found at the crime scene..."

"Oh, okay. That shouldn't be a problem."

Ian realized he'd been holding his breath as he now let it out with a loud sigh. "Great! "While you're here maybe we can get a saliva sample as well."

"A saliva sample?" Meg inquired guardedly.

After he explained that the crime lab could derive her DNA patterns from her saliva, her attitude changed abruptly.

"I, uh, think I would be more comfortable after consulting with my attorney about this. Let me do that and then I'll get back to you, okay?"

Shit! he thought, *I should have waited until she was here . . . now I won't even get her fingerprints.*

"Oh sure," he replied, sounding much more positive than he felt.

After promising to call once she'd talked to her lawyer, she ended the call.

He had just begun an internal dialogue about better handling the same request of Gina when his phone rang. It was ten minutes past three and Colleen was here.

He quickly grabbed the tape recorder and a writing pad before dashing down the stairs to greet her.

———————— ((•)) ————————

Of all the people he'd interviewed so far, Colleen seemed the most nervous. He squeezed her hand in greeting and felt it tremble. Her voice shook when she spoke. Her face was so drawn and pale, her angst so palpable, Ian couldn't help but feel sorry for her.

"Please relax," he murmured gently as she preceded him into the interview room.

Colleen nodded but her hands shook as she pulled out a chair and sat. Ian took a seat across from her then leaned in and quietly asked, "Why so nervous, Colleen?"

Fidgeting in her seat, she glanced toward the door then replied, "This is all new to me. I've never even set foot in a police station before . . . I-I don't understand why you want to talk to me anyway."

"As I said before, just to get some background on Dick. And, you have to admit it was a bit of a coincidence that you were in town the night of the incident."

"I explained that to you . . ." she faltered. She sat back and crossed her arms across her chest.

"So you did."

He sat back in his chair and then calmly contended, "Heather doesn't know she's Dick Tate's daughter, does she?"

Her eyes flashed with a mix of anxiety and anger. "What does that have to do with anything?" she snapped, "And just how the hell do you know she's his daughter?"

"One of his ex-wives told me," he said matter-of-factly.

Her jaw dropped. She just looked at him for a minute and then slowly asked, "How would she know that?" Then, as if the thought suddenly occurred to her, inquired, "*One* of his ex-wives? How many did he have?"

"Three that we know of." He then repeated the story Jordan had told him about the little girl in the picture.

Colleen frowned and said, "I sent a picture to his mother . . . I thought maybe she would want some involvement in Heather's life . . . after all, she's Heather's grandmother. But she never responded and eventually I gave up on that notion."

"So what did you tell Heather about her father?" he questioned.

The door suddenly opened and in walked Mike, startling both Colleen and Ian.

Reading the look on his partner's face, O'Reilly proclaimed, "I'm sorry to interrupt. I just got back and thought I'd join you."

"No problem," said Buchanan. He looked at Colleen. "You remember Detective O'Reilly."

Colleen peered up at Mike and murmured, "Yes . . . hello."

Mike lowered himself into the chair at the head of the table and said, "Please carry on."

Ian cleared his throat and then explained, "Colleen was just about to tell me what Heather's been told about her father . . ."

Focusing on the table in front of her, Colleen murmured, "When she was very small it wasn't an issue, so I told her nothing. Then, when she was almost three, I married Jake Monroe. Dick had never seen Heather - he wasn't involved in her life in any way. So, when Jake said he wanted to adopt her, I was thrilled. As far as Heather knew, Jake was her father."

"Was?" asked Mike.

Colleen glanced in his direction and replied, "Jake passed away . . . when Heather was about ten."

"And you still didn't tell her about Dick?" questioned Ian.

"N-no, Jake's death was very traumatic for her. It took her years to get over it. I saw no need to tell her about Dick. What good would it have done? It would have shattered her to find out the man she'd loved so much, the only father she'd ever known, wasn't her dad after all."

"So, she had no inkling? I mean, could someone else have told her?" Buchanan probed.

"No. She didn't. I shouldn't have taken her to Dick's funeral.

I guess I thought somehow it was the right thing to do – even if she didn't know who he was. It's hard to explain . . ." Her eyes pleaded for their understanding.

"Shit," she uttered under her breath as she once again studied the table.

No one spoke for a long minute. Finally, Ian leaned in and touched her arm.

"Tell us what happened, Colleen. In college, I mean. How you met Dick, your pregnancy . . . what happened between the two of you."

Her head jerked up. Her eyes met his. "Why?"

Ian was momentarily taken aback but quickly recovered and replied, "Because we're trying to understand the man he was. It would be very helpful to us . . . Please, Colleen."

She appeared to be mulling over the idea. Ian held his breath. If asked, he wouldn't have been able to say why, but he had the feeling Colleen's story might contain some valuable information.

Colleen suddenly sat forward and placed both elbows on the table. Ian was surprised to see she was no longer trembling.

Her voice was surprisingly calm as she cradled her chin in her palms and sighed, "Fine."

Buchanan and O'Reilly leaned in to hear her story.

~ COLLEEN ~

"A slighted woman knows no bounds."

Sir John Vanbrugh
The Mistake, I, II, I

Chapter 34
San Jose, California;
Early Spring, 1973

Colleen had just completed ten freestyle laps. Next up was the breast stroke, for which she had set a record at her Palo Alto high school. She'd claimed the fastest time in the 100-yard event in the history of her school, which had attracted recruiters from several colleges offering scholarships. San Jose State had been her choice for two reasons; she liked their swim program and it was close to home.

Colleen shook the water from her short blonde hair as she pulled her 5'6" frame from the university pool. She could feel someone watching her and turned to see a blonde boy with intense blue eyes. He was wearing a blue Speedo bathing suit and, judging by his bulging muscles, had spent some time in the weight room. Colleen flushed as she looked toward her coach who was giving instructions for the upcoming meet.

Glancing his way a few minutes later, she realized he was gone. She was surprised at the disappointment she felt. Although she had dated in high school, she was so focused on her swimming she didn't have much time for boys.

In 1962, when Colleen's father had accepted a job with Hewlett Packard as a Research and Development Engineer, the family had moved from Texas to Palo Alto, which lies fourteen miles north of San Jose.

San Jose, located about fifty miles southeast of San Francisco, was California's first incorporated city and the site of the first state capital.

Because they had arrived in early summer, making it difficult for her to meet kids her age, Colleen's mother had signed her up for a youth swim program. She'd been involved with swimming ever since.

Colleen strolled out of the locker room an hour later to find the boy standing outside the door. Her heart skipped a couple of beats. She continued past him toward the bike racks, a slight smile on her lips.

"You've got a great stroke," he called after her.

She stopped and peered over her shoulder at him.

"Thanks," she said shyly. She rubbed her suddenly sweaty palms along the sides of her jeans.

"I'm a breast stroker too," he continued with a wide grin, "Maybe we should practice together and you could give me some tips."

Colleen laughed as she replied, "Well that's quite a compliment but I think I'll leave the hot tips to your coach.

He walked toward her then and peered down into her blue eyes. Still smiling, he said, "Okay, then how about a movie?"

"I-I don't know you," she stammered.

"I'm Dick Tate," he said, "and if you prefer we can get a bite to eat before the movie and I'll tell you all about myself. Then you *will* know me."

She stood and looked at him for a moment, not quite knowing what to say to this boy who was bolder than any she had met before. She quickly sized him up. *He looks like the All-American boy next door*, she thought. *Besides, Colleen, you are in college now and this is how grownups meet new people!*

Sounding more confident than she felt, she answered with a giggle, "Well in that case, okay!"

They made a date for Saturday night. When she gave him directions to her dorm room, she realized he resided in the building next to hers. He waited while she climbed on her ten-speed then waved as she rode away.

Saturday is only two days away, she mused as she peddled toward the dorm, *and I don't know what to wear.* Other than swim attire, her wardrobe mainly consisted of jeans and peasant tops.

Dick took Colleen to dinner at Joe's restaurant, a popular hangout for college kids in downtown San Jose. As was usual for a Saturday night, the place was packed, so they opted to sit up at the bar for their meal.

While they munched on hamburgers and fries, he described his childhood. He told her he had originally lived in Napa Valley, where his father had sold insurance. In the middle of his eighth grade year, his dad attained his stock broker license, joined E.F. Hutton, and moved the family to Alameda.

"I have a brother and a sister," he explained. "My brother Allen is a year older than me and attends San Jose State too. He's also my roommate."

Her eyes lit up as she registered the name. "You mean Allen

Tate is your brother?" she squealed.

Dick frowned as he looked down at the table.

"Yeah, he's my brother," he said in a weary tone that let her know he had encountered her reaction before.

Allen Tate was a junior at San Jose State and one of the top swimmers in California. He was also very popular with the girls, for both his good looks and his fun-loving personality.

"And you were suggesting I could give you swimming tips, with Allen Tate as a brother!" she laughingly scolded. "So now be honest, how many medals have you accumulated so far?"

A smile replaced the frown on Dick's lips as he boasted, "Enough to fill a wall!"

The wistful tone returned to his voice as he went on to describe his early days of swimming. He explained that it was Allen who originally got involved in the sport, with the rest of the family following suit later.

"I played baseball," he told her, "and was actually quite good."

His lips curled into a pout as he continued, "But swimming was everything to my dad and mom. They proudly displayed Allen's medals and that was the sole topic of discussion at the dinner table. Neither one of them ever came to one of my games. Once I stopped playing baseball and joined the swim team, I fit in with the rest of the family."

Colleen felt a pang in her heart as she listened to this boy go on to describe a very dysfunctional family. It was apparent to her he'd grown up in Allen's shadow. He described their constant battles, to which she attributed Dick's envy. From the stories he told her, it was obvious that Allen received the parental attention Dick longed for but never got.

"As a matter of fact," he told her, "the only reason I'm here is because my dad told the recruiters if they wanted Allen they had to give me a scholarship as well."

Colleen reached out, took his hand and fixed her eyes on his as she murmured, "I'm sure they wouldn't have accepted you on the team if you weren't a good swimmer in your own right."

He stared back at her through watery eyes and then smiled softly. "I guess that's true."

Chapter 35
Spring, 1973

Colleen and Dick began to see each other regularly. Most of their Saturdays were devoted to swim meets so they usually planned their dates for Sunday. When they did get together, it was to see a movie or take a walk in Kelley Park. On several occasions, they visited the newly-opened San Jose Historical Museum.

As college students, neither had much spending money, although Colleen seemed to be better off financially than Dick. One weekend, Dick asked her if she would like to go with him to the Winchester Mystery House, a 160-room Victorian mansion designed and built by the Winchester Rifle heiress. However, when he realized there was a charge for admittance, Dick claimed to have no money with him, so Colleen offered to pay. Though she hadn't minded paying, she was a bit put-off by Dick's readiness to let her do so. Inwardly she wondered if he really had not known they would have to purchase tickets.

They also saw each other at daily swim practice and he called her on the phone every evening. Although she had grown quite fond of Dick over the past two months, he was placing more and more demands on her time. Between her responsibilities to the swim team and her part-time job in the women's department at Sears, she didn't have much free time. Dick's frequent phone calls were interfering with her studies and her grades had begun to suffer.

One evening, she and her roommate Stacey were each lying on their bed studying when there was a knock on the door. Stacey threw her a puzzled look then jumped up to answer it.

Assuming the visitor would be one of Stacey's friends, Colleen redirected her attention to her Math assignment.

She was startled from her reverie when her roommate yelled, "Colleen!" She snapped her head up to see Dick standing just inside the door and Stacey with an amused expression on her face.

Colleen's surprise quickly gave way to irritation. She rose and walked to the door, then snapped, "What are you doing here?"

His face fell. He stood there and looked at her, slack-jawed, without answering. Out of the corner of her eye, Colleen saw Stacey slink back toward her bed. Feeling a pang of guilt, Colleen reached out and placed the palm of her hand on top of his muscular bicep.

"I'm sorry, Dick," she said softly. "I guess I'm a bit irritable because I have a lot of studying to do and I'm feeling frustrated because I don't have enough time to do it."

Dick nodded his understanding then said, "Yeah, I do too, Colleen. But, well, the thing is, Allen has some girl in our room and I can't study there. I was kinda hoping you'd let me study in your room with you."

Colleen glanced downward at his empty arms and asked, "Well, where are your books?"

He shrugged and then grinned. "Okay, you got me. I just

wanted to see you, but Allen really does have a girl in our room. In fact, he does most nights."

"I can go get my books, though," he suggested eagerly.

Tugging on his sleeve to follow, she walked out into the hallway and closed the door behind her.

"I really don't' think that's a good idea," she murmured as she glanced up and down the hallway to see if anyone was around. She didn't want to risk embarrassing him in front of others.

Then she smiled up at him. "I have enough trouble keeping my mind on my assignments without being distracted by having you in such close proximity."

His grin broadened as he reached out and pulled her toward him. Hugging her tightly, he said, "It's just that I love you Colleen and I want to spend every spare minute with you."

Colleen wriggled out of his arms and peered up at him.

"Dick, really, don't you think it's a bit early to talk about love?"

He looked at the floor. His head appeared as if it were attached to his neck by a thread as his chin bounced against his chest. When, after what seemed an eternity, he raised his head and looked at her, she instantly regretted the harshness of her words. The intense pain she saw in his eyes made her feel as if she had just whipped a puppy for messing on the floor.

"I can't help my feelings," he mumbled, "and I guess you can't help it if you don't return them."

Colleen reached up and, standing on the tips of her toes, placed her arms around his neck. "Dick, I really like you, I do. But I think we should just slow down a bit. I mean, at this time in our lives, we should focus on our education, don't you agree? We have plenty of time ahead of us for our relationship to grow."

He nodded his head. "You're right, Coll," he remarked and then turned to head toward the stairs which would lead him down to the first floor. He had only taken a few steps when he turned around and said, "See you tomorrow!"

Colleen was stunned to see his wide grin. *How can he change his whole mood so quickly?*

He stopped at the top of the stairway and stared at her for a moment. He was still looking her way as he began his descent. She raised her hand in a wave and smiled.

<hr />

They continued to see each other off and on over the next few months and Dick's feelings only seemed to intensify. On the other hand, though Colleen liked him, she wasn't ready for such a serious relationship.

Dan and Laura Morgan attended most of their daughter's swim meets and during one of them Colleen had introduced them to Dick. At her mother's insistence, she'd taken him to Sunday dinner at her parents the next week. That had been a disaster.

Her parents had met in college and were married shortly after graduation. Colleen's older brother Dave had come along a year later. Dave had been drafted into the Army soon after his high school graduation. He'd died in Binh Dinh Province in South Vietnam when his engineering unit came under light fire in 1970. Colleen had witnessed her father's devastation. She saw the light leave his eyes completely the day he received the news.

Dan Morgan was a quiet, no-nonsense type. Although he was a strict disciplinarian, Colleen knew she had her father wrapped around her finger. He was also very protective of her, particularly since Dave's death. She was daddy's girl but had a close relationship with Laura as well. In fact, when she'd introduced her mom to Dick, she'd referred to her as her "best friend".

During dinner that night, Dick and Dan were discussing the sport of swimming when Dick began to boast of his athletic abilities.

"I've been lifting weights since my junior year in high school, which has made me the strongest swimmer on the team," he crowed, adding, "except for my brother Allen of course."

Her father raised an eyebrow but didn't comment. *He couldn't get a word in edgewise anyway*, she thought with embarrassment. It was obvious Dick enjoyed being the center of attention. Everyone sat and listened as he told them one story after another, smiling broadly throughout.

It was his remark about Mark Spitz that set her father off.

"Yeah, I swam against him in high school . . . came within seconds of beating him too," Dick blustered.

Dan rose from his chair and walked across the room, stopping at the living room's picture window to gaze at his front yard. In a tone dripping with sarcasm, he said, "Well I had no idea my daughter was dating the original boy wonder!"

He slowly turned, fixed his eyes on Dick's face and scoffed, "Since you would have been about 13 when Mark graduated from high school."

A deafening silence blanketed the room. Dick's face turned a crimson color.

Finally, after a long awkward silence, Laura cleared her throat and said, "Well, anybody up for some ice cream? I have rocky road and chocolate."

"Actually, we both have studying to do so we better get going,"

Dick muttered. He grabbed Colleen by the hand and pulled her up from her chair.

"Um, yeah, Dick's right. Do you mind if I don't stick around to help you clean up, Mom?" Colleen asked as she hurried to keep up with Dick, who was pulling her toward the front door.

"Oh no, honey, you two run along," Laura said. Glaring at Dan, she continued, "I'm sure your father would be happy to clean up."

Neither of them spoke during most of the drive back to the dorm, but as they neared the university, Colleen turned to Dick and said softly, "I'm sorry my father embarrassed you, Dick . . . but why did you lie like that?"

After a long pause, Dick muttered, "I don't know. I guess I was trying to impress your dad. Guess it didn't work, huh?" One side of his mouth curved upward in a poor attempt at a smile.

She gave him a half smile in return and said, "Well, my dad isn't one to hold grudges. He'll soon forget about the whole thing." But she knew in her heart that wasn't true. Later that night, while tossing and turning in her bed, she reflected on the evening and wondered what she could do to change her father's obvious disapproval of Dick.

When she next spoke with her father, the subject of Dick never came up, much to her relief.

—◦((◦))◦—

A little more than a month had passed since the dinner with her parents. They were sitting on a blanket in the park, Dick's head in her lap, when he said, "Allen was asking me the other day if you and I had slept together yet. When I told him we hadn't, he laughed and said that either you didn't really like me or there was something wrong with me!"

Colleen had been staving off his sexual advances for several months. Now, she pushed him off her and moved to the other side of the blanket. "Oh, so I'm supposed to sleep with you so you can prove something to your brother?" she asked crossly.

"Come on, Colleen, you know that's not what I meant. But, you know, this is 1973!" He shook his head as if perplexed by her resistance to his advances. Sometimes you can be such a prude," he accused.

His comment irritated her. "I'm not a prude, Dick," she voiced angrily. Then, looking directly into his eyes, she asked, "Is this what you call good Christian morality?"

He glowered at her. She felt an unwelcome shiver run up and down her spine as his eyes darkened and seemed to bore holes right through her.

He gritted his teeth as he responded frostily, "Don't ever mock my spirituality!"

Colleen sensed she was seeing a dark side of Dick she'd only had glimpses of in the past. Goose bumps suddenly appeared on her arms. She hugged herself to dispel the cold that enveloped her like a dense fog.

In a shaky voice, she softly uttered, "I meant no offense, Dick. But you need to honor my values as well. As I've told you before, I plan to maintain my virginity until I'm married. That's something I feel strongly about. I'm sorry if that seems old fashioned to you."

Once again, his mood completely changed before her eyes. His eyes returned to their normal soft blue color and he emitted a low chuckle as he murmured, "Okay, then let's get married."

Colleen said nothing. Instead, she scanned his face for some sign of the complete fury that had been there moments ago. Once again, she watched as his temperament changed from near demonic to almost giddy.

Colleen looked away, then stood and began to fold the blanket. Dick was rooted to his spot. She could feel his eyes piercing through her and realized he was waiting for her response to his proposal. A foreboding voice within told her to avoid raising his ire again. Her voice wavered as she said, "Well, yeah, I guess that's an option."

She continued to gather her belongings, stuffing them back into the paper bag she'd brought them in. She heard a roaring in her ears from the pounding of her heart. In as casual a voice as she could muster she'd called over her shoulder as she walked toward the parking lot, "It's getting chilly out here – let's go home, okay?"

Dick picked up his empty soda can and followed her, tossing his refuse in a garbage can as he passed. "Okay," he called after her, and then, "I guess we'll talk about the possibility of getting married later . . ."

Chapter 36
Winter, 1973

Colleen had been avoiding Dick for more than a week. She'd instructed Stacey to tell him she was out if he called. Swim season was over, which meant she didn't have to contend with him at practice or swim meets.

She told herself she just needed some time to think. His chameleon-like moods bothered her but it was more than that; she sensed a simmering just below the surface, like a volcano that could erupt at any moment. Although he had never touched her in anger or been rough with her in any way, she feared him.

She also knew she wasn't in love with him, while it seemed his feelings had only grown deeper. The idea that he actually wanted to marry her was agonizing. She knew she needed to talk to him in person, to break off their relationship, but the very idea of seeing him left a bitter taste in her mouth.

Colleen's Economics class had just let out. As she joined the throng of students making their way to their next class, she was jolted by the sound of his voice behind her. Her heart raced as she slowly turned to face him.

"If I didn't know better, I'd think you were avoiding me," he said through a cockeyed grin.

Colleen studied her feet as she uttered, "Hi Dick."

His expression grew serious and he peered into her eyes, asking, "*Are* you trying to avoid me, Coll?"

"Uh, no, I've just been busy," she lied.

After a moment's pause, during which Dick studied her face, she said, "Listen, I'm gonna be late for my Calculus class . . . but we do need to talk . . . so, um, call me later and we'll plan something, okay?"

"What do we need to talk about?"

She wondered if he could hear the pounding of her heart. She shifted from one foot to the other as she answered, "Us, I guess. But, I really need to go . . . I'll talk to you later."

She turned and walked away. As she scurried down the pathway, she had the disconcerting feeling he was watching her.

———※《◎》※———

The phone was ringing as Colleen walked into the room. She dumped her books on the bed then reached for the phone.

"Hello?" she said into the receiver.

"It's me," said Dick glumly.

Colleen glanced at the alarm clock next to her bed and noted it was only 4:30, less than an hour and a half since she had seen him outside her classroom.

Without waiting for her to acknowledge him, he said, "We can go to the park and talk, maybe go to Joe's for dinner first - if you want."

She told him that was fine and they made plans for him to

pick her up at 6:00 p.m.

Moments after she hung up, Stacey dashed into the room.

"Hey!" she exclaimed, "I'm only here for a sec – my study group meets at six o'clock, so Amy and I are gonna grab a bite to eat first. Wanna join us?"

Colleen explained about her date with Dick.

"Oh, that's gonna be rough," Stacey sympathized. She gave Colleen a quick hug then continued, "Well, good luck. I'll be home around eight o'clock if you need a shoulder."

Colleen smiled. "I may take you up on that. Thanks."

———————

Colleen sat on the edge of the bed contemplating the evening before her. She practiced telling him she didn't want to see him anymore, which only seemed to increase her anxiety. She glanced down at her trembling hands and thought, *This is ridiculous. Just get it over with, Colleen, and then you can put it behind you.*

She decided a hot shower might help ease the tension building in her neck and the throbbing in her head. Peeling off her clothes, she tried once again to think of a way to let Dick down easy. She had glimpsed his potential for anger and did not want to wake a sleeping giant.

The shower's warmth welcomed her as she allowed the spray to temporarily douse her worries. She closed her eyes and leaned her forehead against the tile letting the force of the water pound away the pressure in her muscles.

To further ease her tension, she used a technique she learned from her high school swim coach. She imagined herself at the beach. In her mind, she could see the waves pounding against the shore. She felt the sand crunch between her toes and the warm sun baking her skin . . .

Colleen didn't know how long she'd been in the shower since she'd been lost in her daydream, but judging by her prune-like skin, she was fairly certain it had been more than a few minutes.

She pushed the shower curtain aside and reached for her towel. It wasn't there. Exasperated, she combed her fingers through her wet hair to get it out of her face and wiped the excess water from her eyes. She stepped out onto the bath mat and out of the corner of her eye caught a movement to her right. Quickly turning in that direction, she was startled to see him standing there.

Her heart leaped into her throat as he slurred, "Looking for this?"

Dick was standing in the doorway, her towel draped over one arm as his eyes scanned her naked body. She wrapped her arms around herself and turned her back to him.

She couldn't speak. She could barely breathe. It was as if someone had stuffed that towel into her throat. Her tongue seemed to weigh 100 pounds.

Suddenly she felt the warmth of the towel as he wrapped it around her shoulders. He leaned down and whispered in her ear, "You have a beautiful body, Colleen, don't hide it from me." A shiver ran down her spine.

He turned her around to face him and then leaned down to kiss her. His breath, which reeked of alcohol, made her gag. She tried to pull away but his fingers dug into her shoulders, holding her close. His eyes held hers for a moment.

"I know you love me, Colleen, and I know you want to give yourself to me. You're just shy. But you don't need to worry. I love you and I'll be gentle," he murmured indistinctly. He had a strange, slightly crazed look in his eyes. He continued to ramble, his speech garbled. It was as if he was talking to himself, as though she weren't in the room.

She was trembling. Her voice seemed to come from outside of her. "D-don't, Dick, please" she started.

He covered her mouth with his. Again she tried to wriggle away from him, but his strength prevented it.

He pushed her to the floor, his body enveloping hers. She was aware of the cold tile beneath her, but when he entered her she was only conscious of the extreme sense of violation she felt. She cried out, futilely hoping someone would hear, that someone would rescue her. The room began to spin. Her last thought before the lights went out was, *This is the side of him I was afraid to see.*

———◈———

She woke to find Dick holding her. She was lying on her bed, her head resting against his chest. She realized she was wearing her robe and that he must have put it on her. His hand was stroking her face as he whispered, "I'm sorry, Colleen, please don't hate me."

When she turned her head to look up at him, his face brightened. "Are you okay?" he asked.

She jerked away and tried to stand, but the room was whirling around her so she sat down on Stacey's bed. As her senses returned, Colleen glared at him, her mouth twisting into a grimace. For the first time in her life, she had the urge to violently hurt another human being. Her mouth tasted as if she had consumed something rancid.

"No," she hissed, "I'm not okay!"

The words were barely out of her mouth when the door opened. Stacey stopped just inside the door with a puzzled look on her face.

"Um, is this . . . a bad time?" asked Stacey. "Do you want me to come back later?"

No one said a word, but Colleen looked at Stacey, her eyes pleading for help. Stacey appeared to sense that something was wrong. She suddenly turned to Dick and, opening the door further, said in a firm voice, "I think maybe you need to go, Dick."

Dick stood and looked down at Colleen. "I'm going now," he murmured. He turned and walked toward the door. He stopped in the doorway, turned around and quietly said, "Please don't hate me."

<hr />

Colleen had missed a week of school. She'd been unable to bring herself to leave her dorm room. Stacey's presence had been her only saving grace. She had tended to her as if she had the flu. She'd brought her food, she'd intercepted phone calls and she'd made excuses for her to her instructors, to her friends and to her parents.

And though Stacey had urged her to go to her parents and tell them what had happened, Colleen would not, could not, confide this horror to them. Though her head told her she had not asked for nor encouraged Dick's sexual assault, she still felt a deep sense of shame and humiliation. She knew Stacey didn't understand nor agree with her decision, but she had honored her wishes and kept quiet. For that, Colleen would forever be grateful.

This morning, when she awoke, the sun was shining through the window above her bed. She lay there for awhile, soaking up its warmth and realized that for the first time since that awful day, she almost felt like herself. That she could enjoy something as simple as the feel of the sun on her face was a good sign.

Stacey stepped out of the bathroom where she'd been drying her hair. She seemed to sense the change in Colleen and smiled brightly.

"Well, look who has rejoined the human race!"

Colleen's lips moved into a slight smile as she said, "I think I better get a move on if I'm going to make my first class."

Stacey walked over, leaned down and hugged Colleen tightly. "Oh, Coll, I'm so glad!" she exclaimed.

Colleen hugged her back and smiled. Then her face darkened as she dropped her arms and said, "I just don't know what I'll do if I run into Dick."

"You'll keep walking, away from him. You are strong, Colleen. You can deal with this. I know you can," Stacey asserted. "Tell you what - let's plan to meet at the cafeteria for lunch, okay?"

Colleen embraced her roommate again. "Thanks Stacey, for everything," she murmured.

Chapter 37
Early Spring, 1974

Her period was two weeks late, and though Stacey had encouraged her to go to the university clinic to be tested, she already knew she was pregnant. The very idea that she was carrying Dick's child was almost more than she could bear. Every time she thought about him, about what he had done to her, she felt as if someone was tightening a vice around her chest.

Fortunately, she had not seen Dick since that fateful day.

"I truly hate him," she admitted to Stacey. "I've never wished harm on anyone before, but I admit, if I knew he was in real pain I would feel a twisted sort of joy. That he has caused me to have these feelings only makes me detest him more."

Stacey told her she had every right to feel that way. "But what are you going to do if you're pregnant?" she asked. "Colleen, you need to tell your parents. You'll need their help."

Colleen knew what Stacey said was true. Still, she dreaded it. She wept then and Stacey held her, rocking her in her arms, telling her in hushed tones that everything would be okay."

"I-I guess I'll go to the clinic today. No point in putting it off any longer."

———— ⟨●⟩ ————

She bowed her head as she told her parents she was indeed pregnant, a revelation that resulted in a long silence. Colleen studied her hands while she waited for them to absorb her words. Suddenly her mother was seated next to her, embracing her, stroking her hair.

"The last time we talked about Dick, you indicated you were planning to end things with him," her father asserted from across the room. "What happened?"

She peered up into her mother's eyes. The understanding she saw there enabled her to look at her father. But instead of the anger she expected, she saw pain etched on his face.

"Daddy . . . I . . . um . . . Dick raped me," she whispered.

She felt her mother stiffen beside her and watched her father's expression turn from shock to anger within seconds.

"That son of a bitch!" he growled through his teeth, "I'll kill him."

Dan started toward the door. Laura cried after him, "Honey, wait! Let's discuss this calmly. Right now what Colleen needs most is to know we love her and that we'll stand by her no matter what."

Dan stopped but didn't turn around. Instead he stared at the entry wall, the one that housed the family's photo gallery. He seemed to be studying Colleen's baby picture.

Colleen spoke softly to her father. "I'm so sorry, Daddy."

He turned then and she saw the tears glistening in his eyes. "There's nothing for you to be sorry for, baby. I love you, you know that," he muttered. "Your mother's right and I hope you know we'll be here to help you through this. But we'll have to talk about this later. Right now, I need to deal with the slimy bastard who did this to you."

With that, he spun on his heels and crashed out the front door. The next sound they heard was the revving of his car's engine. Laura looked at Colleen and said, "I'm afraid your father is going to have to deal with this in his own way. As wrong as I think it is, I must admit I also have the desire to cause physical harm to Dick Tate."

———————

More than four hours passed before Dan returned home. Colleen was both shocked and heartbroken by his appearance as he slowly walked through the front door. His clothes were in a state of disarray and he looked as if he had been rolling in mud. Traces of tears streaked his mud-caked face. He stood just inside the front door, breathing heavily.

Colleen ran to him and threw her arms around his neck. "Oh, Daddy, are you okay?"

Her mother scurried out of the kitchen to join them. "Dan, what have you done?" she cried.

Colleen followed her mother's eyes downward to Dan's hands. His knuckles were scraped and bloody. Then she noticed the blood stains on his shirt. He stood so still, only his deep breathing distinguished him from a statue. She jerked her head up and searched her father's face for some clue as to what he was thinking.

Finally his breathing slowed and he uttered hesitantly, "I –I'm sorry. When I went to his dorm room, he ran from me . . . ran from me!" He looked up at them, his eyes wide with incredulousness.

"I chased him. We ended up in an orchard. I reduced myself to his level," he babbled. He was silent for several minutes and then, staring into space, declared, "I beat the crap out of him."

His chin met his chest; he crumpled against the wall. Raising his fist toward the ceiling he lamented, "God, why are you punishing me? What sin have I committed? First my son and now my daughter. . . " His body slid down the wall to a seated position. He dropped his head to his knees and wept in despair.

Colleen didn't know what to do. She had never seen her father this upset. In fact, she had marveled at her father's ability to handle highly stressful situations with a certain ease. In most cases he did so without a hint of emotion. Even his grief over Dave's death had not manifested itself in such a manner. She was rooted in place as her mother slowly walked toward her husband. Laura knelt on the floor before him. She pulled his head to her bosom and held him.

Tears welled in her eyes and rolled down her cheeks as she looked up at Colleen and whispered, "He'll be okay . . . Why don't you go check on dinner?"

Colleen realized her mother wanted her to leave them alone. Forcing one foot before the other, she shuffled toward the kitchen, glancing back once at the huddled heap that was her father. She was overcome by an excruciating sense of guilt, thinking, *I'm to blame for my father's anguish.*

The chair slid backward as she plopped down on it. Placing her elbows upon the kitchen table, she pressed the palms of her hands into her eyes. She harbored a deep and abiding hatred for Dick Tate. *Somehow, someday, he will suffer a tortuous death for the pain he's caused me and my family.*

———◈———

Ten days later, Dick's father called Dan at his office.

"Dick told me about his indiscretion with your daughter," he started.

"His *indiscretion?*" Dan interrupted angrily, "That's how you see it – as an *indiscretion?* Your son raped my daughter. That's a crime and a far-cry worse than an indiscretion. If not for the humiliation my daughter would suffer, we'd be pressing charges against him."

"Still might," he added.

Dan's words were met with a long silence. The phone line was so quiet he began to wonder if they'd been disconnected. Just as he decided that was indeed the case, he heard a loud sigh on the other end.

"My son is a screw-up," Richard, Sr. said flatly. "I realized that long ago and I can't do a goddamned thing about it. But that's not why I'm calling."

Dan moaned. "Then why, pray tell, are you calling?"

"To encourage an abortion and offer monetary assistance toward that end," he replied dispassionately.

Dan was stunned; Tate's words rendered him speechless. A deafening silence ensued.

Several minutes passed before Dan answered resolutely, "My daughter is going to have the baby. She . . . doesn't believe in abortion."

"Oh Christ," Richard responded with the most emotion he'd displayed throughout the conversation.

"As for monetary assistance . . . I'd say your son should plan on paying for all expenses associated with the birth, in addition to child support."

"My son has no money," hissed Tate, "he's a fucking college student!"

Dan leaned back in his chair, his forearm shading his eyes. He shook his head in utter disgust. "Like father, like son," he muttered under his breath.

After a momentary pause, Dan sat up in his chair and leaned into the phone, his voice steely as he proclaimed, "That's your problem, not mine. As a matter of fact, the longer we talk, the stronger my proclivity toward reporting this crime to the police."

Once again his words were met with silence, prompting Dan to say, "Figure it out and get back to me. If I don't hear from you within three days I'll personally escort my daughter to the police station."

Dan slammed the phone into its cradle.

———◦((◦))◦———

Colleen was sitting at her desk, trying to concentrate on her Economics book. Final exams would begin the day after tomorrow. She was relieved that the school year was nearly complete. Between the traumatic memories of that awful night and the knowledge that in less than nine months she would be a mother, she'd been unable to keep her mind on her studies.

After a long, emotional discussion with her parents, and an agonizing week of meditation, she had decided to keep the baby. She couldn't explain her reasoning.

Just a year ago, she'd advised a close friend to have an abortion.

Although in a committed relationship, Colleen had thought her friend too young to have a baby and had been convinced doing so would ruin her life. Now, in a similar predicament, she found herself unable to heed her own advice. Inwardly she knew that having a baby was going to change her life dramatically but she couldn't bring herself to do otherwise.

She planned to finish out the school year and then take some time off. Although she told herself she would complete her college degree after the baby was born, deep inside she knew that was only a pipe dream.

Although her parents proclaimed their willingness to help in any way they could, she didn't want to burden them with this. She'd agreed to stay with them throughout her pregnancy, but planned to find a job from which she could make enough money to move out on her own and support her child.

All these thoughts raced through her mind, over and over like a hamster on a wheel, making it difficult to focus. Try as she might to keep her worries at bay, once again she found her mind wandering. She was startled from her abstracted state by the ringing of the phone. She shook her head, admonishing herself yet again for allowing her mind to stray, and reached for the phone.

"Hello?" she chirped into the mouthpiece.

"Oh," he stammered, "I was just getting ready to hang up . . . the phone rang so many times . . . I thought you weren't there."

Her heart leaped into her throat. Her hands began to shake so badly she could barely hold onto the receiver.

"Dick," she whispered feebly.

"I-I called to t-tell you again how sorry I am," he stuttered.

Without thinking, Colleen quickly answered with, "It's okay." She could have kicked herself. *It's not okay*, she told herself.

Why would you say that?

Apparently he was encouraged by her words, as his nervousness seemed to subside a little. "I heard you're planning to keep the baby," he said more as a question than a statement.

She squeezed her eyes shut tightly and gritted her teeth as she breathed, "Yes, I am."

Her heart was pounding now and butterflies fluttered across her abdomen. Her knees felt as if they were made of rubber. She tried to speak, to tell him she didn't want to talk to him, deal with him, only to find her voice had abandoned her.

No sooner had these thoughts crossed her mind than he said, "I'll marry you, Colleen."

She was flabbergasted. The dread that had taken hold of her dissipated as a sense of rage coursed through her. Seething with anger, the lump in her throat subsided just enough for her to snarl through her teeth, "Get the hell out of my life!"

The phone receiver collided into its cradle with a resounding bang.

＝━》《◎》《━＝

Her father's reaction to the phone call was much calmer than she had expected. Since the day she had informed him of her pregnancy, she'd watched with relief as he'd returned to his rational, imperturbable self.

He peered at Colleen over his reading glasses, his brow furrowed.

"If he calls again, hang up," he said grimly.

"But Daddy, I tried . . ."

Holding his hand up to quiet her, Dan told her, "I know,

honey, and I know how upsetting it must be to hear his voice. I'll do everything I can to stop his phone calls. But it really doesn't take much effort to hang up a phone.

Colleen nodded while nervously playing with her fingers as her father continued.

"I told you I'm dealing with his father. He's pulling Dick out of school at the end of the semester. We're dealing with the financial aspect of this. It's going to work out . . . you'll see."

He rose from the couch and walked across the living room toward the picture window where Colleen was standing.

Taking her in his arms, he spoke over her shoulder, "I'll threaten them with a restraining order if Dick tries to contact you in any way."

Colleen closed her eyes and placed her cheek against her father's chest, drinking in his strength. Her tears dampened his shirt.

As she stood there, cocooned in her father's embrace, she began to wonder when she had become so weak. A feeling of self-disgust washed over her. At that moment, she vowed to stop wallowing in self-pity and deal with this problem head on.

She willed herself to smile.

Colleen looked up at her father and, with false bravado, declared, "That's it. I'm not gonna let that son of a bitch get to me anymore. I'm taking back my life!"

Dan gazed at her for moment, an amused smile appearing at his lips. Suddenly, he threw his head back and burst into laughter. Colleen began to giggle and then joined him in his mirth.

They were holding onto their sides, tears streaming down their cheeks, when Laura walked into the room. Although she didn't understand their hilarity, their laughter was contagious; she stood looking at them with a large grin on her face.

"Vengeance is in my heart, death in my hand.
Blood and revenge are hammering in my head."

William Shakespeare
Titus Andronicus, Aaron at II, iii, I

Chapter 38
San Diego, California;
July 25, 2003

"I need a drink," claimed Mike.

Buchanan smiled at his partner, who was seated across from him, head in hands, elbows resting on the desk in front of him.

"I hear ya," muttered Ian. "I'm beginning to hate this case. We've got four women with both motive and opportunity. All these women are intelligent and, with the possible exception of Gina, appear to be the antithesis of a violent criminal. . ."

O'Reilly shook his head. "Yeah, it's a lot easier when the suspect is some coked-up asshole. When we collar 'em for the crime, I go home and sleep like a baby knowing I've helped rid the world of one more bad mother fucker."

Buchanan peered at his partner. "My point exactly."

Mike stood and said, "Tell ya what . . . let's finish this discussion at Mahoney's. It's five thirty and I do believe I hear an ice cold brew calling my name!"

Ian used both hands to push himself away from the desk and

then rose to his feet. "Okay," he replied, "But I'm not going to stay long. I think I need some time to mull over all this shit."

"Mind if I join you?"

Buchanan looked over to see Ben Li standing just inside the office doorway.

"Hey Ben, whatcha know?" asked Ian with a smile.

"Buy me a drink and I'll tell all," Ben grinned and waved a small stack of papers in the air.

"What's that?" asked Mike.

"Firearms Examination," answered Ben, handing the papers to O'Reilly.

"Great," said Ian. He walked over and slapped Ben on the back. "We'll take it with us to Mahoney's. Come on, first one's on me."

As the three headed down the stairs, Buchanan quipped, "Don't s'pose that report's gonna tell us who dunnit . . ."

Li chuckled in response.

———=»«(●)»=———

Mahoney's, a bar and grill located two blocks from the Sheriff's office, was the main hangout for county law enforcement types. Every stool at the long, mahogany bar lining the redbrick wall was occupied. Buchanan, O'Reilly and Li had found an empty table in the back near the kitchen. To the right of their table was a row of dartboards, each in use.

Between the clanging noises from the kitchen and the rowdy Friday night crowd, Ian was forced to shout as he read from the information contained in the report compiled by the Crime Lab's Firearms section.

"As suspected, our perp used a semi-automatic pistol . . . says here a Beretta Model 84 . . . with a .38 caliber full jacket cartridge," summarized Buchanan. "Trajectory and distance analysis also confirms Doctor Epstein's suggestion that the body had already hit the floor before the shot to the chest, which was fired from about two feet above."

Ian paused in thought and then continued, "That could suggest a woman shooter . . . or a short man."

Mike frowned and said, "Well, this is all well and good but unfortunately doesn't help pinpoint the suspect." Glancing at Ben, he explained, "None of our suspects have guns registered in their name."

Ben nodded. "So, you're thinking borrowed or stolen?"

"Probably," answered Mike, eyeing first his empty beer bottle and then the bar. "I'm dry . . . anybody need another brew?"

Both Ian and Ben shook their heads.

"I gotta get something to eat first . . . stomach's already feeling like crap," groused Ian.

Li suddenly sat forward in his chair and said, "Oh shit, that reminds me – Ritter said to tell you he's got the Forensic Biology Section working up your DNA analysis."

Buchanan raised both eyebrows. "That's good news."

"Yeah, he wanted me to ask if you've got any comparison samples yet."

Ian's smile was quickly replaced with a frown as he shook his head, "I haven't had the chance to call Gina yet . . . and since the other two ex- wives won't commit without attorney approval – which we both know is doubtful - I'm not holding my breath."

He described the information they had derived from the victim's phone bills and then said, "Based on that, the ADA is requesting a warrant for prints and a saliva sample from Gina."

He glanced at his watch then crinkled his brow. "Matter of fact, I thought I'd have heard from him by now."

O'Reilly returned to the table with a full beer. Buchanan turned to him and broached, "Remind me . . . did you ask Jordan if she talked to her attorney yet?"

Mike nodded his head and quickly swallowed the gulp of beer he'd just taken. "Asked her . . . she said her attorney advised her not to." He barely stifled a belch while adding, "Said she'd still think about it though."

Buchanan slapped the table with his hand. "Shit! I knew it!" he exclaimed. "We'll probably get the same answer from Meg."

"By the way," added Mike, "They're flying home tomorrow morning."

Ian shrugged and said, "At this point, we've got nothing to keep 'em here."

He turned back to Ben. "Did Ritter say when he expected the results of the analysis?"

"Should be a couple days."

Ian ordered a hamburger at the bar. When he returned to the table Mike was telling Li why he thought Gina was their prime suspect.

"Yeah, she's got some 'splainin to do," quipped Ian, "but you know, after hearing Colleen's story, I'm kinda liking her too. I still think it's more than a coincidence she was in town the night of the murder."

Mike nodded and said, "Yeah. Shit . . . we could go round and round about all of 'em. Like you said before, they all got motive. Hell, after hearing their stories, I couldn't much blame any of 'em for offing the mother fucker."

"Not a nice guy, eh?" asked Ben.

Buchanan shook his head and said, "If you met his fucking parents you'd know why. Shit, if you looked up dysfunctional family in the dictionary, you'd find their picture."

O'Reilly and Li both laughed.

"What about the vic's kids . . . are they as fucked up as he was?" asked Li.

"We only met his sons . . . from his first wife," claimed Ian. "Which reminds me," he turned and looked at Mike, "we still need to talk to Meg's daughter . . ."

"Yeah, we do." Flashing a large grin in Ian's direction he continued, "I'll try to do that tomorrow while you're getting Gina's prints . . ."

Buchanan chuckled then looked at Li and explained, "In case you hadn't noticed, O'Reilly and Gina don't exactly have a love affair goin' on."

Ian's pager began to beep. He reached down and pulled it from his belt.

"Ah, it's Clyde – the ADA. Good, maybe he's got our warrant." He stood up, mumbling, "I gotta go call him."

Ben lifted an eyebrow. "Can't you just use your cell phone?"

Mike began to laugh, then pointed at his partner and said, "This guy? You gotta be kidding . . . He's technologically challenged. Hell, he never even turns the damn thing on!"

Buchanan shook his head and declared, "If anybody needs to get in touch with me they can page me. Besides, I hate those fucking things! Everywhere you go these days, that's all you see - in restaurants, people in their cars - they all have this stupid appendage hanging from their ear. Fucking annoying if you ask me."

"We didn't," bantered Mike.

Ben chuckled. "Wanna use mine to call him?"

"Yeah, okay," murmured Ian, to the delight of his partner.

Buchanan dialed the number displayed on his pager.

After a cursory greeting, Clyde informed him he had obtained the warrant for Gina's fingerprints and saliva sample.

"I know it's late . . . I got tied up and couldn't call before now," said Clyde. "Tomorrow's Saturday and I'm going out of town for the weekend . . . How can I get the paperwork to you?"

"I can come get it," offered Ian, "or come by Mahoney's and I'll buy you a drink."

Clyde laughed. "Thanks for the offer but the wife's holding dinner. Mahoney's is on the way, though . . . I'd be happy to drop it off."

"Thanks," said Ian.

He pulled the phone away from his ear and stared at it. After a moment, he muttered, "How do you turn this fucking thing off?"

"Case closed," sputtered Mike, to which Ben roared with laughter.

Chapter 39
July 26, 2003

The muscles in Ian's upper back and shoulders were killing him, a common occurrence when he was on a particularly difficult case. Although he kept meaning to go to the gym, his long work hours usually prevented it. He made a mental note to go tomorrow - Sunday.

He rolled his shoulders foreword and then back in an attempt to get the kinks out.

"Morning," commented Mike as he walked through the doorway with a cup of coffee.

"'Bout time you got here," replied Ian.

O'Reilly furrowed his brow and opened his mouth to speak but Buchanan ignored him and kept talking. "I called Gina to tell her we were coming by. She wasn't exactly keen to the idea but I didn't give her much choice. Got a little pissy with me but finally said she'd wait for us. I think the only reason she agreed was because she doesn't want the Navy to think she's involved in this in any way."

"Yeah, well they'll find out eventually anyway," responded Mike.

I didn't mention the warrant," added Ian. "I figured if I did, she'd really balk."

Mike nodded. "Probably a good call."

"Li's coming with us . . . to collect the prints and saliva sample," Ian conveyed.

"Whatchoo mean us?" Mike asked with raised eyebrows. "I've got a call into Meg about meeting with her daughter . . . I was gonna do that while you talked to Gina, remember?"

"I remember. But I want to be there when you do. Since the daughter is a minor, Meg will have to be there. So I'm thinking if we take Ben with us, maybe we'll be able to convince her to provide her fingerprints. The daughter's too . . . what's her name again?"

"Caitlin."

Then, as if the thought suddenly occurred to him, Mike flashed a toothy grin and ribbed his partner, "Sure this isn't just an excuse to see Meg again?"

Buchanan shot back, "Don't start . . ." In an attempt to hide the uncontrollable grin creeping onto his lips, he turned away and busied himself at his desk.

"How is Meg gonna get in touch with you?" asked Ian.

O'Reilly held up his cell phone and bantered, "Well you see, I've got this newfangled contraption. You ought to try it sometime."

While Mike snickered, Ian countered with, "Bite me, O'Reilly!"

⊜»(⦿)«⊜

Buchanan was just merging with the I-15 southbound traffic

when Mike's cell phone rang. Ian glanced his way and his partner waggled his eyebrows at him. Buchanan couldn't help but smile as he turned his eyes back to the road.

Ian listened as Mike spoke into the phone. After declaring their desire to meet with Caitlin today, O'Reilly was silent for several minutes.

Then he said, "Okay, we'll do that," and hung up.

Mike rolled his eyes in Ian's direction. "That was your girlfriend . . . "

"Yeah, yeah, yeah. Just fuckin' tell me what she said."

"Apparently Caitlin is out with friends but is due back around three o'clock. She suggested we stop by some time after that."

Buchanan smiled. "That'll work."

"Yeah," joked Mike, "She said she can't wait to see you . . ."

Ben Li chuckled in the back seat. A crooked smile graced Ian's lips as he slowly shook his head.

———◦((◦))◦———

Buchanan was reaching for the doorbell when the front door flew open. He swung his head around to see Gina, wearing white shorts, a navy blue sweatshirt with *U.S. Navy* displayed across the front and a scowl on her face.

"I hope this will be quick," she snapped, "I have much to do today."

Ian crooked an eyebrow at her. "Uh . . . Good morning Commander Rodriguez . . . nice to see you again."

She stood motionless with her arms across her chest and glared at him. For a brief moment, no one said a word. Mike finally broke the silence by suggesting, "If we may come in, it will certainly speed things up."

Gina stood back and waved her hand in resigned invitation.

As Li entered the doorway, she questioned, "Who the hell are you?"

Ian answered, "Commander Gina Rodriguez, this is Ben Li, our Forensic Evidence Technician."

She nodded but looked confused as she briefly shook Ben's outstretched hand.

"Ben is here to collect your fingerprints and a saliva sample for DNA analysis," added Ian.

Gina's eyes grew wide. She jerked her head in Ian's direction and said, "Why do you want my fingerprints?"

Buchanan's voice was tinged with sarcasm as he answered, "To eliminate you as a suspect, of course."

Vehemently shaking her head, she growled, "I don't like this one bit. You never said anything about collecting my fingerprints!"

Ian responded by handing her the warrant. "I'm afraid you don't have much choice, Commander."

Gina's brow furrowed as she perused the document before her. "You told me you just had a couple more questions for me . . . why did you not tell me about this on the telephone?" she demanded.

Ian pointed toward her living room and suggested, "Why don't we sit down and discuss this calmly?"

A sense of foreboding coursed through Ian as it occurred to him that the furious look now blemishing Gina's face might have been the last thing Richard Tate ever saw.

"If it's all the same to you, Detective, I don't feel much like entertaining at the moment." Her jaw was rigid as she turned toward Li and said, "Let's just get this over with."

Li shot Ian a questioning look and then offered a slight smile to Gina, murmuring, "Thank you, Ma'am," He looked down at the large black case dangling from his left hand. "Um, is there a table I might use?"

Gina responded by pointing her chin toward the dining room table.

While Ben unpacked fingerprint cards, inkpads, sterile swabs and vials, Buchanan said, "Commander Rodriguez, we have evidence that you lied to us when you said you hadn't spoken with Mr. Tate since your return to the San Diego area."

Gina's head jerked up. "Wha—what evidence?"

Ian ignored her question and continued, "As you can imagine, Commander, I get rather suspicious when a witness lies to me . . . I mean, I figure the only reason someone would attempt to deceive me would be to cover up their guilt . . ."

She began to shake her head slowly from side to side. She opened her mouth as if to speak but nothing came out.

"Gina . . ." he paused because until now he had not called her by her first name. She had not invited him nor encouraged him to do so. When she didn't rebuke him, he continued, "If you had anything at all to do with the murder of your ex-husband, you need to tell us . . . we may be able to help you – but only if you're honest with us."

She remained motionless and slack-jawed while continuing to stare at him. Buchanan looked at her intently but said nothing, giving her time to respond.

Ben finished laying out his forensic tools and turned to look in her direction, then at Ian. He stood by the dining room table, waiting, saying nothing.

After what seemed an eternity, Gina looked at the floor and

spoke so low Ian had to strain to hear her. "He called . . . he left a couple of messages . . . I didn't return his calls. He . . . I . . . finally one night he called and I answered. It was . . . last Thursday . . . or maybe Friday. I told him I wanted nothing to do with him, to leave me alone . . ." Her voice trailed off.

Without lifting her head, Gina peered up at him, her eyes filled with fear. "I-I didn't kill him, Detective."

Ian was surprised by her obvious discomfort. He could hardly believe this was the same woman who was so confident, so arrogant, just moments ago.

"Gina, why did you lie?" he asked.

"B-because . . . I-I don't know," she murmured. A flush crept from her neck to her cheeks. "You said you thought I had dinner with him that night. I didn't. I thought if I told you he'd been calling . . . that I talked to him . . . you wouldn't believe me and you would make something out of it that wasn't there." She stared at her feet.

Buchanan slowly turned, looked at Li and nodded.

Ben cleared his throat and nodded. "Commander Rodriguez . . ."

She turned and looked at him blankly for a moment then walked to the dining room table. "What should I do?" she quietly asked.

Ian looked on as Li first explained the procedure then helped Gina roll her right thumb over the inkpad and then the fingerprint card. The process continued through the fingers on her right hand and then her left.

Buchanan felt his partner's eyes on him and returned his gaze. Mike's eyes were as big as saucers. A stunned smile playing at his lips prevailed when he realized Ian was looking his way. He shook his head and mouthed, "Amazing." Ian smiled.

The detectives turned and watched as Ben set the fingerprint card aside, snapped on a pair of rubber gloves and asked Gina to open her mouth. He removed a swab from its sterile packaging then mopped it across both inner cheeks. He carefully placed the sample in a plastic vial, securely tightened the lid then picked up a black marker and wrote a description on the outside.

Ian was astonished to see tears welling in Gina's eyes and almost felt sorry for her when Mike remarked, "Well, Commander, I expect that will provide the proof we need. We don't need to contact the Navy to ensure you don't leave town, do we?"

Gina's eyes flashed pure hatred as she gritted her teeth and said, "No."

Showing Mike her back, she looked at Ian and declared, "The only thing this will prove is that I had nothing to do with Dick's death."

———— ✦ ————

It was only 1:45 when the three men left Gina's house, so they decided to get some lunch before driving to Poway for their interview with Caitlin. Not wanting to risk any accusations of evidence contamination, they first drove to the Crime Lab where Li logged in the saliva sample.

"After we collect fingerprints for Meg and her daughter, I'll run the fingerprint analysis," explained Ben.

"That reminds me," broached Ian, "did you compare Carter and Brett's fingerprints yet?"

"Yeah, I did first thing this morning . . . Sorry. I thought I'd told you. Brett's matched a set we lifted from the front door. No match at all with Carter's."

Ian nodded as he maneuvered the car into a tight parking space outside a coffee shop on Balboa Avenue. "Well, that pretty much goes along with what both of them told us. Carter told us he hadn't been to his dad's house and reiterated that when Mike interviewed him yesterday."

"Yeah, we actually had a pretty good conversation," added Mike, "He's fairly quiet but when you get him one on one he opens up a lot . . . rather fuckin' witty as a matter of fact."

As they climbed out of the car, Ben mentioned, "Ritter is running their DNA as part of the analysis he's working up for you."

"Ian pursed his lips and said, "Well, hopefully we'll get samples from Meg and Caitlin today. Then we'll have all the ex-wives except Jordan. If there's a match with those we have, then we're sitting pretty. If not . . . well, I guess we'll focus in on Jordan . . . and Colleen."

Mike interjected, "I'm banking on Gina."

Buchanan chuckled. "I know you are . . . and I hope you're right because not only would we have our suspect, but it would be a lot more fun to arrest her than any of the others."

O'Reilly nodded vigorously then out of the corner of his mouth, muttered, "No shit."

Ben asked, "Is Meg as difficult as Gina?"

Mike guffawed. "Difficult? That word is much too mild for Gina."

"To answer your question," proclaimed Ian, "Meg is fucking angelic compared to Gina."

"Yeah, well . . . after listening to O'Reilly, I've kinda gotten the impression you're enamored with her," joked Li. Turning toward

Mike, he asked, "What's your opinion?"

Buchanan rolled his eyes and muttered, "Shit."

Mike chortled. "Actually, she ain't too bad."

⸻ ◈ ⸻

Ian's pulse quickened at the sight of Meg standing in her front doorway. As he and the other two men followed her into the living room, he tried to calm his rapid breathing by inhaling deeply. He heard a muted chuckling next to him. Out of the corner of his eye he glimpsed O'Reilly's grin, then felt the heat rise to his face. He was mortified at the thought that Meg might have noticed his reaction to her and was relieved that she didn't turn to look at him.

When she did turn, instead of looking at him, she directed her eyes toward Ben Li. Smiling, she said, "We haven't met."

Buchanan once again found himself tongue tied in Meg's presence and was grateful when Mike introduced Li.

She wrinkled her brow and asked, "So, what is your purpose here?"

Ian found his voice and quickly said, "We thought - since we were coming anyway – we'd go ahead and get your fingerprints."

When she frowned, a sense of dread coursed through him. Although he berated himself for letting his attraction to her interfere with his job, his desire for her to like him took over.

"Meg," he murmured, "You agreed on the phone to provide your fingerprints – for elimination purposes. This way, you don't have to go all the way down to our office . . ."

The lines between her eyebrows softened slightly. A smile teased her lips as she said, "Why do I have the feeling you're

— 308 —

trying to dupe me?"

Hard as he tried, Ian couldn't control the hooks pulling the corners of his mouth upward.

"I wouldn't do that, Meg."

"Hi. I'm Caitlin," said a voice from behind him.

Buchanan turned to see a teenaged girl with strawberry blonde hair and Dick Tate's face breeze into the room.

Meg crossed the room and, because Caitlin was three to four inches taller, had to reach up to place her arm around her daughter's shoulders. She swung her hand toward Ian and said, "Honey, this is Detective Buchanan."

Ian walked over and shook her hand. Meg proceeded to introduce the other men and then suggested they all sit. Caitlin dropped onto a wing chair, behind which Meg stood protectively, both hands clutching the back.

Ian started, "Caitlin, let me start off by telling you how sorry I am for your loss . . ."

"Thank you," replied Caitlin. She reached up to wipe away the moisture accumulating in the corners of her eyes. "My dad and I weren't very close . . . in fact I haven't seen him or even talked to him in a couple of years . . ."

"I see," murmured Buchanan, ". . . so you haven't been in his townhouse in awhile?"

Caitlin shook her head. "It's been probably five years since I visited him," she answered.

"Mind if I ask why?" asked Ian.

She shrugged and focused her eyes on the floor. In a voice barely above a whisper, she said, "My father wasn't a very nice man. H-he told me about his own childhood once . . . how Grandpa beat him up and stuff . . ."

Caitlin lifted her eyes and looked directly at Ian. "He told me how awful it made him feel. So how could he turn around and do that kind of stuff to his own kids?"

Ian frowned. "Your dad was abusive with you?"

She shook her head. "Not really bad with me . . . but my brothers . . . have you met Carter and Brett?" When Ian nodded, she continued, "He was really mean to them. Mostly, I watched . . . it made me so sad." A tear trickled down her cheek.

"I also saw him hit Gina," she went on, "When I told my mom about it, she said she didn't want me to witness that stuff anymore. I didn't want to either, so I told my dad I didn't want to see him anymore."

"How old were you then?" asked Ian.

Caitlin pursed her lips in thought and then turned to peer up at her mother.

"She was twelve," Meg answered matter-of-factly.

Buchanan returned his gaze to Caitlin and questioned, "Have you talked to him since then?"

Caitlin nodded and said, "Yeah, but it's been a couple of years." She studied her lap for a moment then stammered, "I-I feel kinda g-guilty now. I guess I wasn't very nice to him." Looking once again at Ian, she added, "He kinda deserved it but I'm not proud of myself."

Meg leaned down and hugged her from behind, "Shh honey, don't beat yourself up. You did nothing wrong."

Caitlin's bottom lip protruded slightly. Tears streamed down her face. No one spoke for a moment.

Ian stood and said, "Tell you what . . . let's go ahead and get your fingerprints." Glancing at Meg, he added, "Yours too. Then we'll get out of your hair."

Ben asked where he could set up his equipment. They all followed Meg into the kitchen.

Li opened his bag and withdrew his fingerprinting paraphernalia. Without looking up, he asked, "We're getting a saliva sample as well, correct?"

Buchanan reddened as he murmured, "Might as well."

Meg swung her head around and looked daggers at Ian, causing the blood to rush to his head.

"Ian, I thought we had an understanding," she snapped. "Was I not implicit enough when I said I wanted to consult my attorney first?"

He felt as if someone had lit a match to his face. "I-I'm sorry Meg . . . I take it you haven't talked to your lawyer yet?" he asked gently.

"No, I haven't. I will. But, for now, neither of us will provide anything except our fingerprints." She peered into Ian's eyes and added, "And I'm beginning to waver on that."

Buchanan turned to Ben and nodded, "Let's get this done, Li . . . before the lady changes her mind."

He felt his heart race when he saw Meg's gaze on him.

Chapter 40
July 27, 2003

Ian's legs rapidly pumped the pedals of a stationary bike. Using his already-drenched towel, he mopped the sweat off his face and neck. As he glanced around the gym it seemed as if he was the only person perspiring. He shook his head. *Why*, he wondered, *am I dripping wet while everyone else seems dry as a bone?*

After seven miles, he decided he'd had enough for one day. He climbed down from the bike and reached for his water bottle, taking a large swig of the ice cold liquid. Using the back of his hand he wiped the excess from the corners of his mouth.

Ian was looking forward to his usual twenty minutes in the sauna. As he dragged his tired body toward the locker room, he had the sudden feeling that someone was watching him and straightened his posture. He slowly turned his head and spied a tall blonde woman staring at him. *Well*, he thought as he smiled to himself, *guess I still got it.*

He walked on but, just as he reached the entrance to the men's locker room, it occurred to him that the woman looked familiar. He turned back around and peered at her. She hadn't moved. She was still staring after him but was too far away for him to make out her face. Chalking it up to wishful thinking, he decided he didn't know her after all.

After rinsing off in a tepid shower, Buchanan donned his bathing suit and headed for the spa area. He opened the sauna door and was glad to find it empty. He climbed to the top of the wooden-slatted seats then closed his eyes and rested his head against the wall. The dry, hot air filled his lungs.

Going over the previous day in his mind, his heart pounded when he remembered how quickly Meg had become angry with him. On the way back to the station, Mike had teased him about giving in so easily. Even Ben added to the ribbing. He'd laughed it off and asked them what they would have done differently. When neither of them could come up with a good answer, they'd relented.

He sighed audibly as he thought of Meg's face, her smile, and the way she'd said his name. At that moment he hoped beyond hope that she was not involved in Dick Tate's murder. Ian's cynicism about people had grown over the years, but he didn't think he could handle the idea that Meg was capable of violent thoughts, let alone actions.

His mind continued to wander, thinking about this case, going over the facts and evidence accumulated thus far and ruminating over not having more to go on. He was still convinced the vomit was important and that having the material to complete a full DNA analysis was key.

He wasn't as convinced of Gina's guilt as Mike apparently was. Although she wasn't particularly pleasant about providing the saliva sample, she'd appeared fairly confident it would clear her of suspicion.

He shook his head. *If only I could get samples from Jordan . . . and Meg . . . he thought ruefully . . . and Colleen, for that matter.*

———⇒)((◦))(⇐———

A half hour later, Buchanan emerged from the locker room, feeling physically tired but mentally refreshed. He meandered through the maze of weight machines and past a small row of cubicles that housed the gym's sales and personal training staff.

Once again, he experienced the prickly feeling on his neck that indicated someone was watching him. He turned his gaze to see the same young blonde woman peering out from behind a pane of glass that separated the cubicles from the rest of the gym. This time, when she saw him looking at her, she averted her face, but not before he recognized her.

Ian walked toward her and said, "Nice to see you again, Ms. Monroe."

Heather's face reddened as she responded, "Detective . . . I thought that was you but wasn't sure."

It was then that he noticed she was wearing a shirt bearing the gym's logo. "Do you work here?"

"Yes, I'm a personal trainer," answered Heather with a seemingly reluctant smile.

"Wow," he grinned, "And to think we've probably passed each other a zillion times in the past. I mean, I've been a member here for at least five years . . . How long have you worked here?"

"About a year."

"Well, I don't get in here as often as I should but I'll look forward to seeing you when I do."

He raised his hand in a brief wave and said, "Until next time."

Heather nodded. "Goodbye, Detective."

As he dropped into the driver's seat of his car, it occurred to him that Heather had not been particularly friendly. He mentally revisited his conversation with her. Starting the engine, he shook his head and said aloud, "Knock it off, Buchanan. You know a lot of people aren't comfortable around cops . . . Goes with the territory."

Chapter 41
July 28, 2003

Buchanan hung his wrinkled sport coat on the back of his desk chair then headed toward the break room for a cup of coffee.

He hated Mondays. Especially those following a weekend during which he'd had to work. It seemed whenever he was able to get away, however briefly, from the arduous work of a homicide detective, his desire for more time to enjoy life only increased. Ian resented the hours wasted with people he considered to be the dregs of society rather than enjoying the Southern California coastline or playing a round of golf.

His father had taught him to play golf when Ian was a teenager, claiming that conquering the game, though impossible, was the goal of any true Scotsman. Now, as he poured a cup of lukewarm and sludgy coffee, he realized how long it had been since he'd been on the golf course and how much he missed it.

Mike entered the break room and muttered, "Morning . . ."

"You look like hell," Ian noted his partner's bloodshot eyes with a frown. "Too much partying yesterday?"

O'Reilly nodded. "Went to a barbecue at my brother's house. Started drinking at noon . . . didn't leave until 10:00 last night." Placing palm to forehead, he added, "My fuckin' head feels like it's gonna explode any second."

"No sympathy here," replied Buchanan with a shake of the head. He turned and walked out of the break room.

When Ian sat down at his desk, he noticed two pink slips of paper bearing Cheryl's writing. Jim Ritter had called at 8:10 this morning, Ben Li at 8:45. He glanced at his watch, which read 9:15.

Just as he reached for the phone to call Ritter, Mike walked into the office area. Buchanan finished dialing then lifted his eyes to observe his partner.

Plopping into his chair, O'Reilly offered a crooked smile and said, "I'm fine," to which Ian rolled his eyes.

O'Reilly changed the subject. "Who're you calling?"

Ian picked up the phone messages and tossed them onto Mike's desk. Ritter wasn't at his desk, so he left a message on his voicemail and hung up.

"Do you think he had the chance to run Gina's sample yet?" asked Mike.

"Doubt it," replied Ian with a shake of the head, "But hopefully, they'll get to it today. According to Li, Ritter was successful in creating some urgency with the lab's forensic biology section, so keep your fingers crossed."

Buchanan reached for the phone. "Maybe Li will know something. Let's see."

Ben Li answered the phone after two rings. "Hey Ben, what's up?" greeted Ian.

"Wanted to let you know I ran those prints for you," replied Ben.

"Yeah?" asked Ian, "and . . . ?"

"No match on any of them."

Ian slammed his fist down on his desk and exclaimed, "Shit!"

In a low voice, Ben uttered, "Sorry."

"That really sucks," declared Ian with a frown.

"Maybe something will show up from the DNA analysis."

"Have you talked to Ritter?" asked Ian, adding, "He left a message this morning, but we haven't been able to connect yet."

"Nope. Found a note from him on my desk when I came in this morning, though. It said our DNA guy would run Gina's sample and that he expects the analysis to be complete sometime today."

"Well, I hope his news is better than yours. If you see him, tell him to call me ASAP, will ya?"

"Sure thing," answered Ben, "I'm kinda anxious to know myself. Talk to you later."

Ian hung up, turned to Mike and muttered, "Damn, we need Jordan's prints."

O'Reilly shrugged.

He closed his eyes, leaned back in his chair and pondered this current dilemma. Suddenly, an idea hit him.

Wearing a huge grin, he turned to Mike and said, "I know how we can get her prints!"

Mike raised an eyebrow in inquiry.

"She was in the Army, right? Let's send the unidentified prints from the scene to the Army CID folks . . . they should have her prints on file and can tell us if there's a match," suggested Ian.

O'Reilly smiled. "Shit, Buchanan, just when I was beginning to wonder why the hell they made you a fuckin' detective, you actually have a good idea."

Buchanan lifted the phone receiver with enthusiasm. "I'll call Li."

Ian began explaining his idea the minute Ben answered the phone. When he was done, he waited for Li's response but only heard silence.

"You still there?"

Ben answered haltingly, "Yeah, I heard you. I can certainly do that . . . but, well, I just talked to Ritter . . . he said he was going to call you in a few minutes . . . I think you need to hear what he has to say first."

Ian felt a tingling sensation in his spine. "What's going on?"

"It would be better if you talked to Jim. I don't want to talk out of school. But suffice it to say, he has some very interesting news for you."

"C'mon Li," coaxed Buchanan, "You can't leave me hanging like this . . . Where's Ritter now?"

"Well, like I said, he's planning to call you. He may be trying right now," said Ben quietly, leaving Ian with an uneasy feeling.

He hung up and repeated the conversation to Mike.

"Well shit," complained O'Reilly, "This is getting ridiculous. I say we get in the car and drive over to the fuckin' lab."

Buchanan glanced at the phone, willing it to ring. After a minute he looked at Mike. "Okay, let's do it."

The detectives took two stairs at a time as they raced to the parking lot. Ian was breathing fast and hard as he slid behind the wheel and muttered, "I don't know what the big fucking secret is!"

The San Diego Crime Lab was less than four miles from their office but due to heavy traffic on Balboa Avenue it took the detectives nearly ten minutes to get there. While Ian drove, Mike groused about the many frustrations they'd encountered while trying to solve Richard Tate's murder.

"It's not often we have this many suspects so early in a case. Yet, we've been stymied at every turn. There's no doubt in my mind that one of the ex-wives is behind this thing, fingerprints or no."

Ian pressed his lips together and then said, "Well, I have a feeling what we're about to hear may just be the evidence we've been looking for. That's the impression I got from Li anyway."

O'Reilly shook his head. "As much as I dislike Gina, I can almost understand why she, or any of the others, might be driven to kill the son of a bitch. You have to admit, from what we've heard, he was a total asshole!"

"There's no doubt in my mind," replied Buchanan. "I mean, if one wife had told us some nasty stories about him then I would have chalked it up to bitter ex-wife syndrome. But all three related some pretty horrific stuff. Even Colleen - and that happened what, thirty years ago?"

Mike nodded vigorously and said, "That's what I'm talking about. What a mother fucker! He gives the rest of us men a bad name."

Ian chuckled. "And in your case, that's no easy task."

<hr />

Buchanan pulled into a reserved parking spot in front of the Crime Lab, which is located inside a former hospital in the

Clairemont area of San Diego.

He quickly shut off the engine and threw open the car door. Opting to present a calm, professional demeanor, he resisted the urge to run into the building. O'Reilly followed suit.

The detectives walked through the glass front doors, signed in at the security desk and then turned down the wide hallway leading to Ritter's office. Jim shared the sizeable workspace that once was a hospital patient room with Ben Li.

Li sat at his desk scrutinizing his computer screen, while Ritter was perched on the edge, with his back to the door, talking on the phone.

Ian called from the doorway, "Okay, what's the story?"

Ben's head jerked up. He smiled as he leaned over and jabbed Ritter in the ribs.

Jim turned to look at them and then murmured into the phone, "Oh, here they are now. Thanks for your help." He stood as he slowly replaced the phone to its base.

"You gonna tell us what the fuck's going on?" quizzed O'Reilly impatiently.

Ritter chuckled and said, "Calm down, guys . . . I have good news for you. No need to get testy."

Ian and Mike stood quiet, staring at Jim, waiting.

When Ritter finally spoke he simply said, "Got the results of the DNA analysis."

It became apparent to Ian that Jim was toying with them - and enjoying it. After about thirty seconds of silence, Buchanan blurted, "And . . . are you gonna clue us in on the results?"

Ritter laughed. "Well, since you obviously are in no mood to wait for the written report, I guess I will. The vomit didn't come from the victim, nor from Gina Rodriquez."

"Oh, goddamn it!" muttered Ian, "Then just what the hell is the good news?"

"Steve – that's our DNA expert - was able to determine that the *vomiter* was related to the victim."

Ian's eyes grew wide. He turned to look at Mike, who stood next to him gaping at Jim.

"Holy shit," whispered Buchanan, ". . . don't tell me it was Brett."

"Or Carter," O'Reilly quickly added.

"It wasn't either of them."

"How do you know that?" Ian questioned.

"I know because Steve was also able to determine the sex of the person who discharged the odorous liquid. According to the DNA, that person was of the feminine persuasion."

Ian wrinkled his brow and asked, "And she was definitely related to Richard Tate?"

"You got it."

"Son of a bitch," uttered Mike, "That boils it down to three people . . . not the same three we've been investigating, I might add."

Buchanan held up his hand then bent his index finger in half as he began, "Mommy Dearest," then continued with the next finger, "Caitlin . . . Who else?"

"His sister," answered O'Reilly.

"Hmmm," uttered Ian, ". . . and Heather makes four."

"Heather?" asked Mike, "But if she didn't even know he was her father, why the hell would she want to kill him?"

"We don't know for sure that she didn't know. Maybe Colleen was protecting her or maybe Heather found out and never let on to her mom."

Ian told the others about running into her at the gym and about the lack of friendliness on her part.

"Ever think she might just hate cops?" Ritter put forward with a smile.

"Well, let's go find out," Mike said as he slapped Ian on the back, "But if you're taking bets, place mine on Mom. That woman gives me the creeps."

Ian snickered. "From the beginning you were certain it was Gina for the same reason."

Ben interjected, "You that certain the person who vomited is your killer?"

"Well, you know as well as I that nothing's ever certain in this line of work," answered Ian. Glancing at Ritter, he smiled and added, "Except DNA evidence . . . Thanks Jim."

"You're welcome. But Steve's the one who performed the analysis so I'd say you owe us both a drink."

"You got it," replied Ian, then turning to his partner, exclaimed, "Let's go find Ms. Monroe."

"Right," replied Mike as he turned toward the door, "And after that, we'll check out dear old Mom. Now that I think about it, we haven't heard from her since the funeral. Don't you find that odd?"

Ian waved at Ritter and Li and followed his partner out the door, muttering, "Everything that woman does is odd."

Chapter 42
July 28, 2003

Buchanan walked to the car with a lilt in his step. From the beginning, he'd thought the vomit found at the scene would lead them to the perpetrator of this crime. So, though they hadn't yet solved the case, he just knew they were very close. He felt it in his bones.

He grinned at Mike and said, "Okay . . . first off, let's get Heather's address."

O'Reilly settled into the passenger seat and reached for the laptop computer.

"Okay," he murmured as he typed, "Let's see here . . . Heather Monroe." After a minute he muttered, "Okay, there's two of 'em."

Mike continued to click on the keyboard. "This one is forty three years old . . ." Then he smiled and uttered, "Bingo! Heather L. Monroe . . . birth date . . . November twenty first, nineteen seventy four. That would make her . . . 29 years old."

Buchanan grinned. "Certainly fits."

"Yep," agreed Mike, "Okay . . . address is 6600 Olive Street, apartment number fourteen in Lemon Grove."

"That's only a couple miles from the gym where she works -it's gotta be her."

He pulled out of the Crime Lab parking lot, turned right on Genesee, then took Balboa Avenue toward I-805 heading south.

———⟫(⦿)⟪———

The detectives parked on the street parallel to a 1960s-era apartment building. Ian noted the owner's attempt to keep the mature property in good condition. The small lawn fronting the rental office was recently mowed and a hedge of agapanthus sprouted healthy lavender flowers.

Three recently-painted apartment buildings formed a U shape around a gated swimming pool. They found Heather's apartment in the building on their right. Mike knocked on the door bearing a black metal number fourteen. The door swung open and there stood Colleen wearing a pink chenille bathrobe.

She stared at them for a moment, wide-eyed.

"Detectives…" she said haltingly, "What are you doing here?"

"Actually we're here to speak with Heather," Buchanan explained then with furrowed brow added, "I didn't realize you were still in town."

She continued to stand in the doorway, holding the door open just far enough to look out at them. "Well, Heather's not here right now."

"Where can we find her?"

"W-well, why do you want to talk to her?"

Ian frowned and replied, "Heather is an adult, Colleen. We don't need your permission to talk to her. We have some questions for her . . . now, where can we find her? Is she at work?"

Colleen studied the floor for a minute then in a voice barely above a whisper said, "She had an appointment with her therapist. She should be back soon."

Mike gently inquired, "May we come in and wait for her then?"

She lifted her eyes to his but said nothing.

A moment later, she stepped back from the door, murmuring abstractedly, "I guess it would be okay."

They entered into a tiny living room just off an even smaller kitchen. Colleen motioned toward an old and threadbare, brown plaid couch and said, "Please, have a seat."

Ian noticed Colleen's hands were shaking. She saw him looking at them and clasped them together.

Reaching up to pull her robe closed over her chest, she muttered, "I-I'm going to go get dressed . . ." then turned and walked through a door just off the living room.

O'Reilly suddenly announced, "I gotta make a phone call."

Buchanan lifted his eyebrows in surprise. "To who?"

Mike waved his hand through the air as if to say *never mind*, then walked out the front door, leaving Ian alone in the tattered apartment. He glanced around the room. A television sat under the window to his right. The local news flickered on the screen, but the sound had apparently been turned down because he only heard the low buzzing of voices.

An oak paneled bookshelf occupied the other wall. He walked over to get a closer look at the books and pictures that sat haphazardly on its shelves. Most of the books pertained to health and fitness, although a few paperbacks – mostly mysteries – lie on their side on the bottom shelf.

Ian picked up a silver-framed picture and gazed at Colleen as a young bride, smiling brightly beside a tall, dark man he assumed to be Jake Monroe. Placing it back on the shelf he perused the rest of the photos. Other than one picturing an older couple, the rest were of Heather – in cap and gown, lifting weights in what looked to be some sort of tournament, with a group of young women . . . Buchanan noted the fact that none of the pictures portrayed Heather with a smile. He took a second look. She wasn't frowning, but staring expressionless at the camera.

How odd, thought Ian with a shake of the head. *It would appear she doesn't particularly like having her picture taken, yet she displays them on her shelf.*

Just as Colleen returned, wearing blue jeans and a pale blue tank top, O'Reilly walked through the front door.

Mike must have seen the confusion in Colleen's eyes. He held up his cell phone and uttered, "Phone call," to which she nodded.

Colleen looked over at Ian. "Heather should be here any minute. Her appointment was at 11:00 and her therapist is only ten minutes away."

Buchanan checked his watch and realized it was nearly 12:30. "Why is she in therapy?" he asked.

Colleen looked startled by the question. She fidgeted with her hands, gazed in Mike's direction and then back at Ian.

Finally, in a near whisper, she said, "I'm not really sure but, frankly, I don't think it's any of your business."

Ian raised an eyebrow and pursed his lips then nodded in concession.

"Do you know why she owns a gun?" questioned Mike.

It was Ian's turn to be startled. He jerked his head toward Mike and stared, with his mouth open.

"I don't think she does," Colleen answered with a frown.

"She does. She has a Beretta Model 84 semi-automatic pistol registered in her name."

A stunned silence permeated the room.

The front door abruptly flew open. Ian turned to see Heather standing just inside, a puzzled look on her face.

"What the hell's going on here," she growled, swinging her head in her mother's direction.

"Th-they said they want to ask you some questions," answered Colleen.

Heather stepped away from the door then raised her arm and pointed outside. "I have nothing to say to you so you may as well leave right now!"

Ian stepped forward and looked directly into her eyes. "Heather we have evidence that implicates you in Dick Tate's murder. We'd like to give you the opportunity to clear this up. If you don't wish to, well then –that's your prerogative. But, if that's your decision, we'll have no choice but to place you under arrest."

Heather's eyes grew wide.

Colleen spoke from behind him. "Other than her owning a gun, what evidence do you have?" she demanded.

Heather swung her head from Ian to her mother then back again. She began to walk backward, flailing her arms through the air, stopping only when her back banged against the cabinets separating the kitchen from the living room.

"What the fuck are you talking about?" she shouted.

"Heather!" Colleen admonished, "Watch your mouth."

Heather turned a ferocious scowl in her mother's direction.

"Shut the fuck up, *Mother*," she snarled.

Colleen's mouth flew open. She held her palm to her cheek as if she'd just been slapped, audibly sucking air into her throat.

Buchanan looked on with astonishment as the young woman mimicked, "Watch your mouth, Heather. Don't talk to your father that way, Heather. Show some respect, Heather."

"H-honey . . . ," stammered Colleen.

Heather's eyes grew dark as they continued to focus on her mother. "Just going through the fucking motions doesn't make you a fucking mother. A mother is supposed to protect her child . . . and I don't mean by lying about who her goddamned father is!"

Ian made eye contact with Mike. Both detectives stood by quietly, watching the drama unfold before them.

Colleen gasped, her eyes filled with horror. With tears streaming down her face, she breathed, "Heather, don't."

"Don't?" screeched Heather, "Don't? That word didn't work when I fucking pleaded with my so-called father so why should it work for you?"

"What are you talking about?" Colleen asked haltingly.

"Oh, now you're going to pretend like you knew nothing! Shit, Mother, it's all your fucking fault!"

Colleen vigorously shook her head from side to side. "Please, Heather, I don't know what you're talking about . . . please," she choked.

Heather suddenly collapsed to the floor, buried her head between her knees and began to sob. No one said a word. Ian studied the huddled form, fascinated by her transformation from a determined young woman to a tragic, pitiful child.

Colleen walked slowly across the room then kneeled down, wrapped her arms around her daughter and murmured, "As God is my witness, I don't know, baby, I truly don't. Please tell me . . . oh, please."

They sat like that for several minutes, neither of them speaking. Struggling to regulate her breathing, Heather gradually raised her tear-streaked face and looked at her mother.

In a tiny voice, she asked, "Y-you really didn't know that your husband raped me every night of my life, from the time I was six years old until he died?"

Colleen caught her breath, her eyes as big as saucers. "Oh, dear God!" she whispered. Her body trembled as her tears began anew.

Ian felt like an intruder. He knew he needed to be here, to do his job, but what he was witnessing seemed such a private matter, it made him uncomfortable. In an attempt to be as unobtrusive as possible, he slowly made his way to the couch and sat down. He glanced at Mike who stood rooted to his original position, looking just as uncomfortable.

Colleen continued to hold her daughter in her arms while murmuring, "Oh my sweet baby, I didn't know . . . I swear I didn't know."

Heather sniffed, "How could you not know, Mommy? He came into my room every night. I-I hated you for letting him do that to me."

"D-did you talk about this with your therapist?" Colleen asked quietly.

She nodded. "It was only a few days ago that I remembered. I guess I blocked it out. S-she hypnotized me . . ." Tears continued to stream down Heather's face.

Colleen pulled back and looked into her daughter's face. "When Jake died, you were so upset for such a long time. I-I thought that was because you loved him so much . . . I don't understand . . ."

"I think that's when I started blocking it out – when he died,"

Heather tearfully explained. "But my therapist helped me under-stand . . . For years, I prayed that something would happen to him. I wished him dead. When he did die, I felt responsible."

"I'm so sorry," uttered Colleen, "I'm so sorry I didn't protect you from him."

A long silence ensued, during which Ian pondered man's in-humanity to man . . . or in this case, to woman. At times like this he wondered why he had chosen his profession. His shoulders sagged under the weight of the incomprehensible evil he'd wit-nessed too often over the years.

Finally, realizing he had a murder to solve, he spoke softly, "I'm sorry . . ." Both women raised their eyes to him. Fighting to keep his emotions at bay, he continued, "How long have you known that Dick Tate was your real father, Heather?"

Colleen swung her head around to look into her daughter's face as Heather quietly answered, "Since shortly after Daddy . . . er . . . Jake died."

Colleen gasped. "How?"

Heather looked at her mother. "I overheard you and Grandpa talking one day. He said his name . . . actually I think he said, 'If it weren't for that son of a bitch, Dick Tate, you would have finished college.' Then he said that if it weren't for Dick you wouldn't have me either."

"How did you find him?" inquired Mike.

Confusion was etched on the faces of both mother and daughter as they looked up at Mike.

Heather focused her gaze on her trembling hands as she said, in a surprisingly steady voice, "I started looking when I was seventeen. I went to San Jose State . . . I found an old yearbook that had his picture in it. Then I looked at school newspapers from the early seventies. There were several articles about the swim team that mentioned both my mom and Dick Tate."

She paused and then looked at Colleen, who said, "I had no idea . . . you never let on in any way that you knew."

"So how were you able to trace him to San Diego?" asked Mike.

"A few years ago, I hired a private detective. He searched military records, driver's license information and other stuff . . . then he found Dick's address. That was a year ago."

Colleen exhaled loudly and remarked, "That's when you moved to San Diego!"

Heather spoke in monotone as she said, "I came down here for a week . . . remember? I said I was spending a week with my friend Carol?" Colleen nodded and Heather continued, "I was really watching him. I found out what gym he belonged to and applied for a job there."

"Dick Tate was a member there too?" asked Ian incredulously.

Heather turned to him with veiled eyes, a malapropos smile etched on her lips. "I thought you knew that, and that was why you were there yesterday."

Ian shook his head and said, "I assume Dick didn't know he was your father," his voice tilting upward with the last word, turning the statement into a question.

Heather continued to smile abstractedly as she whispered, "Not until last weekend."

His ears felt hot and a tingle ran down his spine as her words sunk in. Ian quickly raised his palm in the air in an effort to halt any further utterance on her part.

"Ms. Monroe, before you say another word, I must inform you of your Miranda Rights . . . You have the right to remain silent and refuse to answer questions. Do you understand?"

Heather nodded and climbed to her feet.

"Anything you do or say may be used against you in a court of law. Do you understand?"

"Detective Buchanan," Heather interrupted, "I understand what you're telling me and I also know I have the right to consult an attorney. . ." She glanced at her mother and then, in a small voice, said, "I want to talk about it. As my therapist repeatedly tells me, before I can get better I first have to confront what has happened to me."

Colleen jumped up and grabbed her daughter by the shoulders. "Heather," she shouted, "Look at me! Don't say another word. We'll get you an attorney . . . Let me call Grandpa . . ."

Heather pulled away from her mother and briskly shook her head from side to side. "No!" she screamed, "I know what I'm doing and I don't need your help – or Grandpa's."

"Maybe you should listen to your mother in this instance," murmured Ian, ignoring the grimace on Mike's face. Though he realized he could be jeopardizing their chances of getting a full confession from Heather, he didn't feel right about how it was coming about.

"Detective!" He heard his partner's admonishment and turned to look at him. "Let her talk," Mike said sternly.

Ian shook his head sadly and looked at the floor.

He heard O'Reilly speaking as if from a distance, "Heather, we're required to read you all of your rights . . . If you cannot afford an attorney . . ."

As Mike continued, Ian studied Colleen's face. Tears poured from red and bewildered eyes, dark creases seemed to have affixed themselves permanently to her forehead and around her tight lips.

He couldn't help but feel sorry for her. Not only had she

suffered a vicious rape as a young girl, but because of her love for her child – the product of that rape - she'd also sacrificed her dreams. And now, within a matter of minutes, she'd learned of her child's ultimate violation by another man she'd presumably loved and was about to hear what Ian felt certain would be Heather's confession of murder.

His mind wandered back in time, to a conversation between his mother and his sister, who at the time was suffering from a broken heart. When Ian overheard his mother declare women as the stronger sex, he'd laughed, mocking her. Now, he felt a sudden urge to see his mother, to hug her and apologize for his insensitivity.

Buchanan came back to the present just as Mike finished, "Knowing and understanding your rights as I have explained them to you, are you willing to answer my questions without an attorney present?"

Heather nodded. O'Reilly held up the miniature tape recorder and said, "Ms. Monroe, I need you to say yes or no out loud."

The young woman leaned forward and evenly stated, "Yes, I'm willing to answer your questions."

Mike smiled encouragingly and prompted, "You were about to tell us how Dick Tate found out you were his daughter . . ."

In a dispassionate tone, Heather stoically related her account of the previous weekend.

"I always made it a point to talk to Dick whenever he was in the gym. We sorta became friends . . . A couple weeks ago I decided the time had come to introduce myself. But I didn't want to just blurt it out while he was lifting weights, ya know?"

O'Reilly nodded.

Ian noted that Colleen's haunted eyes hadn't left her daughter's face. *What must be going on in her mind?* he wondered.

Heather continued, "So, I offered to come by that weekend and drop off a fitness book we'd discussed. He suggested I go on Sunday, because on Saturday he'd be with his son who was visiting from out of town. That made me feel . . . I don't know . . . kinda sad, I guess, because his son could visit him anytime and I . . . well, I was born first – ya know? And I never had a relationship with him."

Without thinking, Ian blurted, "Shit, from what I've heard, you're probably better off!"

Mike narrowed his eyes and glared at him, silently saying, "If you aren't going to help, then shut up."

Buchanan hunched over, placing his elbows on his knees and burying his head in his hands. The cop in him was urging him to set his feelings aside and do his job and he couldn't understand why he was having so much trouble doing that. He'd always considered himself the consummate professional.

It's because I've never had a case like this, he told himself. *Because, in reality, Dick Tate was an evil man who spent his entire life wreaking havoc, creating victims at every turn. He wasn't the real victim here . . . this tragic figure before me is but one of them.*

As she persisted with her story, Ian felt as if he were stuck at one end of a tunnel with Heather speaking to him from the opposite side.

"I had to work until eight o'clock on Sunday . . . didn't actually get out of there until eight thirty. I didn't want to wear my uniform to his house and I wanted to shower first, so I went home. I called him and asked if it would be okay to come by later. He said he was in the middle of a movie on television that wouldn't get over until eleven o'clock. He said he was really into it and asked if I would wait until then . . . "

"He wanted you to come to his house at that time of night?" Mike interjected skeptically.

Heather acknowledged Mike with a flicker of her eyes but kept on talking, her voice maintaining the same robotic tone.

"It took me longer than I'd expected. I got there about eleven thirty. When I arrived, the porch light was on but the house seemed dark. I thought maybe he'd fallen asleep. I didn't want to wake him if that was the case, so I knocked lightly on the door. But he wasn't sleeping. He answered the door right away. I propped my bike against the shrubs and took the book out of my saddle bag."

Mike interrupted to ask, "You mean you rode your bike there . . . at eleven thirty at night?"

Heather slowly turned her gaze toward Mike. She stared at him for a minute, furrowing her brow as if trying to remember who he was.

"How else would I get there? I don't own a car."

She hesitated a moment before continuing, "He led me into his living room. The lights were dim. I almost expected to hear soft music on his stereo . . . you know, as if I was there for a romantic tryst or something. I sat down on the couch while he went in to the kitchen. He returned a few minutes later with two glasses of wine. I was starting to get a bad feeling and his presumptuousness really bothered me. So, I said I didn't want any wine. I told him it was late and that I had something I needed to talk to him about."

Heather paused long enough to lick her dry lips before carrying on, "So, he set the glasses down on the table and then reached for the book. I could tell he was irritated because he was frowning, but he didn't say anything. We talked about the book a little and then I stood up and told him I really had something important to tell him. He asked me what that was and that's when I informed him that I was his daughter."

She stopped talking and turned to look at her mother.

"What was his reaction to that?" Mike prodded.

"At first he just stared at me, like he couldn't believe what he was hearing. But when I told him I was Colleen's daughter, I knew he believed me. He started to smile and he said he should have known because I look just like her."

For the first time since she began her narration, Heather showed some emotion. A single tear trickled down her cheek as she continued, "Then he told me I was beautiful."

Her voice began to quiver; her eyes welled with tears as she murmured, "He walked toward me with his arms open and said, 'Well aren't you going to give Daddy a hug?'"

Heather stopped speaking. For several minutes the room was silent. Realizing he was holding his breath, Ian suddenly expelled the air from his lungs.

Mike asked gently, "What happened then, Heather?"

Colleen wrapped her arms around her daughter's trembling body. Finally, in a muffled voice, Heather said, "I don't remember."

"What?" O'Reilly asked incredulously, "What do you mean you don't remember?"

Heather began to sob, gasping for air.

Colleen glowered at Mike and hissed, "Leave her alone, damn you!"

Buchanan watched his partner's expression change from irritation to puzzlement and then sympathy. Finally, when Mike glanced in his direction, Ian placed his index finger to his lips and nodded.

Nearly five minutes passed before Heather was calm enough to speak.

"The next thing I knew," she began, modulating her voice for the first time, "I was looking down at his body. I knew he was dead. He wasn't moving and there was all this blood! I-I felt sick to my stomach. I knew I must be responsible but I didn't remember doing it. I ran into the bathroom and threw up."

She looked at Ian and said, "I thought about calling the cops, but then I realized that you'd know I did it and that I'd probably spend the rest of my life in jail. So, I ran out, grabbed my bike and rode home."

Looking at Colleen, Ian finally spoke up, "Where was your mother through all this?"

"She was asleep," answered Heather. Lowering her voice to a whisper, she added, "She thought I was out on a date. That's a rare thing for me, so she was really happy . . ."

Colleen's eyes were a scarlet color, her cheeks raw from crying. She peered at Ian and simply nodded her head.

Mike pulled out his handcuffs as he walked over to Heather. When she turned to look at him, he murmured, "I can't tell you how sorry I am about this, but I'm afraid I have to place you under arrest."

Heather held out her wrists but said nothing. Colleen threw her hands to her face and began to wail.

Ian felt as if someone had stabbed him with a knife. At that moment, he hated his job, he hated his partner and he hated himself.

"Oh, I have suffered
With those that I saw suffer!"

William Shakespeare
The Tempest, I, ii

EPILOGUE

He sat at a table on the restaurant's patio, patiently waiting her arrival. He closed his eyes and tilted his head back, savoring the sun's warmth on his face. The low din of conversation from nearby tables slowly receded as his mind began to wander.

Ian could hardly believe only two weeks had passed since Heather's dramatic confession and resulting arrest. He'd spent that entire evening contemplating her circumstances, wondering what would become of the young woman who was in custody for the crime of murder, a woman who had been violated by one father and disregarded by another.

He'd finally dragged his tension-filled body to bed and tried to put the day's events out of his mind, to no avail. Tossing and turning, he'd watched each hour tick by on the clock beside his bed.

A deep and abiding sadness coursed through him. Never before had he been so tortured by a case. It wasn't just the outcome; it was his inability to reconcile himself to the idea of Richard Tate as the victim.

The following morning Ian had stopped by to see his parents on the way to the office. While his mother plied him with blueberry pancakes and bacon, he'd discussed his feelings with his father.

"From my first days with the Sheriff's Department, I've felt proud of what I do. I mean, I catch the bad guys, you know? But now . . . I feel like I'm helping to victimize this young woman even more than she already has been."

He'd buried his head in his hands and then dug his palms into his eyes. He couldn't remember the last time he'd experienced such emotion, and felt shame at displaying it in front of his tough-minded father.

He'd been stunned when his father said, "You aren't the first cop who has struggled with a case like this and you won't be the last."

Ian had jerked his head up and peered into his father's eyes.

Bob Buchanan had awarded him with a gentle smile. "The main thing you need to remember is that ninety nine percent of the time you *are* getting the bad guy. That's what makes it all worthwhile. We chip away one case at a time with the hope of one day ridding the world of evil."

Ian had focused his eyes on the table before him and remarked, "We're never going to rid the world of evil, Dad . . . because every day more people that shouldn't be parents are having babies. They go on to mistreat them, abuse them or neglect them . . . then we end up with a new generation of criminals."

His father had chuckled softly and dryly commented, "A chip off the old block."

Though his father's words had helped ease the heaviness in his chest, it was his chance meeting with Colleen that had dispelled his gloom.

Two days later, while visiting Heather at the County Jail he'd run into Colleen in the waiting room. When she'd seen him, she'd greeted him with a smile, much to his amazement. He'd been certain she would harbor harsh feelings for him, that she'd blame him for Heather's incarceration. Instead, she'd thanked him for his gentle treatment of her daughter.

"Heather is being released on bail today," she'd explained. "My father hired an excellent attorney who thinks she has a good chance of beating this thing."

"I'm very glad to hear that."

"I know you are," she'd said, before continuing, "Her therapist has been wonderful as well. With her assistance, we were able to determine the actual events of that night."

Raising an eyebrow, Ian had quietly asked, "Can you tell me?"

Colleen had a sparkle in her eye as she said, "Detective Buchanan, believe it or not, I think of you as a good guy in all this."

After a moment's pause, he'd smiled for the first time in days.

According to her therapist, Colleen had told him, Heather was suffering from Posttraumatic Stress Disorder, brought on by the sexual molestation she'd suffered at the hands of her stepfather. Apparently, Jake had frequently initiated sex with Heather by saying, "Come give Daddy a hug." That night, Dick's utterance of similar words had caused Heather intense psychological distress. She'd reached into her purse and retrieved the gun she carried for protection. By that time, Dick was close enough to embrace her. Heather had jammed the pistol into his abdomen and pulled the trigger.

When Ian later learned the name of Heather's attorney, he'd been pleased. Grace Scott, a savvy, San Diego criminal defense attorney, was well known for her successful representation of several clients who'd been victims of child abuse. If anyone could obtain an innocent verdict from a jury, it was Grace.

He was suddenly brought back to the present, her silky voice causing a stir deep down inside as she whispered in his ear, "It's so good to see you smiling."

He lost his battle with the hooks pulling the outer corners of his mouth upward when he opened his eyes to Meg's angelic face.

"I didn't realize I was," he chuckled as he got to his feet and pulled out her chair, "Guess I must have sensed you."

She grinned. "Careful Detective, these days I tend to shy away from men who ooze charm."

Ian laughed. "Now *that's* something I've never been accused of."

ACKNOWLEDGEMENTS

I am indebted to Santa Clara County Forensic Chemist Ann Im-Obersteg and to Celia Hartnett, Director of Forensic Analytical Specialties Inc. for explaining complex toxicology and DNA processes in layman's terms.

I also appreciate the invaluable information provided by staff of the Sacramento County Laboratory of Forensic Services and the San Diego County Medical Examiner's Office.

Much gratitude goes to my cousin, Charol Page, for providing color and authenticity to police procedures and those who practice them.

Most especially, enormous thanks to my husband, Tim, whose patience, encouragement and support helped make this novel a reality. Thank you for showing me that true love does exist.

Breinigsville, PA USA
03 August 2010
242975BV00001B/2/P